THE DUKE'S ENFORCER

The Duke's Guard Series,
Book Eight

C.H. Admirand

DRAGONBLADE PUBLISHING, INC.

ARE YOU SIGNED UP FOR DRAGONBLADE'S BLOG?

You'll get the latest news and information on exclusive giveaways, exclusive excerpts, coming releases, sales, free books, cover reveals and more.

Check out our complete list of authors, too!

No spam, no junk. That's a promise!

Sign Up Here

www.dragonbladepublishing.com

Dearest Reader;

Thank you for your support of a small press. At Dragonblade Publishing, we strive to bring you the highest quality Historical Romance from some of the best authors in the business. Without your support, there is no 'us', so we sincerely hope you adore these stories and find some new favorite authors along the way.

Happy Reading!

CEO, Dragonblade Publishing

Additional Dragonblade books by Author C.H. Admirand

The Duke's Guard Series
The Duke's Sword (Book 1)
The Duke's Protector (Book 2)
The Duke's Shield (Book 3)
The Duke's Dragoon (Book 4)
The Duke's Hammer (Book 5)
The Duke's Defender (Book 6)
The Duke's Saber (Book 7)
The Duke's Enforcer (Book 8)

The Lords of Vice Series
Mending the Duke's Pride (Book 1)
Avoiding the Earl's Lust (Book 2)
Tempering the Viscount's Envy (Book 3)
Redirecting the Baron's Greed (Book 4)
His Vow to Keep (Novella)
The Merry Wife of Wyndmere (Novella)

The Lyon's Den Series
Rescued by the Lyon
Captivated by the Lyon

Dedication

For DJ ~ Love of my life and keeper of my heart

Acknowledgments

A special thank you to Arran McNicol, my wonderful editor! Your attention to detail, and ability to find those loose ends that need to be tied up, is greatly appreciated.

For my loyal readers and new-to-me readers, thank you for reading my books and letting me know how much you love The Duke's Guard Series *and my handsome-as-sin Irishmen. A special shout out to Sandra, Jackie, Fredine, Millie, Wendy, Mariah, Anne, Sherry, Linda, and Suzonne!*

PROLOGUE

MISS AIMEE ANDERSON stood off to the side of the busy inn yard with her small, battered portmanteau clutched in her left hand. She heard the carriage and turned to watch its approach. Fear curdled in her belly. The last time she stood in this spot, her dreams had been crushed by the man who'd professed to love her.

He'd lied.

The coach slowed down and entered the yard. Her heart beat faster, and she could not catch her breath. Would this decision be a mistake, too? Should she have listened to the innkeeper's wife? The last time she had taken a chance, and believed in a dream, she had lost everything—her reputation, her self-respect…her virtue. All of it taken from her within the confines of a coach just like the one slowing to a halt in front of her.

She tried to remember the earnest expression on the handsome, dark-haired lord's face as he swept her off her feet, declaring his love and promising to take her away from her menial existence to live a life in the lap of luxury. But all she could recall was the menacing expression on his patrician features, and his warm, dark eyes hardening at her refusal of his offer, not of marriage, but as a kept woman—his mistress.

Abandoned and alone, she had trembled as he sneered at her, reminding her that she was now damaged goods. No one would want her if she did not accept his offer. He may have taken her virtue, but she still had what was left of her tattered pride. When she refused for the second time, he ordered his coachman to drive on as he slammed the carriage door in her face.

"Miss?"

Ruined, beyond redemption, she'd watched his carriage drive away. She had no money, nor connections, but she had a strong will to survive and was unafraid to return to the life of drudgery she had thought she could not bear.

"Miss?" The voice was louder this time.

She blinked, and her past vanished—though still in the inn yard, she was about to embark on her last chance at the life she had once dreamed of while polishing silver and changing her cousin's bed linens.

"Are you Miss Anderson?"

Digging deep for her courage, she drew in a breath and walked over to the carriage. "Yes, I am."

The burly man tied off the reins and stepped down from his perch atop the coach. "I'm required to verify that you are indeed the same Miss Aimee Anderson who answered the advert. Do you have the letter Mrs. Underwood sent to you?"

She reached into her reticule and pulled out the folded bit of foolscap she'd received after applying for the position and handed it to him. He examined the handwriting on the front before unfolding and scanning the letter. With a nod, he folded it and handed it back to her.

"Very good, Miss Anderson. I shall see about changing the horses for the return trip and be with you shortly. You have time for a cup of tea before we leave."

Mouth dry, insides shaking, she licked her lips to moisten them. "Thank you for the suggestion, but I had a cup a little while ago."

His gaze swept from the top of her head to the toes of her half boots. She wondered what possible reason he would have to study her person so closely. Mayhap it was part of his instructions when picking up newly hired shopworkers, and the reason she had dressed in her best gown, a deep gray—the color of winter storm clouds. A darker thought occurred—mayhap he wanted to ensure she did not pose a threat to his precious carriage.

Finally, he said, "You can wait inside the carriage, if you wish. I'll let the hostler know you are inside and caution him not to jostle the carriage when changing the horses."

"Thank you."

He nodded and opened the door for her.

She hesitated for a brief moment, gathered her courage, and stepped into the carriage. Lowering herself onto the squabs, she was pleased to note the worn leather was quite comfortable. Wear wasn't as important as cleanliness. The inside of the carriage was spotless. Relieved to finally be leaving her past behind her, she set her portmanteau on the seat next to her. It would be within reach, should she decide to read on the way to London.

London! she thought with a nervous smile. She was changing her life for the better…again. Aimee Anderson—the much-maligned poor relation with a tattered reputation—had had the good luck to secure a position that would not include cleaning up after her betters. She was to be employed in a fashionable merchant's shop in London! She could not wait to begin her apprenticeship working at the milliner's. Visions of the varied textures she would use—the ribbons, feathers, and furbelows in an array of colors—filled her. She let her mind wander, imagining what it would be like immersed in her new role, while she waited for the horses to be changed and the coachman to return.

"Ready, Miss Anderson?"

She had not realized he had been watching her through the carriage window. Unease slithered up her spine, then slid down to curl low in her belly. She bravely ignored the feeling. "Yes. Thank you, sir."

His speculative gaze further unnerved her, but his words were innocuous, "Well then, let's be on our way!"

The coach shifted as he heaved his considerable bulk onto the bench atop the coach. The carriage rocked as he released the brake.

She glanced out the window for a last look at the safe haven where she'd recovered from her ordeal. Working for the innkeeper and his wife had restored her faith in humanity. All at once, she noticed Mrs. Potts waving a handkerchief. "Don't forget to write," she called to Aimee. "Let me know you've arrived in one piece!"

Grateful for the woman's kindness and protection at a time when she had needed it most, she replied, "I will!"

Aimee continued to watch the innkeeper's wife waving. The coachman guided the carriage onto the main road, and the team picked up the pace. Still, she watched until Mrs. Potts was an indistinct speck in the distance. With the crack of the coachman's whip, the team responded, picking up even more speed.

With a prayer in her heart, she whispered, "For better or worse, London, here I come!"

CHAPTER ONE

DARBY GARAHAN, ONE of the Duke of Wyndmere's private guard, was a few minutes late for a meeting in the offices of Gavin King of the Bow Street Runners. The duke's London man-of-affairs, Captain Coventry, would also be in attendance. After greeting the Runner stationed outside the door to the building, he strode along the darkened hallway until he reached King's door.

"Ah, Garahan." The older man nodded to him. "Am I taking you away from an important assignment?"

"Well now, as I have been known to juggle more than one duty at a time for His Grace," Garahan replied, "I cannot say that ye are." He grinned at the captain, adding, "Besides, ye must know that the captain here repeats everything we say and do to His Grace."

Coventry coughed to cover his snort of laughter, while King chuckled. "Close the door behind you."

Garahan complied and walked over to stand in front of King's desk. When King did not motion for him to be seated, he knew the meeting would be short.

"I received a message from Miss Michaela," King began. "You will recall she has saved more than one young woman from the streets of London." He handed a sealed note to Garahan.

He frowned. "'Tis addressed to me brother, James."

"The messenger advised that it should be passed on to you, if

James were not available," Coventry said.

Garahan took note of the intensity of the captain's gaze. "James mentioned a number of his London contacts would be aware I would be arriving, now that me brother and his bride would be permanently stationed at Chattsworth Manor."

He still had difficulty absorbing the fact that all three of his older brothers had been hit between the eyes by an emotion they had danced around for years—*love*. He highly approved of his sisters-in-law but had no intention of following in his brothers' footsteps.

"Do ye mind if I open it now? I may be needing yer assistance with whatever Miss Michaela needs."

Coventry answered, "Not at all. We're aware of the promise James made to Miss Michaela to send for him should she ever need his assistance. Tremayne offered the same to her, after her aid in locating—and sheltering—Miss Melinda Waring."

"'Tis *Mrs.* James Garahan now," Garahan reminded the captain.

Coventry smiled. "How are Melinda and James? Have you heard from them lately?"

Garahan shook his head. "I'm thinking he's too busy balancing married life and carrying out his duties to write a note to his youngest brother."

"It is an adjustment, and not without compromise on both sides. Best decision I have ever made. I'm certain your brother—rather, all of your brothers feel the same."

Garahan wasn't listening as he scanned the note from the mysterious woman who had made it her life's work to rescue young women off the streets of London. Miss Michaela tended to their injuries, and either helped them find work or spirited them away to safety. Add in the rumor that she studied medicine at her father's side, and she was an enigma to be sure.

"What does she need?" King asked.

Garahan answered, "A Miss Anderson is being held against her will at a boarding house. One that has a reputation for placing adverts claiming to have well-paying positions with fashionable London merchants." Coventry narrowed his eyes, and Garahan said, "I take it ye've heard of this before."

"Aye," Coventry answered. "Far too many young women who have either lost family, or lost their way, are willing to start a new life in London."

"When the young women arrive in London," King said, "they find they will not be working at a fashionable shop at all."

Garahan crushed the note in his hand, his insides churning. He didn't need to ask—he knew. "'Tis a front for a brothel, isn't it?"

"Aye," Coventry answered. "I can send Bayfield or Hennessey with you tomorrow, if you wait until they return from their current assignment."

"I'll be leaving at once," Garahan informed him.

King rose and walked to the door. Hand to the doorknob, he cautioned Garahan, "Rein in your temper and remember that you must exercise caution approaching Miss Michaela's building. You cannot afford to be seen."

"Ensure you are not followed," Coventry added. "For Miss Michaela's sake."

"Is that all?" Garahan asked.

King nodded and opened the door.

Garahan strode from the room, his pounding footsteps along the hallway the only reaction he allowed himself as he fought to control his anger. The lengths the depraved would go to sickened him.

He took the necessary precautions to ensure he was not followed. Half an hour later, he entered the seedier side of London, as familiar to him as his family's home back in Ireland. He reined in his horse outside of a run-down building with dark curtains blocking the windows. Unlike the buildings on either side of it, the windows were intact.

He knocked twice and waited for the single responding knock

he was told to expect...the signal. When he heard it, he opened the door and paused to take the measure of the behemoth holding it open before ascending the stairs two at a time. The door opened as he gained the top step.

"Mr. Garahan," the mysterious angel of the streets greeted him.

He nodded to the petite woman illuminated by the candle-light behind her, framing her in a halo of gold. For a moment he wondered if she were a heavenly apparition, or real. He blinked, and thankfully, she did not disappear.

He cleared his throat. "Miss Michaela."

She smiled, and he could not help but think that the rumors of her strength were either exaggerated, or magically hidden somewhere within her tiny frame. Mayhap 'twas her courage that his brother and Tremayne had commented on more than once.

"Just Garahan, if ye don't mind," he added.

She waved him into the room. "You remind me of James. Thank you for coming so quickly. Please come in."

He'd heard as much most of his life. Each of the four Garahan brothers had been blessed with dark hair and eyes, a broad, well-muscled build, and an extra dollop of charm to offset their hair-trigger tempers.

As he stepped inside, she reached around him to close the door behind him. "I need to explain the delicacy of the situation you are walking into."

He listened to her describe how young women from the country were lured by adverts, and what was often the deciding factor—transportation to London would be provided. His hackles rose at the description of the boarding house where Miss Anderson was being held against her will. Neither King nor Coventry had needed to confirm his supposition that the boarding house was a front.

"From what ye're not saying, I'm guessing 'tis a stopping point and not a final destination."

Tired eyes met his. "Yes, and it could not be further from

what these poor young women were promised when they answered the advert."

His gut churned and his blood began to boil. "They're being groomed for another type of work."

She answered, "Two brothels in particular." Before he could ask, Miss Michaela added, "Miss Anderson is uncommonly tall and slender, with platinum hair and blue eyes."

"What if Miss Anderson is no longer at the boarding house?" Her troubled gaze was his answer. Miss Anderson would disappear into the maw of lost souls in the bowels of the city.

She handed him a scrap of foolscap with an address on it and a small leather bag of coins. "When you speak to the owner of the boarding house, tell her Lord Atwell sent you. She knows what Atwell prefers...blue-eyed blondes. Show her the coin," she urged, "but don't hand it over until she produces Miss Anderson."

He clenched his jaw, mentally preparing for what could be a tenuous situation bartering for Miss Anderson's release. "Ye have me word."

"No matter what state Miss Anderson is in, promise you will bring her back here as quickly as possible."

The weight of the coins in his hand had his gut churning at the prospect of an innocent young country lass being forced to work in a house of ill repute. "I promise to return with the lass— even if I have to haul her over me shoulder kicking and scream-ing."

Michaela frowned at him. "She may have sustained injuries either on the journey to London or since arriving. I will treat her myself."

He'd heard about the woman's healing capabilities...and limitations. "What if she has a separated shoulder like me sister-in-law, Melinda, had? Will Alasdair Cameron be here to assist ye? James mentioned the Scot was adept at setting bones and putting shoulders back into the socket."

She smiled at the mention of Cameron. "He was a godsend and very protective of the young women I rescued, and myself.

But he has recently married and is temporarily living with his wife's family. His father-in-law was quite ill but is recovering."

"I had heard, but forgotten, that Cameron married. Tremayne mentioned 'twas Cameron's sharp eye that detected his wife's father—his former superior in the dragoons—had been poisoned." He waited a beat to add, "As to being a godsend, I don't believe that was the expression James used to describe the Scotsman."

Michaela sighed. "They disliked one another on sight, but then overcame their prejudices to work together for the greater good."

Garahan slipped the bag of coin in his waistcoat pocket. "By all counts, the greater good would be yerself, and the invaluable work ye do for those less fortunate who, for one reason or another, have ended up in the bowels of London in situations not of their own making."

She placed her hand on his arm and started to speak, but hesitated.

"Is there something else I need to know?" he asked.

"No matter what questions the boarding house owner asks—especially if they have to do with Lord Atwell—do not answer. Stare her down until she agrees."

"Has this tactic worked in the past?"

"Yes." Her grip on his arm tightened. "I must caution you, Mr. Garahan—"

"Just Garahan."

Her lips curved into a small smile, which quickly faded. He suspected the wee lass was exhausted. Mayhap his cousin Emmett O'Malley would know of an herbal concoction that would set the woman to rights. He'd make a point of mentioning her to O'Malley...*after* he rescued Miss Anderson.

"As I was saying, Garahan, use extreme caution."

"Ye have me word. If there is nothing else—"

She wrung her hands together, and he added nerves on top of her exhaustion. He'd definitely be speaking to O'Malley about her.

"Be on guard—the boarding house owner hides a small blade in her sleeve, and a larger one in her apron." She released her hold on him as if she'd only just realized what she'd done. "Do not hand over the bag of coin until Miss Anderson has been turned over to you."

"Have no worries. I'll exercise caution approaching and dealing with the owner of the boarding house. Ye have me word of honor that I'll return with Miss Anderson." Staring at the way she absently massaged her temples, he added, "See that ye take whatever herbs will help with the pain in yer head."

She dropped her hand and lifted her chin to study his face. He had no idea what she hoped to see, other than the determined set of his jaw, which he hoped she understood indicated that he meant every blessed word he'd said to her.

"Trust me, lass."

Michaela's heavy sigh indicated that she was not quite ready to do so. Only the mention of Cameron had had the lass truly smiling—a smile that reached her eyes. One more item to add to the growing list of reasons to convince his cousin that he needed to meet the lass. Whether she knew it or not, she needed Emmett O'Malley.

Garahan descended the stairs, nodding once again to the large man guarding the door. No words were necessary. Garahan knew what was expected of him. He'd given his word to Miss Michaela. When the door closed behind him, he waited to hear the snick of the lock before reaching for the reins and untying his horse.

He stroked the roan gelding's neck and whispered, "We've been charged with an important rescue, laddie."

The horse's ears pricked up at his words. Satisfied that the animal understood, he mounted and guided his horse into the darkest bowels of London.

CHAPTER TWO

G ARAHAN KNEW WORD would have spread through his contacts, and those of his cousins, that he was in the darkest part of the stews. Keeping an eye out, he recognized more than one of the men loitering in a doorway here, an alleyway there. Relieved that his horse would come to no harm while he was otherwise occupied, he lifted his chin and made eye contact with the third man.

The dip of the man's head indicated that he would watch out for Darby's horse, as he had for other members of the duke's guard when necessary. Their network of contacts in the poorer sections of the city were as essential to performing their job protecting the duke and his family as the duke and the earl's contacts within the higher echelons of Society. Good thing, because he had little respect for most of the useless members of the *ton* who spent their days huddled in their clubs, swilling brandy, speaking of their wealth, their women…and their wives. The few exceptions were the duke and his family.

He shuddered just thinking of the foul brew and the *ton's* propensity for keeping more than one mistress. Irish whiskey— and not brandy—was the true water of life…*uisce na beatha*. When an Irishman married, 'twas for life, and God help the man if his wife suspected he had even *looked* at another woman. Da never had.

The empty feeling in his gut caught him off guard. Was he wrong to dismiss the happiness his brothers—and O'Malley cousins—had found?

A slight movement in his peripheral vision had him pulling on the reins. "That's Burke over there, in the shadows," he told the gelding. "He'll be watching out for ye till I'm back with Miss Anderson." As if the animal understood every word, he lifted his head and snorted at Garahan, who chuckled softly. "There's a lad."

Highly aware of his surroundings, Garahan was confident in his ability to fend off any thickheaded thug who thought that he would be an easy mark. He cracked his knuckles and relished the idea of going a few rounds with anyone who tried. They had no idea they'd be dealing with Tipperary's youngest bare-knuckle champion.

The outside of the boarding house was nondescript, identical to the other buildings surrounding it—drab, worn, with an air of neglect. Ma would say all it needed was a good cleaning to set it to rights. Preparing to be accosted the moment he opened the door, he knocked first, then entered.

A hulking brute strode toward him. "We got no rooms."

The man's first mistake was to think he could intimidate Garahan. His second was to lay a hand on him. Before the man could blink, Garahan had the thug in a headlock. "Tell the owner of this establishment that Lord Atwell sent me." The man struggled, but Garahan increased the pressure on his throat. "Tell her, or ye'll be waking up an hour from now."

To Garahan's immense pleasure, the man continued to resist. He waited a moment more, and the man went slack in his hold. When he loosened his grip, the thug fell unconscious to the floor. Expecting to be surrounded, Garahan was surprised when a gray-haired woman strode toward him from the other end of the hallway.

He sized her up immediately. Squarely built—as wide as she was tall. There was a fair chance she had muscle hidden beneath her bulk. She was the woman he needed to speak to. The person responsible for stealing young women's hopes and dreams, kidnapping them, forcing them into a life of prostitution. A life they may never have the courage to leave.

She kicked the fallen man with the toe of her boot as she passed him, but he didn't budge. Lifting her dark, empty eyes, she stared at Garahan. "No one has ever gotten past Stark before. How did you manage it?"

Garahan stared back, sending a silent message that she was no longer in charge. Her very stance indicated that the woman would not back down.

Her eyes slid to his neck. *Bloody hell!* She would go for his throat if he left it unprotected.

The man at his feet hadn't stirred yet, and Garahan had no time to worry about going against what Miss Michaela advised. He had no choice—he had to tell the owner who'd sent him in order to whisk Miss Anderson to safety. "Lord Atwell sent me."

She spat on the floor, crossed her arms in front of her, and blew out a frustrated breath. "Well, I changed my mind. Atwell can't have her!"

Garahan raised an eyebrow in silent question, hoping she could see his expression in the dim light of the hallway.

"Leave now," she warned, "while you are still breathing."

Garahan was pleased to note the anger flaring to life in the woman's all-but-dead, black eyes. His silence was having the desired effect...it unnerved her.

He narrowed his eyes, letting the woman see the contempt and determination in his gaze as he sent a chilling message and promise of his own—*I'll see ye in hell first!*

She took a tiny step backward, and he knew he'd succeeded in intimidating her. Still, he did not advance. He waited to see how long it would take for her to brandish one of her knives. Shifting from foot to foot, she finally whipped the small blade from her sleeve and waved it at him.

Silently challenging her with the intensity of his gaze, he

watched her anger building to the point where he knew she would charge him. He kicked out with his right foot, and her weapon flew from her hand, landing a few feet away.

Eyes wide with shock, and a hint of fear, she reached for the blade in her apron and rushed him.

It would be too easy to rid her of the second knife. He decided to let her think she had the upper hand by not moving. Luring her closer, allowing her to think she had the drop on him, he let her take three steps before flicking the knife out of her hand with the back of his. He felt the nick of pain as the sharp blade sliced his hand. *Bugger it!* An injury, from a blade that long, was inevitable. The warmth of his blood seeping from the wound irritated the hell out of him. He glared at the woman he'd disarmed, but she didn't notice…she was staring in fascination as he slowly bled.

Never taking his eyes off her, he whipped his handkerchief out of his frockcoat pocket and wrapped it around the wound, curling his hand into a fist to keep the makeshift bandage in place. With his other hand, he reached into his pocket and retrieved the bag of coin, holding it up for her to see.

He expected a reaction, and got one. Her eyes were riveted on the bag and glazed over with greed. She reached for it, but he stuffed the bag back into his waistcoat. Staring at the slight bulge in the pocket, she grumbled, "I could have made a fortune with this one."

So close to achieving his goal, he had to assume the detached manner he and the other members of the duke's guard employed in difficult situations. Patience in the face of danger was another tactic they employed.

Just a little longer.

The woman's greedy expression shifted to one of malevolence. He felt pity for those who had been lured and trapped by this harpy. 'Twas coin she worshiped. The woman placed a value on human life as if it could be bought and sold. What had others suffered at the hands of this wretch?

After he delivered Miss Anderson to safety, he'd return and free any others being held here. And when he did, he would have the satisfaction of seeing this despicable woman being clapped in irons and hauled away.

His neutral expression did not change, as he hid his thoughts. No matter how long it took, he knew the lure of the coin would win the day for him. Waiting for her to make the exchange, he wondered if the woman would try to pass off another young woman in Miss Anderson's place. The only description he'd gotten from Miss Michaela was that the lass was uncommonly tall and slender, with platinum hair and blue eyes. He'd seen a number of blonde-haired women with blue eyes since he'd been in London—of all shapes and heights. What if the woman she produced only claimed to be Miss Anderson in order to escape? From the look in the boarding house owner's eyes, Garahan suspected she would lie if it suited her needs.

He clenched his jaw, to keep from telling the woman to hurry it up. Finally, his patience won out, and she spun on her heel, retracing her steps. She stopped to kick the still-unconscious man in the stomach, smirking when he emitted a groan of pain, warning Garahan that he'd be rousing soon. No matter—Garahan planned to be long gone by then.

Revealing her true colors, the woman deliberately stepped on the man's hand, cruelly pressing her considerable weight on it, before marching down the darkened hallway, mumbling to herself. She wrenched the door open and screamed, "Anderson, get out here…now!"

Nothing happened for a few moments. The boarding house owner screamed again and slammed a fist on the open door before stomping over the threshold, disappearing from sight. A loud commotion ensued, punctuated by a resounding crash. He rushed toward the door, but stopped in his tracks when the owner returned, dragging a tall, slender, blonde-haired, blue-eyed angel with a dirty face and a red handprint on her cheek.

His protective streak rushed through him at the rough treatment of the lass, and he nearly bit his tongue to keep from demanding to know who'd struck the young woman. But bloody hell, he'd given his word to remain silent, and except from being forced to speak when there was no one to deliver his message, he had and would continue to keep quiet.

He resumed his neutral expression, vibrating with the need to ask if she was indeed the Miss Anderson he'd come to rescue. Their eyes met across the room, and he knew that he would not leave without the poor young woman. He waited for the pair to reach his side before digging into his waistcoat pocket a second time for the bag of coin.

As she drew nearer, he noted the lass's eyes were wide with shock as she stared at him. Did she think he was paying to have her for the night? Had the poor woman been abused? He silently cursed a blue streak, waiting for the older woman to speak, while the need to spirit the lass away before the wretched woman changed her mind grew. He could explain things to her afterward.

"Tell Atwell this is the last time I'll accept payment to divert our fresh young women from Scarlet Ribbons or The Scarlet Boudoir!"

He motioned for the woman to release Miss Anderson to him with his injured hand. The lass blinked, finally breaking eye contact, only to stare at the blood-soaked handkerchief. What little color she had drained from her face. He hoped she wouldn't swoon; he still had to complete the transaction and get her out of here. He jiggled the coins.

The older woman grabbed hold of the leather bag and yanked, but he refused to let go until he had Miss Anderson in his protective custody.

"Those coins are mine!"

Garahan shook his head, and the woman shoved the lass at him. He wrapped a protective arm around her slender waist, cradling her to him, and had to call on all of his control to keep his mind off the woman nestled against his heart. He let go of the bag. While the harpy was occupied opening it and drooling over the coins, he ushered the lass outside, and shut the door behind them.

Leaning close, he rasped, "I was not at liberty to speak until I had ye safe in me arms, Miss Anderson. Me name's Garahan. 'Tis a short ride to Miss Michaela's. She's the one who asked me to liberate ye. From the fear in yer eyes, I'll be asking ye one thing only. Trust me, lass, and know that I mean ye no harm."

She gave him a speculative look, as if deciding whether or not to trust him. Unable to wait, he decided to go on faith that she would. Untying the reins, he introduced her to his horse. "This fine roan gelding is on loan to me while I'm stationed here in London. Laddie, meet Miss Anderson. Miss Anderson, me horse."

She gently stroked the horse's neck and whispered, "I have never met a horse as fine as you." His horse whickered in reply, and she added, "You are so beautiful."

Garahan struggled to break the spell her husky tone had woven around him. Clearing his throat, he urged, "We need to leave immediately." He put his hands around her lean waist and hid his shock—he could feel the lass's ribs! She needed a few of Mrs. O'Toole's hearty meals to gain her strength back. He lifted her onto the horse's back, pausing when a thought struck him. "Do ye need me to go back inside and collect yer belongings?"

"I no longer have belongings." A hint of worry flashed in the depths of her eyes before it disappeared. "How long will I be gone?"

Her question surprised him, as did his need to soothe her worry. "Ye'll not be returning here."

"I won't?"

"Nay, lass. As I said, Miss Michaela sent me to rescue ye."

A flicker of hope appeared and quickly died. "What of the others? There are three other young women who were tricked by the advert and promise of employment." She shifted as if she were going to dismount, and he stopped her, placing his hand on her leg. She stiffened, and what little color remained on her face vanished. "If you are going to go back inside, couldn't you free the others? Their freedom is more important than what little I brought with me on the journey."

"I do not have the coin to pay for their freedom, too."

Still, she shook her head. "They are younger than I, and innocent. Please take me back—mayhap Mrs. Underwood would take me in exchange for two, or all three!"

Her plea scraped across his raw gut. "If I give ye me word to return and free the lasses, will ye come with me now? The coin may not hold her attention as long as we need it to. If we linger, we may be putting the others in danger, lass."

She stopped squirming beneath his hand and sat still. "You promise to return for them?"

"I promise. Me word is me bond."

Finally, she inclined her head, agreeing.

He mounted behind her. Scanning the alleyway, he nodded to Burke, who lingered in the shadows as they left. "If it'll ease yer mind, I'll see to it what ye've lost is replaced."

She trembled in his arms. "You will never be able to replace what has been taken from me."

A combination of sorrow and anger filled him. The lass had all but told him she'd been taken against her will. He didn't know what to say to her, but he knew what his ma would have done. He pulled her onto his lap and held her to his heart. She did not resist—but he did not know if it was because she had learned not to resist, or because she felt safe with him. He hoped the steady beat of his heart would in some way calm her. She needed to understand that no matter what happened before this moment, it was now her past.

A sudden realization struck—he not only felt protective of her, he wanted to help her put her past behind her.

When he gauged that they were a safe enough distance away, he said, "As of right now, lass, yer past is just that. Ye have the rest of yer life ahead of ye. Don't be wasting it living in the past, holding the hurt to yer heart. Forgiving is hard, but possible if ye ask the Lord's help. Forgetting… Well now, that's something I've not yet mastered. But…I'm working on it. Open yer heart to the promise of the future." He could all but hear his words rattling around her brainbox. "I don't expect ye to agree yet, lass, but ask that ye think long and hard on me advice. 'Twas given to meself, and me older brothers, by the very wise woman who raised us and reminded us of her advice too many times to count growing up."

She quieted in his arms, and he hoped she believed him. He hadn't the first few times Ma had tried to convince him that a person could change—if they had faith in God, hope in their heart, and the courage and strength of a people who had suffered for years at the hands of their oppressors and had never given up!

Miss Anderson shivered again, and he tightened his arm around her. "I need to ask a favor of ye, lass. Are ye up to holding the reins for me? I couldn't tie off the handkerchief with one hand. It's slipping and needs to be tightened."

She shifted on his lap and did as he asked, while he brought his hand up to his mouth and clamped one end of the handker-chief between his teeth, yanking on the other with his free hand. He stifled a groan at the pain, not wanting to frighten the lass. The slash was deeper than he'd realized.

"Let me tie it off for you." Looping the reins over her arm and tucking them tight to her side, she reached for his hand and expertly tied off the bandage. Her eyes lifted to his, and she appeared to want to say something, but held back.

Humbled that she would offer to help him, he said, "I'm in yer debt, Miss Anderson." The unasked question in her eyes had him adding, "I always keep me promises and pay me debts, lass."

They fell silent as he led his horse through the darkened streets, winding their way through to a slightly better section of the stews where a few lampposts lit the way. He noted her slight weight against his chest and felt the overwhelming need to protect the lass. What surprised him was the need to do so for more than just tonight. It strengthened, deepened as they rode.

Though she may not have uttered the words, the way she leaned against him told him that she had begun to trust him.

Her breathing slowed, and he knew she slept. Unable to help himself, he lowered his chin to the top of her head and whispered, "Ye're under me protection now, lass. 'Tis yers, whether ye accept it or not."

As they rode, he wondered how long she had been held against her will. Now wasn't the time to question her, but he would be asking eventually. He knew Miss Michaela found positions for those she had a hand in rescuing. Whatever employment the angel of the streets found for the lass, he would pay the employer a visit to discern for himself whether he judged the person trustworthy. With his current assignment still in the early stages, he may not be able to visit the lass right away. He had yet to pinpoint the source of the most recent threat against one of the duke's distant cousins, Baron Summerfield.

As they approached the building, he gently woke her. "We're here, Miss Anderson." He dismounted and tied off the reins before sweeping her off the horse and into his arms. Her sharp intake of breath could mean one of two things: she was over-whelmed with his manly face and form—his preference—or her ribs were injured.

He quickly set her on her feet, and watched as she bit her bottom lip. The need to reassure her was nearly as strong as the need to protect her. "Miss Michaela will bind yer ribs for ye, lass. Then they won't pain ye as much."

She lifted her chin and met his gaze, and his body nearly betrayed him. He calmed the rapid beat of his heart and quelled the desire pulsing through his veins. Beneath the smudges of dirt across her forehead and chin was a beautiful woman. "Thank you for rescuing me, Mr. Garahan, but you should not have both-ered."

When the light in her eyes dimmed, he told her, "Try to remember the advice I gave ye, and remember, no one in this life deserves to be held against their will. We Irish know what it feels like to be held under the boot heel of our oppressors. Ye're well worth the bother, lass. And 'tis just Garahan...no mister." She nodded, and he said, "Now then, hold on a moment while I give the signal."

"Signal?"

Her interest eased his mind—the lass hadn't given up on the prospect of freedom...yet. "Aye." He gave three short raps with his knuckles against the door and waited. The single knock on the inside sounded, and the door opened.

The burly guard told him, "Miss Michaela was starting to fret."

Garahan frowned. "She needn't have. I told her I'd return with Miss Anderson."

The guard noticed the bloody bandage on Garahan's hand and nodded. "She expected something like this. She'll insist on tending to that knife wound after she sees to Miss Anderson."

"No need. I'll have me cousin tend to it when I get back to the duke's town house."

"Duke?" the lass asked. "I thought Miss Michaela was a woman from my class, not the upper class."

"I'll ask ye to kindly keep what I say between us. Miss Michaela could be in danger otherwise."

Eyes wide, the young woman nodded. "I will. I promise."

Garahan inclined his head and motioned for her to precede him up the staircase. He wanted to be prepared to catch her in case she swooned. He needn't have worried—Miss Anderson made it to the top without swaying. She was pluckier than he thought.

At the door, he greeted the petite woman holding it open. "Miss Michaela, meet Miss Anderson. I...er...need to tell ye that I mostly kept me word and didn't say anything to the woman."

Michaela motioned for Miss Anderson to enter the room, before meeting Garahan's gaze. "Oh?"

He had to get it off his chest. "I had to dispatch the only person available to deliver the message about Atwell."

Instead of upbraiding him, as he thought she might, she searched his face, then stared at his hands. She reached for his wrist and yanked him into the room. "Didn't I warn you about her knives?"

"In me experience, there are times when ye're bound to get nicked disarming a miscreant."

"That amount of blood is not from a nick." She turned to Miss Anderson and said, "I need to unwrap this to see how deep the slash is before I check you for injuries. Would you please have a seat?"

"I'm fine," the lass assured her, glancing about the room. He watched her stiffen and then sigh when she spotted the blue and white ceramic pitcher and bowl. "Would you mind if I washed my hands and face first?"

"Not at all. There is hot water in the pitcher, two rounds of soap, and fresh linens next to the bowl."

"Two?" she asked.

"Rose and lavender scented."

The lass's voice broke. "And I may use the soap?"

Garahan noticed the tears welling in her eyes—and understanding in Miss Michaela's.

"Of course—use both if you wish."

"Thank you," Miss Anderson whispered.

"You're welcome."

Now that she had been safely delivered to Miss Michaela, Garahan needed to leave and give his report to King and Coventry—in person. If the wrong person intercepted a missive discussing Miss Michaela, she would be in grave danger. The temptation to pull his arm out of her grasp was great, but he could not. To do so may inadvertently cause her injury. He'd been raised to never harm a lass—whether she be Irish or not!

"Please sit down, Garahan. This will only take a moment." True to her words, Miss Michaela had the bloody cloth removed quickly and was studying the wound. "I'll need to sew this closed."

"I appreciate the offer, but me cousin'll tend it for me when I return to the town house."

She placed her hands on her hips and glared at him. "You may be bigger and far stronger than me, Garahan, but you run the same risk of losing too much blood, as I would, from such a wound."

When he reluctantly sat, she gently pressed a thick, folded linen on his hand and turned to gather what she needed.

"Ye'll see to the lass first." When she didn't answer, he rose to his feet, pressed a hand to the linen so it wouldn't fall off, and took a step closer. His hope to intimidate the woman failed. He had to swallow his snort of laughter, watching her green eyes flash with temper.

"Fine!" She reached for a length of linen, wrapped it around his hand, and secured it. "Please wait downstairs while I examine Miss Anderson for injuries."

"Oh, but I'm fine," the lass said.

"What about yer ribs?"

"Garahan, please leave—now!"

He ignored Michaela and stared at Miss Anderson. "When I put ye on me horse, ye gritted yer teeth and drew in a sharp breath, while yer face lost what little color it had. Ye could have cracked a rib."

When it looked as if the lass would continue to contradict him, Miss Michaela spoke up. "Do you realize this is only the second time I have had difficulty doing my job in the past few years?" Her cheeks flushed and her eyes gleamed with temper. "Do you want to know why, Garahan?"

Faith, she was just the woman to stand up against his cousin! He couldn't wait to introduce Miss Michaela to Emmett. "I have a feeling ye'll be telling me no matter if I want to hear it or not."

"It was the day your brother arrived to in answer to Alasdair's summons to collect Miss Waring—"

He interrupted, "'Tis *Mrs. Garahan.*"

The soft gasp had him glancing at the lass, who stared at him wide-eyed. He winked at her and turned back to Miss Michaela. He really should stop riling the woman. Her only crime was disagreeing with him. "Beg pardon for interrupting—ye were saying?"

She raised her eyes to the ceiling and her lips were moving—was she counting, or praying? Finally, she said, "Miss Anderson, when you are finished, please take a seat." She turned back to Garahan. "You have a head of granite just like your brothers James and Alasdair!"

He smiled. "Granite, is it? Well now, since ye've complimented me—rather than insult me with the comparison—I believe I'll go speak to yer man at the door while I wait for yer summons."

Michaela narrowed her eyes. "Greenwood will know to use force, if necessary, to keep you here until I see to your hand."

He met her direct look with one of his own. He was about to disagree when the musical sound of water distracted him. Miss Anderson's soft sigh of pleasure had him wondering if she'd been denied clean water and soap to wash with.

The lass finished her ablutions and turned around. Her gaze met his, and it felt as if one of his brothers had plowed their head into his gut. While he struggled to drag in a breath, he could not help but stare. Scrubbed clean, her face was the color of fresh cream, with a sprinkling of freckles across the bridge of her nose. The only thing marring her beauty was the deep purple bruise forming on her cheek, where the red handprint had been.

She wrinkled her nose. "Did I miss a spot of dirt?"

Michaela shook her head. "No, but you have a deep bruise forming on your cheek. I'll prepare a compress for it. Have a seat, please." Turning to Garahan, she said, "Before I forget, ask Greenwood about the two men lurking nearby right after you left."

Surprise mingled with irritation, but he knew he'd already pressed Miss Michaela harder than he should have. Still, he had to remind her, "Ye should have said something earlier."

"You need that poor excuse for a bandage changed. And

before you think to chase off in the direction the men headed, I'll have your word that you will not leave here until I have sewn that wound closed. If it is not cleaned out properly—"

Garahan interrupted before she worked up another head of steam. "Ye sound just like O'Malley. He blathers on about dire consequences, and wound care, until the lot of us give in and do what he asks."

Michaela lifted her chin to a defiant angle. "I suggest you do the same for me. I seem to recall the story that O'Malley saved your cousin Sean's life, as well as his arm."

Chastised, he sighed. "Forgive me, Miss Michaela, for sounding exasperated with ye. Ye have the right of it. I wasn't there at the time, but we've all heard 'twas Emmett's skill, the duke's physician, and a former surgeon in the King's Dragoons, combined with Mignonette's care, that saved Sean's life—not to mention his arm."

"Mignonette?" Miss Anderson asked.

He smiled at her. "Aye, Sean's wife."

"Such a lovely name."

Michaela studied Miss Anderson before replying, "So is your name, Aimee. You aren't going to be leaving until I check for injuries. Sit before I am compelled to make you sit, while I shoo Garahan downstairs."

The lass sat.

Garahan walked to the door, and Michaela reminded him, "Do not leave, Garahan!"

"Faith, woman, ye sound just like me ma. Even she knows not to ask after I've given me word."

Miss Michaela preened. "What a lovely compliment."

He stood on the threshold and grumbled, "'Twasn't a compliment."

◆◇◆◇◆

CHAPTER THREE

AIMEE CLENCHED HER hands in her lap to keep them from shaking. She had heard whispers of the angel of the streets, but she had not believed them until Miss Michaela had opened the door.

She was still in a state of semi-shock from all that had transpired in the last few days, and her rescuer's presence rattled her. His dark hair and dark eyes—so similar to the man who'd taken everything from her—had her stomach threatening to rebel. In the last few years, she had learned to distinguish truth from lies— but only after she had suffered the consequences of her naivete. She would be forever regarded as damaged goods, not fit to employ in one of the better households—nor would she ever be considered fit to be the wife of a good man. Her shame would follow her to the grave.

She hadn't realized Miss Michaela had spoken to her until she felt the slight weight of the other woman's hand on her shoulder. "I was woolgathering," she fibbed.

"You are safe now," Michaela told her. "Remember that. You never have to go back to that boarding house, nor to the life you were escaping by answering that advert."

Shocked, Aimee asked, "How did you know about the advert?"

"You would be surprised what facts I glean while helping

those in similar situations."

Aimee needed to ask, had to know: "Why are you so willing to help, when others are so quick to condemn?"

Michaela sighed. "When my mother passed away, I was lost. My father is a renowned physician, and he let me stay by his side while he treated members of the *ton*. I soaked up everything he said and did, and begged him to let me study further, rather than be forced to set my knowledge and training aside to wed a man who expected me to grace his arm and his table when entertaining his peers."

"Then you are not one of us," Aimee murmured.

"I beg to differ. Over the past few years, I have used every means necessary—monetarily and with my knowledge of healing—to help young women who have been cast aside, injured, violated, and treated as if they were of no consequence. It is my life's ambition and work. I am definitely one of you."

Miss Michaela's words soothed Aimee's fears, as did the lack of venom in what should have been a proper dressing-down from her savior. Aimee had been on the receiving end of many since the accident that left her a poor relation, dependent upon the largesse of her relatives.

"The only thing I ask of those I aid is that they do not speak of me, or what I have done for them," Michaela continued. "I would be labeled a charlatan for doctoring others, and a woman of loose morals for allowing a handful of men to protect the women I save—and myself—from those who enslaved them."

Tears filled Aimee's eyes, and she let them fall. "I am sorry to have passed judgment without knowledge of who you are and what you have done for those before me. Forgive me."

Michaela rubbed her eyes and the back of her neck. "I am normally not so easily agitated. I recently lost a gifted healer and protector. I miss his ability to remain calm no matter the circumstances." She slowly smiled. "He would have had something pithy to say in his Scots burr if he heard how I spoke to you just now. I am terribly sorry."

"There is no need to apologize. What happened to him? Was it a carriage accident or footpad?"

Michaela's eyes lit with merriment. "Nay, he recently married."

Aimee laughed, then gasped, as a sharp pain sliced through her.

"If it pains you to draw in a breath, you could have a cracked or broken rib. No more of such talk until after you describe what happened to you on your journey to London and since you arrived. I need to ensure you do not have any other injuries."

Aimee did not quite know where to begin—should she mention the dark-haired lord who'd swept her off her feet, the one she'd pledged her heart and her life to?

"Please remember I have never, and will never, judge anyone I rescue. I am a healer—I am not your judge, nor jury. I am a good listener and have heard so many stories of young women like yourself who have been misled and mistreated. Some abused emotionally, more that have been abused physically…" Michaela paused, and for a few moments she was silent, until she cleared her throat and rasped, "Many, so many more who have been violated through no fault of their own."

Aimee did not realize she was weeping until Michaela handed her a large handkerchief and sat on the chair beside her. Unable to hold back, she gave in to the tears. As she cried, she realized the wisdom in Mrs. Potts's advice to let the tears come. She had foolishly ignored the advice, holding her pain close to her heart.

Michaela gently took the soaked handkerchief from her, replacing it with a dry one. Exhausted, but no longer bitter or angry, Aimee realized the tears she'd bottled inside of her for the last few years had begun to cleanse the wound to her body, and the black mark she felt on her soul. She blew her nose and met the petite woman's gaze. "Thank you. I had been shuffled about as the poor relation for more years than I can remember. I was desperate to escape the life I had been expected to lead as a scullery maid to my distant cousin. When I met Lord Wolfingham—" Her voice hitched, and she dug deep to continue. "He was a friend of my cousin, so charming and handsome. He sought me out, not the other way around. I knew it would be frowned upon not only because I was a poor relation, but also because my cousin's peers thought I was a member of his staff. But he was so charming."

She closed her eyes to collect herself, and to speak of a time that had cruelly scarred her. "I was seven and ten at the time. No one had ever paid such lavish attention to me before. It went to my head and my heart so quickly, I could hardly speak, let alone put two thoughts together."

When Michaela reached for her hand, Aimee sensed it was not only to offer comfort, but to share something from her past.

"If my head and heart had not been swept away by the need to doctor those in need," Michaela confided, "I may have lost it to some titled gentleman who would never care what my dreams were, nor what I hoped to accomplish in life. It would be expected that I bow to his dictates and do whatever my husband told me to do."

Aimee saw a fleeting glimpse of pain quickly covered, and said, "You deserve to have happiness, too, Miss Michaela. I often wondered if my cousin would have kept his promise to find a suitable husband for me. But I couldn't wait—I had to follow my heart, though I knew he would never accept me back into his home if I eloped."

Michaela tightened her grip. "Wolfingham never married you, did he?"

Aimee bit her lip to keep from dissolving into more tears. *Will I ever run dry?* "We were halfway to the inn at Gretna Green when he spoke of love and the years we would be together…and then he—" The urge to shut down and not speak of what happened was great, but the need to unburden her soul and leave it in the past, as Garahan had advised her to do, was greater. "He anticipated his vows and forced himself on me. When he was finished, he buttoned the placket on his trousers and spoke of the gowns and jewels he would shower me with—the house he would set me up in."

"The blackguard never intended marriage, did he?"

"I thought he was the answer to my prayers—instead, he was the instrument of my ruin." She lifted her gaze to Michaela's, relieved to find understanding, not condemnation. "I'll never be seen as anything but damaged goods."

"From the moment Garahan liberated you from that den of iniquity, you have been given a second chance at life—a chance to reach for happiness. If not happiness...at least contentment. If you are brave enough to grasp it with both hands."

Aimee shook her head. "It sounds as if it is attainable, but you do not understand what it feels like to suffer the shame, the degradation."

"I was eight and ten the one time I decided to appease my father and allow myself to be courted by a gentleman he approved of."

Aimee's gut twisted. Had this beautiful woman—the angel of the streets—suffered as she had? She wrapped her hands around Michaela's.

Tear-filled eyes met hers as understanding flowed between them.

"He waited until my head was in the clouds after my first waltz with him before he led me into the garden, luring me the promise of listening to my dreams—in the privacy of the gardens."

Aimee squeezed Michaela's hands and let them go so the woman could dry her own tears. "He lied to you."

"The bastard."

"He took you against your will." It wasn't a question.

Michaela nodded. "He seduced me with soft kisses and whispered words until I shared my dream of healing others. He was incensed, accusing me of playing fast and loose with him and his reputation. Then he accused me of never intending to become a proper wife, as Society dictated. After...after he was through, he adjusted his clothing and told me no one would ever want a woman who thought herself intelligent enough to seek what was a man's profession…let alone damaged goods. He spun on his heel and walked away."

"He stole your dreams, your dignity, and your virtue," Aimee rasped. "I am so sorry I doubted that you understood. Thank you for being so courageous in sharing your story with me. I vow to tell no one, nor will I ever breathe a word about those you save from the streets. Garahan is right—you are an angel."

Michaela stood. "We'd best see to your ribs and whatever else is paining you, Miss Anderson—"

"Aimee. I'd like to think that we are kindred spirits, forged by the dire circumstances we both suffered."

The other woman nodded. "We are. Please call me Michaela."

Aimee was subdued while Michaela bound her cracked ribs. Finding no other injuries, she prepared the poultice for the bruise on Aimee's face. "Do you recall a specific shop name in the advert?"

"No. Just that it was a fashionable London shop. On the carriage ride, I dreamed of the millinery where I would begin working as a shopgirl and eventually be apprenticed, helping to create beautiful hats."

"Were you forced against your will at any time on the journey here, or after?"

Aimee shook her head. "No. It was just the one time."

Michaela nodded. "As it was with me. You do not have to give up hope of finding someone who will love and care for you, Aimee. There are many good and kind men who will not censure you for being an unwilling victim. In fact, once you are brave enough to share what happened to you, they will be fierce in their protection of you. If you find a man of compassion and strength that you are willing to trust, you will discover that what you experienced had nothing to do with love, and everything to do with control."

"Have you found that someone?" Aimee asked.

Michaela shook her head. "Not yet, but I have someone who encouraged me, as I am encouraging you not to give up hope. To live your life and know that you are not damaged. You are a worthy person from the top of head to soles of your feet."

Aimee hugged Michaela. "'Thank you' doesn't seem like enough."

"Trust me," Michaela told her. "It is more than enough. I think we can call Garahan back now. Do not think you are required to discuss anything other than the fact that you answered an advert with free transportation to London. He knows that you have been abused from the bruise on your cheek. I have been reassured by Alasdair Cameron that Garahan is a protector of innocents, as are his brothers and cousins. They are part of the Duke of Wyndmere's private guard. The sixteen men who have vowed to put life and limb on the line to see that no harm comes to the duke and his family."

Aimee met her gaze and nodded. "I'm ready to tell him what happened, so he can go back and rescue the others."

Michaela frowned. "How many others?"

"Three, but I overheard Mrs. Underwood mention they were expecting two more…and they are far younger than me."

"You can tell Garahan while I take care of his wound. It will save time, and then he can be on his way."

"Do you think he can manage if injured?" Aimee asked.

Michaela had her hand on the doorknob when she answered, "I do, but it would be best if he had someone guarding his back."

✧◆✦◆✧

CHAPTER FOUR

G ARAHAN CULLED THE information he needed from Green-wood, who hesitated at first, until Garahan mentioned his connection with Captain Coventry. Apparently Coventry had more contacts than either he or his cousins were aware of. As soon as he questioned Miss Anderson, he would be on his way to meet with Coventry and King.

He had to ignore the feelings rioting inside of him concerning the lass. He'd rescued others before and felt protective of them…but not like *this*. The wounded look in her eyes drew him to her. He suspected that she had been compromised by a man she trusted, then lured to London by those not offering gainful employment. What they offered was employment in a far more volatile trade that would add to the heavy burden he sensed she carried…so heavy it could destroy her!

He was still sorting through what he'd witnessed at the boarding house and observed on the ride back to Miss Michaela's. It ignited a fire inside of him to avenge the lass. The conflagration threatened to consume him. Of his three older brothers, James's story was the closest to what he'd encountered a short while ago. Was this what James had felt after rescuing Melinda? Had he felt torn between honoring his vow to the duke, and yet doing all in his power to shield and protect the woman he'd rescued?

Garahan had never experienced this onslaught of feelings

bombarding him, distracting his thoughts—threatening to distract his actions. He called on his steely control and cleared his mind, concentrating on his duty to the duke. As a member of the Duke of Wyndmere's guard, it was expected that he would answer any and all summons from Captain Coventry and Gavin King, while performing his duties to the duke. At times, assignments he received were connected to protecting the duke and his family. To his knowledge, the summons from King to rescue Miss Anderson was not.

He rubbed the back of his neck, but the tension persisted. He'd done as King asked, and the only thing left to do was give his report in person. Committing it to writing and having it intercepted by the wrong individuals could be catastrophic. As much as he wanted to be involved in Miss Anderson's recovery, he would have to leave that in Miss Michaela's hands.

But what then? Leave her to her own defenses? Would Michaela encourage her to return home, or find suitable work that was not tied to the underbelly of London?

"You're not the first man who answered Miss Michaela's plea for help."

Garahan met Greenwood's gaze. "From what I was told, I won't be the last."

Greenwood shrugged. "You can plug one hole in the dam, but another leak will appear. Plug that, and suddenly three more appear."

Garahan appreciated the metaphor—his da had said something similar years ago, when his uncle, Patrick O'Malley, died. Setting the memory of that time aside, he said, "Ye're saying no matter how many times Miss Michaela rescues a young woman, three more will need rescuing."

The other man nodded.

"There are too many participants involved in the luring of young lasses to London."

"Aye. Before Cameron married, he explained that he'd discovered a number of boarding houses suspected to be the first stop when the lasses arrive."

"Go on," Garahan urged.

Greenwood vibrated with anger. "A source told him these boarding houses train the girls for employment in a select few brothels—ones that cater to individuals with *specific* tastes."

Garahan had suspected something like this. Having it confirmed raised a red flag inside his brain. He would not let this happen to the lass—nor the others he suspected had been hidden from sight when he was buying the lass's freedom under the guise of purchasing her for Lord Atwell.

And who in the bloody hell *was* Atwell?

"Thank ye for telling me, Greenwood. Cameron's trusted by me brother and by Tremayne—"

Greenwood interrupted, "One of the captain's men."

Garahan nodded in response. "How much longer before Miss Michaela's finished?"

"Depends on the injuries—physical and emotional."

Emotional. He hadn't thought of that. *Poor lass.*

"Are you in a hurry?" the guard asked.

"I have a meeting shortly and need to report in first."

Greenwood did not ask whom he was meeting, nor whom he would be reporting to. Smart man. The less he knew, the easier it would be to keep Miss Michaela safe.

While they waited, Garahan wondered what information the night would provide. He anticipated a response from one of his contacts on the docks, and was to meet him at midnight. He hoped the man had information about the threat to destroy the duke's cousin. More importantly, whether the threat was physical or verbal. Garahan would be prepared to act in either event.

The last thing he needed was the distraction of the blue-eyed angel with a bruise blossoming on her cheek...and he suspected far more that he could not see on her heart. They said the eyes mirrored what was inside a person—if that were true, the lass's reflected pain and suffering.

At Miss Michaela's summons, he ascended the stairs and

crossed the threshold. The tension surrounding Miss Anderson was gone, and he was glad for it. "Now that Miss Michaela has seen to yer injuries, I need ye to answer a few questions before I leave ye in her care."

Her delicate complexion paled until her freckles were noticeably darker. He reached out a hand to steady her and urged, "Sit down before ye fall down, lass."

She slumped onto the nearest chair, increasing his worry. Did she fear his questions…or him? Instead of asking her outright, he asked Miss Michaela, "Should she not be sitting straight to keep the strain off her ribs?"

"Yes, she should. Miss Anderson, please remember not to bend, even the slightest bit. It prevents the bones from healing properly."

Garahan noticed the lass straightened but did not lift her head. She stared at her hands. He didn't have the time to coax the young woman into trusting him with what may very well have been a horrifying experience for her. "Miss Michaela, would ye reassure the lass that I mean no harm, but need her to answer me questions?"

"Of course. Miss Anderson—*Aimee*, Garahan must report to his superiors before returning to his other duties. Please answer his questions."

The young woman lifted her head and nodded to Miss Michaela, but she had yet to look directly at him. At this rate, it would be another hour before he got the answers he needed. "'Tisn't that I am trying to rush ye, lass, but to tell the truth, me hand has bled through the bandage. 'Tis an annoyance that I don't need."

She stared at the blood-soaked bandage wrapped around his hand and gasped. "Forgive me, Mr. Garahan!" She turned to Michaela. "I did not mean to take so much of your time when poor Mr. Garahan needed you to tend to his wound."

He sighed. "I thought we agreed, 'tis just Garahan."

The lass rose from her seat, ignoring him. "Michaela, what

can I do to help?"

When he rose too, Michaela asked the lass, "Why don't you sit next to Garahan, Aimee?" She complied, and Michaela turned back to stare at him. "Garahan, please sit down. Aimee will be happy to answer your questions." He was about to disagree when the woman added, "He'll need the distraction while I cleanse and stitch his wound closed."

He'd later swear to O'Malley that the lass had faded to the point where he could see the veins beneath her fair skin and the shadow of her bones! "Thank ye for yer concern, Miss Michaela, but 'tisn't necessary. King knows that however long it takes me to do as he asked, I'll be reporting to him on Bow Street."

"Bow Street?" Miss Anderson asked.

"Aye, he's in charge of a group of highly experienced Runners. He's trustworthy and a man ye'd want to have at yer back in times of trouble." He flinched when Michaela began to cleanse the deep wound on his hand. Their eyes met and he apologized. "Forgive me. I was thinking of King and what he'd need to know. I'll hold still for ye."

She inclined her head, then asked, "Do you by any chance have a flask with you? It might help stave off the pain if you have a sip or two."

He smiled. "It so happens that I keep one in the pocket of me waistcoat for times such as these."

Michaela waited for him to take a swig. If he hadn't been in their company, he would have gulped it down. He didn't want them to wonder if he'd become foxed—who knew what really went through the minds of females? He did not want to add to what he imagined both women had gone through. 'Twas rumored that the angel of the streets herself had been ill treated, which explained her overwhelming need to save other young women. "Now then, lass…er, Miss Anderson, do ye remember the wording of the advert, or any name mentioned?"

He was pleased to note Miss Anderson seemed more at ease when she answered, "As I told Michaela, the advert stated it had well-paying positions with fashionable London merchants."

"Was that all it said? No particular shops were mentioned?"

She stared at her hands for a few moments before lifting her head and meeting his gaze. "I should have been more wary of the other part, but I wanted desperately to leave everything behind me."

He wondered what would make a young woman that desperate, but instead asked, "What part?" When she hesitated, he said, "Ye would be helping other lasses like yerself, if ye could trust me enough to tell me the rest. The only way to stop this from happening again is to find the source and put an end to it." Greenwood's words sliced through him—he'd be plugging one, possibly two leaks. How in the bloody hell would he plug them all?

Eyes the color of a summer sky met his, and he had to save himself before drowning in the endless blue. "They were seeking country girls who were not afraid of hard work," she explained. "The advert said transportation to London would be provided."

Suppressing the need to swear, he nodded. But *bugger it*, he wanted to get to the bottom of who was luring these young women to London! "Do ye remember a name or address in the advert?"

"It said to write to Mrs. Underwood, in care of Underwood's Boarding House."

Garahan frowned. Thanks to Michaela, he knew the location of the boarding house and the harpy who owned it. Though the lass did not even have a shawl with her when they left, he needed to ask, "Do ye still have the advert?"

"It was taken from me when I arrived at the boarding house, along with my reticule and portmanteau containing…" Her eyes welled with tears, but she blinked them away. "If you could somehow find my mother's locket… It's all I have left of her."

The abject sorrow in her eyes kicked him in the gut. When he returned to the boarding house to free the others, he'd retrieve her belongings. Mayhap he could convince O'Malley to go with him. From there he could continue to the docks and his late-night meeting. "I cannot make any promises, ye understand, but I'll do me best, Miss Anderson."

Hope shone in the depths of her expressive eyes. "And you'll free the others?"

"Aye, lass."

"Thank you."

"Remember that I cannot make any promises about yer locket."

"I understand. Thank you, Garahan."

"Ye'd be welcome, then—Bloody hell!" The needle piercing his skin hurt like blazes. "Beg pardon, Miss Michaela, Miss Anderson." He clamped his jaw shut and waited for Michaela to finish sewing the wound closed and bandage it. "Thank ye." He rose to his feet and bowed to the women. "Ye may not see the whites of me eyes until tomorrow or the next day, but do not fret. I shall return, Miss Anderson."

He crossed the room and grabbed the edge of the door, but a small sound had him pausing to glance over his shoulder. He froze, captivated by the image of the two women illuminated by candlelight. The purity of their hearts shone as brightly as the flame. In that moment, he silently vowed to do all in his power to help them. One last nod and he closed the door.

His heart raced as his protective instincts roared to the surface once more. His mind made up, he descended the stairs. He'd either break down the door to the boarding house or slip in unnoticed. With God as his witness, he'd not leave until he freed the three young women and found the lass's locket. But he did not relish the thought of a blade between his ribs, so he'd convince O'Malley to accompany him.

He nodded to Greenwood, and for the second time that night, he waited to hear the snick of the lock before mounting his horse. Leaning close to the horse's ear, he said, "King's probably pacing, waiting for me. After I'm finished on Bow Street, we'll head home to yer stable, where there'll be an extra apple and handful of oats."

His horse whinnied, and Garahan smiled. Life should always be this simple. A man talking to his horse...and his horse answering.

KING WAS INDEED pacing when Garahan knocked on the open door. "I was about to send Thompson to see what was keeping you. Did you deliver Miss Anderson to Miss Michaela?"

"Aye, and ye should know by now that if I don't show up in the time frame ye think it'll take me, 'tis because something happened."

King noticed the bandage. "Did that happen at the boarding house or in one of the alleyways?"

"Boarding house. I had no choice but to deflect the fair-sized blade the owner was determined to skewer me with."

The older man studied him closely. "Any other injuries?"

"'Tisn't an injury—'tis an inconvenient scratch."

King chuckled. "One that needed threads, no doubt, or it wouldn't be bandaged. Miss Michaela's handiwork?"

"Aye, she can be a mite stubborn and wouldn't let me leave until she was satisfied it was clean and she'd used twice as many stitches as O'Malley would have."

"I take it there was no trouble locating Miss Anderson."

"After I handled the man guarding the front door, I had a bit of a wait while Mrs. Underwood went into the back to fetch Miss Anderson. I heard other voices, and Miss Anderson confirmed there are three other lasses in need of rescuing and the possibility of two more—much younger—arriving tonight. I gave me word and will be going back to free them...all of them!"

King frowned. "Did you see any of them?"

"Nay, just Miss Anderson, who had a red handprint on her cheek."

"Anything else?"

"I'm thinking her ribs are either bruised or cracked. She flinched when I lifted her onto me horse. I have information I'm thinking will add to what ye need to take down this ring of kidnappers." Garahan filled King in on what Miss Anderson remembered about the advert, and then mentioned his plan to enlist O'Malley's aid and return to the boarding house.

"Will you be delivering the other young women you plan to rescue to Miss Michaela?"

"I think 'twould be best. She has a gentle way about her, and the man guarding her door is no pushover."

King grinned. "Couldn't get the drop on him?"

Garahan shook his head. "Took his measure and decided 'twould be better not to take him out—Miss Michaela and the lass would need him standing guard. By the by, do ye know of a Lord Atwell?"

The tic under King's left eye gave away the fact that he did.

"I'm wondering why Miss Michaela would have anything to do with a man who collects blue-eyed blondes for his personal use."

King rubbed the back of his neck. "What I am about to say must not leave this room."

"Ye have me word."

King nodded. "Atwell is not the man's real name, nor is he a lord at all. His much younger cousin was lured to London under similar false pretenses. He was not able to rescue her in time."

Garahan's heart ached for the man's loss. "Being a member of the *ton* is a ruse, then?"

"Aye. I cannot reveal anything more. Know that he is an ally—not a foe."

Garahan bade King goodbye, but stopped when the older man asked, "Are you expecting trouble?"

"Faith, me ma told the four of us to always be ready for trouble. After I drop off the lasses and enlist one or two of me contacts to stand guard with Greenwood, I'll be meeting another on the docks—at midnight."

"Regarding the threat to Summerfield." It wasn't a question.

"Aye, it has been three days since I asked him to ferret out what he could. He'll have a lead for me. Do ye want me to stop by on me way back to the duke's town house?"

King frowned. "We should have had the culprit pinned down by now. It feels off—someone must be tipping off whoever is behind this."

"I'll return as soon as I am able."

"Excellent."

Garahan was halfway through the door when King called out, "Try not to get stabbed again tonight."

"I wasn't stabbed," Garahan corrected him. "I deflected the blade."

He could hear King's laughter as he strode down the long hallway.

Outside, he nodded to the Runner standing guard and mounted his horse. There were not as many carriages now as there would be later when the evening's entertainments would begin. He urged his horse into a fast trot, mindful of pedestrians and others on horseback.

Garahan found O'Malley where he expected to at this hour of the night—guarding the perimeter. His cousin walked over to him. Noting the bandage on Garahan's hand, he asked, "Where did ye run into trouble?"

Garahan noticed the stable master approaching and waved him over. After ensuring his horse would get the promised treat and a rubdown, he turned to answer O'Malley.

"'Tis a long story. We'd best find Findley to let him know we've a bit of housekeeping to do. Will ye be wanting to choose two footmen to take our shifts, or leave that to Findley?"

"Depends on where we're headed," O'Malley said, "and how long ye expect the chore to take."

"If we're able to sneak in through the back, not long." Garahan met his cousin's questioning look with one of determination. "If we have to break down the door, it may take a bit longer. She'll have had time to replace the guard I took out of commission."

O'Malley grinned. "Did ye now? With a right cross or upper-cut?"

Garahan grumbled, "Neither. The man thought I'd be an easy mark and grabbed hold of me."

"Ah, ye spun around and put him in a headlock." His cousin nodded his approval. "Wise choice, but not as satisfying as a good, clean blow to the face. Does this have anything to do with the missive from Coventry, or the summons from King?"

"King…as a favor to Miss Michaela," Garahan answered.

O'Malley's eyes gleamed with interest. "I've heard yer brother James speak of the lass in hushed tones. She's part healer, part savior of young women."

"That she is. I'll be needing ye to act as me reinforcement. The proprietress carries two blades."

"Ye were in a bawdy house?"

"Nay…boarding house," Garahan replied. "Though I'm thinking 'tis a front for one. They lure country lasses to London with the promise of employment in a fashionable merchant's shop—even provide transportation."

"What lass in her right mind would believe that there wouldn't be strings—especially if the transportation was free?"

"Not a one from back home, Emmett."

His cousin sighed. "There's times it feels as if we've been here for a year—and other times it feels like the dozen it has been. Still, I haven't forgotten the sharp-tongued lasses from County Cork, with their long-lashed, bright green eyes and winsome smiles."

"Aye," Garahan agreed. "Those of us from Tipperary, Dublin, Cork, and Wexford all agree that the lasses back home are sharp-tongued, but God help me, they're strong enough to fight beside their men and protect their families."

"Me brother Finn was lucky to find a sweet Irish lass like Mollie Malloy."

Garahan snorted. "Sweet? I heard she ran the others ragged trying to rescue Finn from the smugglers, when all along it was that crooked excise official that got the better of him!"

"Bloody bugger forced her to stand there on the platform as they placed the noose around me brother's neck!"

Garahan's eyes narrowed. "James was there with Coventry's men to save Finn."

O'Malley curled his hands into fists. "From what Finn said, James, Tremayne, and Hennessey arrived in the nick of time." He slowly relaxed his hands and added, "By the by, Finn's description of his firebrand of a wife was that she's the strongest woman he knows—a warrior goddess, with an angel's face and the devil's own temper."

Garahan sighed. "I'm not ready to even think of following in either of yer brothers' or me own's footsteps by marrying anytime soon. When, and if, I do, 'twill be to a fine and feisty Irish lass."

O'Malley heartily agreed. "One with eyes as green as the hills back home and hair that rivals the setting sun."

"And freckles across the bridge of her nose." The words were out before Garahan could call them back.

His cousin stared at him as if waiting for him to continue, but Garahan would bite off the tip of his tongue before he dug himself a deeper hole. The lass that popped up in his mind was not from Ireland. With a name like Anderson, 'twasn't likely she'd have a drop of Irish blood in the tip of her pinky.

"We'd best let Findley know what we're about, then. Should we alert Mrs. O'Toole to expect us not to come home empty-handed?" O'Malley asked.

Garahan shook his head. "We'll bring any lasses we rescue straight to Miss Michaela. She's a skilled healer." Watching the interest in his cousin's eyes, he added, "I'm thinking she's not only compassionate about saving young women who have been sorely mistreated, or lured into circumstances beyond their control…" He let his words trail off, unsure if he should confide what he thought may have happened. If he was wrong, it may malign Miss Michaela's character.

"Ye know I would never think less of any woman whose been

mistreated. 'Tis our calling to rescue others," O'Malley said. "And more—mine to heal them. Ye think Miss Michaela's been a victim of abuse."

Garahan nodded. "Aye. Though she's risen above it, and made it her life's work to tend to those who have no one else to care for them or about them, pulling them off the streets."

O'Malley met his gaze. "Like James's wife."

"Aye," Garahan agreed. "Like Melinda. And like me sister-in-law, I'm thinking Miss Michaela could use someone strong to protect her. I'll be checking in on her from time to time, but I'm not gifted as a healer like yerself."

O'Malley's eyes narrowed with suspicion. "Are ye after pushing me at the lass?"

Garahan kept a straight face when he answered, "Nay. Ye remember Alasdair Cameron?"

"The Scot. Aye."

"He not only helped her with the more difficult injuries that require strength—like putting Melinda's shoulder back in the socket—but he acted as her protector."

O'Malley's eyes blazed—not with anger, but purpose. "Findley's guarding the interior. Let's have a word with him. He's been working with us long enough to know which footmen we prefer having guard the town house during the evening hours."

A quarter of an hour later, they were on their way to the lair of the woman Garahan thought of as a despoiler of innocents. One who lured young lasses from the country to the heart of London's dark side, where she would sell their bodies—and their souls—to the highest bidder.

※ ◇ ※

CHAPTER FIVE

MICHAELA SIGHED AND shook her head. "Does it matter how I found out you needed rescuing, Aimee?"

"My cousin never bothered to search for me after his friend convinced me to run away with him. I have no idea what Wolfingham told my cousin, but after the way he treated me, I know it was not the truth. As a poor relation, I have no other relatives that would claim me."

Aimee and Michaela had been talking nonstop since Garahan had left a short while ago. They had suffered similarly at the hands of men they mistakenly put their trust in. It bonded them, forming a kinship that was fast on its way to becoming a friendship. Aimee prodded Michaela to tell her who would have been concerned enough to find her.

Finally, Michaela answered, "I have been sworn to secrecy and will not reveal her name. I have contacts at the different coaching inns in London and along the North Road."

Aimee knew then who had been worried about her safety. Her eyes filled with tears. "I promised to let the Mrs. Potts know when I arrived safely."

"You never had the chance, or you would have."

Aimee agreed. "I started to suspect something was wrong when we drove through the part of London I thought I would be going to—while not on Bond Street, not very far from it. The carriage continued. When I noticed the streets were more unkempt, and the buildings more run-down, I feared I was being kidnapped. I had no idea where I was going or what would become of me." She searched Michaela's gaze—when she found no condemnation in the woman's eyes, relief swept up from her toes. "I had no means to write to her either."

Instead of asking more questions about the condition of the building she was thrust into, Michaela said, "Would you like to write to her now? I have a quill, ink, and foolscap."

Aimee sighed. "I would, thank you. I owe her so much for taking me in and giving me a way to earn my keep."

Michaela nodded. "Not everyone has a black heart, Aimee. If I were to confide what happened to me, I know without question that I would be ostracized by my peers and given the cut direct in public. The only reason Lord…" She stopped and shook her head. "I have vowed never to speak his name again. Suffice it to say if my father ever got wind of what happened to me, he would call the man out!"

"Then why didn't you tell him?"

"And suffer from the disappointment in my father's eyes? It would have brought shame to his name—and his noble profession. I could not risk it."

Aimee's heart hurt for the other woman. "So that is why you became the angel of the streets."

Michaela nodded.

"Does your father know?"

"I think he might," Michaela rasped, clasping her hands tightly in her lap. "But he never speaks of it. Father will inquire which evening entertainment I will be attending, and who my escort for the evening will be. From the sadness in his eyes, I think he knows I will only be at the musicale or ball for a short time before I claim to have developed a headache, feel faint, or remember a promise to attend a different function. That's when I slip off to my true calling."

"It sounds as if he would like to support what you do, while at the same time is worried for your safety. If my father were still alive, I believe he would be concerned for my reputation. I truly think your father is concerned and mayhap grows more worried by the day, wondering what would happen if it is discovered that you are the angel everyone whispers about." Aimee paused for a moment for Michaela to absorb her words, then added, "I believe that, above all, your father trusts you, and mayhap has known all along how valiantly you rescue and tend to the abused and mistreated women of London."

Michaela's shoulders slumped. "I hate deceiving him. As long as I continue to serve others in secret, and it does not cast a slur upon the family name, I do not think he will try to stop me. He knows how much I need to use the healing skills I learned at his side. His careful tutoring got the both of us through our grief after my mother passed away."

"You heal more than their bodily injuries," Aimee said. "Your kindness and compassion go a long way toward healing their hearts and souls. Just knowing that someone as lovely and highborn as yourself has suffered a similar fate as me—and not given in to despair—is encouraging. You have made it your life's mission to help those who cannot help themselves, and, in doing so, have become a beacon in the darkness."

Michaela held Aimee's gaze for long moments before saying, "There is a rumor that the proprietress of Underwood's boarding house instructs the women she kidnaps in certain arts before delivering them to Scarlet Ribbons and The Scarlet Boudoir. Is it true?"

Bile bubbled in Aimee's belly and threatened to rush up her throat, but she fought to regain control. She would not cast up her accounts, as she had the night before at the boarding house. Regaining control, she managed to answer, "Yes."

"I have a more difficult question for you—and you have been so courageous already. Please know that you do not have to answer, though it would be crucial information to be able to relay when the authorities clap Mrs. Underwood in irons."

Aimee's stomach felt as if it had been scraped raw at the memory of what she'd been forced to witness. Thinking of the other young woman who'd been there when she arrived and had been shipped off to the two houses of ill repute, she prayed for the courage to answer. She met Michaela's unflinching gaze and asked, "What do you need to know?"

"Had you begun your training?"

"Yes, the observation part of it." She hesitated, then said, "My participation was to begin this evening, when the two Miss Scarlets arrived with their escorts."

The other woman frowned. "Two Miss Scarlets...and their escorts?"

"Yes." Aimee needed Michaela to understand the lengths her captor went to in supplying young women to the two bawdy houses. "Twins, with ebony hair, gray eyes, and lips painted a shocking shade of scarlet that matched their scandalous gowns. They're beautiful, but in a glaring, hard way."

Michaela nodded. "Did their escorts act as their guards?"

A tear escaped while Aimee explained, "Mrs. Underwood told us to consider the sisters and their men as actors in a play." She brushed away her tears and continued, "Before we were to be participants, we were expected to observe. We accompanied Mrs. Underwood and the first couple into one of the locked rooms at the end of the hallway." She trembled at the memory that had been burned into her brainbox, set it aside, and said, "When it was over, we were expected to observe the second couple."

Michaela reached for her hand. "To have been forced to watch something that should never be made into a spectacle must have been terrifying to someone as innocent as you and the others. I hate to ask but need to. Can you tell me what you saw?"

Aimee held tight to Michaela, grateful for the anchor. She dreaded reliving what happened, let alone having to speak of it.

"You do not have to answer, thought it will help immensely when Mrs. Underwood and the others involved in this dastardly scheme are brought up on charges."

She dug deep and thought of the kindly Mrs. Potts, who was no doubt worried after not receiving a letter that Aimee had arrived safely at her destination. "Mrs. Underwood lined the three of us along one side of the bed while the first Miss Scarlet and her escort disrobed, and then got on the bed—" She had to take a deep breath and slowly exhale to finish the telling...to get it over with. "Mrs. Underwood explained as they were...er...performing, reminding us that what Miss Scarlet was doing pleased their customers. We needed to pay close attention, as we would earn a percentage of the coin the men would pay us to do the same." She closed her eyes and gathered what was left of her tattered pride to add, "They demonstrated variations of what Mrs. Underwood laughingly said occurred 'in the marriage bed.'"

Aimee didn't remember Michaela wrapping arms around her, but the warmth finally penetrated the chill in her bones.

"There are some who fall far below the level of depravity I thought existed in this world," Michaela said. "I believe that Mrs. Underwood, both Miss Scarlets, and their escorts are among the worst. What they have done—and are still doing—is far more damaging to you and the other young women they held—and are holding—against their will."

Aimee felt hollowed out from the telling, just as she had after her own experience on the way to Gretna Green. She was compelled to add, "At least it was darker inside the carriage when Wolfingham..." Her words trailed off, and she had to dig even deeper to continue. "That experience was painful and had damning consequences, changing the course of my life. But what we were forced to witness—and then we were reminded by Mrs. Underwood that we would each have a turn, 'rehearsing' with both escorts until we performed to their approval before being sent to earn our keep in that way—was far worse."

Finished, she looked into Michaela's eyes. She saw the shock the other woman was not quick enough to hide. Though, mayhap, Michaela was recalling what happened to herself.

Her next words confirmed it: "It was dark in the garden, too."

A thought occurred to Aimee, and she had to ask, "Will I have to repeat everything I just told you to Garahan?"

Michaela's gaze was steady when she replied, "You have been beyond brave, Aimee. I would not subject you to that, but he does need to know. Would you be willing to write down what you've just told me? You could sign it, and I would sign below your name, attesting that this account was exactly as you relayed it to me tonight. We could hand it to Garahan to read, and if he has any questions, I will answer them."

"I think you are not only a healing angel...but a warrior guardian angel. That you understand has eased my worry. It is one thing to confide in you—another altogether to tell Garahan. Do you think less of me because of what happened?"

"Nay. Do you honestly think Garahan would think less of you if you confided in him?"

Aimee shrugged. "Wolfingham told me that no man would ever want me if he knew the truth. Even though I have a suspicion that if he told any of his cronies, he would lie to them as he lied to me."

Michaela nodded. "'Twas the same with...er... 'Twas the same for me. I have met a few good men since I began my campaign to help others. Alasdair Cameron, James Garahan, Gryffyn Tremayne, and now Darby Garahan. I trust them implicitly, and doubt they would ever blame us for what happened. We were both stripped of our virtue against our will." She paused, then asked, "Did you fight him?"

"Yes, but he overpowered me."

"I fought too, but he was far stronger than I." Drawing in a deep breath and exhaling slowly, Michaela continued, "The only thing we are both guilty of is our naivete and putting our trust in the wrong man. What helped me was praying for the strength to let go of the guilt and to forgive myself for placing my trust where it would not be returned."

Aimee had much to think about. Her reaction to Garahan had been entirely different to Wolfingham. It was not just due to the circumstances when they'd met, but the fact that although the men shared the same coloring, they were completely opposite in every other way. Wolfingham had been polished, arrogant, a bit autocratic, while charming.

Garahan had been rough in his manner and speech, steadfast, and protective of her. The way he held her in his arms when Mrs. Underwood released her had had a tiny crack forming in the wall she'd erected around her bruised and battered heart. His actions echoed his words, yet still she hesitated before realizing she had no other choice but to trust him for fear he would leave her at the boarding house. The way he'd introduced her to his horse tipped the scale in his favor and eased the worst of her fears.

Would she have trusted him if he had been the man to convince her to elope? She wasn't certain.

Michaela patted Aimee's hand and rose to her feet. "I shall gather what you need to write to Mrs. Potts. After you do, you can write down the events that occurred last night at the boarding house."

Aimee's hand shook, but she managed to dip the tip of the quill into the ink without making a mess. Pushing her worries and other thoughts aside, she wrote a note of thanks to Mrs. Potts for alerting the innkeepers along the North Road, so others would be alerted to her disappearance. Then she wrote an account of what occurred the previous evening. It was far easier to commit it to foolscap than to say it aloud again. When she finished, she prayed Garahan would be able to stop Mrs. Underwood and the others from luring any more young women into their clutches.

She signed the document and held out the quill to Michaela. "Your turn." After the other woman signed her name, their eyes met, and Aimee asked, "Is it wrong of me to hope that they will drag that evil woman through the front doors of the boarding house—as I was dragged in through it?"

"Not at all, though I would not put too much effort on thoughts of revenge," Michaela said. "Over the years, I have learned to pray for justice, though it may not come within the time frame one wishes it to."

"Are you hoping the lord who compromised you will be brought to justice?"

Michaela sighed. "To do so, I would have to reveal what he did to me. There are those who feel themselves holier-than-thou and would place the blame squarely on my head."

"But—"

"I have learned to accept the fact that Society is only concerned with its own best interests. I have encountered some men who rise above the rest, in their bid to protect those weaker than themselves, those who put their lives on the line in defense of the indefensible. I trusted Alasdair, James, and Tremayne with my life, and they have upheld each promise they have made—although not without telling me what they thought along the way. After meeting James's brother, Darby, there is no question as to whether to trust him. I do."

Aimee wondered what reason Michaela had for telling her this, and was about to ask, when the woman added, "Trust Darby. He will protect you with his life."

CHAPTER SIX

G ARAHAN LED THE way through the streets and alleyways as they rode to the place where the lass had been kept against her will. He raised a hand, and O'Malley reined in beside him. Eyes narrowed, jaw set, he scanned the perimeter, then stared into the darkened alleyway. A form emerged. The man nodded to Garahan, then shifted so he was concealed again.

O'Malley leaned toward Garahan. "Burke?"

"Aye." Garahan dismounted quickly. The need to rescue the young women inside the boarding house was paramount. He hadn't mentioned to Miss Michaela that he'd be doing so, but he sensed she would not balk when he and O'Malley arrived on her doorstep with a few more lasses who'd been kidnapped.

O'Malley followed Garahan's lead, dismounting. "Are we entering through the front or rear?"

A sound had them turning toward the alleyway where Burke waited. They moved closer but, as was their habit, moved in such a way that it did not bring attention to their contact. Raising his voice to be heard inside the building, Garahan locked eyes with O'Malley. "And I say we should storm the front door! The bloody buggers have our cousin inside!"

Taking his cue, O'Malley replied, "Ye've lost yer mind! No one in their right mind sneaks in through the front door!"

Under cover of the argument, Burke rasped, "Rear door is

guarded by two men. Three guard the front."

"Ye go through the rear door," Garahan told his cousin. "I'll go in the front."

O'Malley grabbed hold of Garahan's arm. "We go together."

The sound of a scuffle from behind the rear door alerted them that their argument had been overheard, as intended. Garahan shook free of his cousin's grip and grinned. "I'm thinking it'll be five guarding the front. We can take care of the bloody buggers all at once. Are ye ready?"

"Aye," his cousin replied.

They slipped around to the front door, Garahan on the left, O'Malley on the right. "The harpy who owns the place is fond of knives—keeps one in her sleeve and another in her apron pocket," Garahan said.

O'Malley nodded, and they kicked the door open. Surprise was on their side, and they easily gained the upper hand, delivering blows to the face and throat before taking down two of the men with solid kicks to the groin.

"Three to one's not much of a challenge," Garahan murmured, eyeing the remaining thugs. "Ye can have the one on the left, and I'll take the other two."

"What if I want the two on the right?" O'Malley argued.

Garahan took out one man with his wicked right cross. "Are ye happy now? We've each got one."

O'Malley snorted with laughter. "Ye always were me favorite cousin."

The two men left standing reached for their weapons. Garahan quickly disarmed the one brandishing a blunderbuss, while O'Malley took away the other's lethal blade. They heard a scream of anger and looked up as the boarding house owner flew at them—a knife in each hand.

"We'd best take care of these two before we deal with that one." Garahan braced as the woman raced toward them. O'Malley nodded and grabbed hold of the two men they'd disarmed, knocking their heads together. When the woman was within reach, Garahan said, "I'll go left, you go right."

The woman was no match for the strength of the Irishmen. Garahan squeezed her wrist until she opened her hand and dropped the weapon. O'Malley did the same. The men who'd been kicked in the bollocks rose slowly and moved to stand behind the woman.

"Did ye remember to bring the rope this time?" O'Malley asked.

"Bugger it!" Garahan said. "We'll have to use our cravats again."

O'Malley sighed. "His Grace will be asking for an accounting of why we go through so many of the bloody things."

While the woman shouted obscenities at them, the duke's men used their cravats to bind the wrists of two men. "What about him?" O'Malley asked, pointing to the third.

Garahan stared at the woman's apron. "Hand me the knife in yer boot—me hand's a bit stiff." While the woman protested, Garahan brandished O'Malley's blade and sliced off enough fabric to bind her wrists behind her back, and then did the same to the third man.

"How long do ye think those two will stay unconscious?" O'Malley asked.

"Long enough." Garahan turned to the woman. "Do ye have more than three lasses in the back?"

She glared in reply.

"We need to search the building," Garahan said. "I'll need a word with Burke. Watch the prisoners."

O'Malley agreed. "Ye'd best have someone fetch the Watch."

Garahan opened the door and disappeared into the alley. Burke materialized from the shadows. "O'Malley and I need to search the building for the lasses. Can ye spare someone to stand guard over the prisoners, and another? We'll be needing the Watch."

Burke frowned. "Two more young women were delivered not long after you left. They're younger than the others." He turned and spat on the ground. "They couldn't be more than three and ten, if that."

Garahan's blood ran cold at the thought of lasses that young being put to work in a brothel. "We'll take care of it, Burke."

The man stepped to the mouth of the alley and whistled. Two men came running from the other side of the street. "Go with Garahan. He needs you to stand guard inside. I'll go for the Watch."

Before Garahan could thank Burke, the man was halfway down the street headed toward the nearest watchman's post. Garahan turned to Burke's men. "We've three men and the owner of the boarding house bound, but ye may be wanting to gag the woman. Two others were still unconscious a few minutes ago."

He opened the door and nodded to O'Malley. "Burke's gone for the Watch. His men here will stand guard while we round up the lasses." His heart ached as he added, "Burke said two more lasses were delivered a short while ago—said they looked to be about three and ten."

O'Malley strode over to stand in front of the woman. "There's a place in Hell for the likes of ye. Ye're lucky I'm a God-fearing man and can control me urge to send ye there before yer time."

Garahan grabbed his cousin's arm. "Ye'll have plenty of time to issue yer threats after we find the lasses." They strode toward the door at the back of the main room. "I'll go in first," he told O'Malley.

"Fine, but next time, I'll be leading the charge."

"God help us if there is a next time," Garahan murmured as he opened the door and stepped inside. "Miss Anderson is worried about ye, lasses," he called out as he walked into the empty kitchen.

"No one's about," O'Malley said from behind him. "Do ye think they heard what happened out front and are afraid?"

"Aye." Pitching his voice to be heard beyond the kitchen, he said, "Me name's Garahan—I was here earlier and rescued Miss Anderson. I've brought me cousin O'Malley with me to rescue the rest of ye."

He heard what sounded like a gasp, followed by someone whispering, "Did ye hear that?"

O'Malley nodded and pointed toward the doorway leading from the kitchen to a narrow hall.

"The Watch has been summoned," Garahan continued as they approached the doorway. "We have two men guarding those who held ye against yer will. We're pressed for time, lasses. Won't ye come out? We'll be taking ye to the angel of the streets."

A dark-haired lass stepped out of the pantry, demanding, "How do we know we can trust you?"

Brave lass. "O'Malley and I are part of the Duke of Wyndmere's private guard. We took an oath to protect the duke and his family—and extended family—with our lives."

A redhead revealed herself to stand beside the dark-haired lass. She was no more than four and a half feet tall and had the temerity to frown at him. "We aren't related to the duke—why would you help us?"

Another redhead, who had to be a blood relative, shoved the shorter redhead behind her and asked, "How do we know you aren't lying to us?"

O'Malley cleared his throat. "Well, if ye'd rather stay here…"

"Ouch!" The taller redhead spun around. "Quit pinching me, Alice!"

Garahan struggled not to laugh. "I'm thinking Alice doesn't want to stay here. Do ye, lass?"

"I want to leave, and so does my sister Beatrice, but she won't admit it because she doesn't trust anyone after…"

Her voice trailed off, and Garahan sensed there was a story he needed to hear—but not right now. "If ye'll come along with us, Miss Michaela will tend to any injuries ye may have." He paused, glanced at O'Malley, who nodded, then asked, "Ye aren't from

London, are ye?" The three young girls shook their heads. "Are ye the only lasses here, or are there others?"

The dark-haired girl spoke up. "There are two more upstairs. That evil woman locked them in the room all the way at the end of the hallway."

Garahan fought to keep his anger from showing. "Ye three wait here with O'Malley—"

"No!" the trio said in unison. "Sally and Jenny won't leave unless we tell them that we're going too," Alice added.

"Why is that?" O'Malley asked.

"They're new here," Alice answered.

"And still think they'll be working for a modiste, sewing lace and ribbons on fine gowns for ladies of the *ton*," Beatrice added.

The lies kept piling up. They'd get to the bottom of this and follow the wicked strands of the web that started with an advert...and ended with young girls collected from the countryside for nefarious ends. "Guard the rear, O'Malley. The rest of ye stay between us until we reach the room. Understand?" Garahan asked.

"I don't," the lass with the dark hair said.

Time was ticking away, but Garahan needed everyone to follow orders. "What's yer name, lass?"

"Mary."

"Well now, Mary, 'tis how me cousin and I will be protecting the three of ye—O'Malley in the rear and meself leading the way. Once ye convince Sally and Jenny we mean them no harm, we'll be leaving."

The three young women formed a single file line between Garahan and O'Malley as they ascended the rickety staircase.

Garahan stopped in front of the room and glanced over his shoulder. "Mary, would ye tell the lasses to move away from the door? I need to break it down."

Three pair of eyes were riveted on him. He sighed at their disbelief. "I may need O'Malley's help, but this door is old. Shouldn't take more than a tap or two with me shoulder to break it open."

Mary moved to stand beside him. "Sally? Jenny? It's me, Mary. We have two of the duke's guard with us. They rescued Aimee. You remember me telling you about Aimee before Mrs. Underwood dragged you up here and locked you in?"

The silence unnerved Garahan. "I need to break down the door. There isn't time to find the key."

"Step away from the door," Mary told them.

"Hurry," Alice implored.

"We need to leave before Miss Scarlet arrives," Beatrice warned.

"We're over by the dresser," a young voice called out. "In the corner."

"Hunker down, then, with yer backs to the door," Garahan told them.

"Cover yer heads," O'Malley added before nodding to his cousin.

Garahan rammed his shoulder into the door and stepped through the splintered wood into the room. "Hurry, lasses! This way!" When the two little mites stood up, he vowed to put a stop to this evil trade—or die trying! The lasses were younger than ten and three—mayhap only nine or ten years old. "Do ye need me to carry ye?"

The girls shook their heads and rushed past him out of the room into Mary and Beatrice's arms. "We're ready," Mary told him.

"I'll need all of ye to follow me downstairs, the same as ye did coming up."

"Single file," O'Malley reminded them.

Everything was going according to plan until they stepped through the kitchen door into the main room of the boarding house. Sally and Jenny froze when they saw Mrs. Underwood.

"She'll whip us," Sally whispered.

"And won't give our things back," Jenny cried.

Burke stepped through the front door and called out,

"There's a hackney waiting outside. Thought ye might be needing it."

"Thank ye, Burke," Garahan said. "I thought there'd only be two or three and could manage that on two horses, but not with five."

O'Malley added his thanks and urged the young girls forward. Sally and Jenny refused to take one step closer to the woman they feared. He knelt beside them. "Why don't I carry ye out? Garahan will see to it that witch of a woman won't lay a hand on either of ye."

Sally nodded, and he scooped her up. Jenny hesitated, but seeing Sally wrap her arm around O'Malley's neck, she changed her mind. He scooped her up in his other arm and stood. "We're ready."

Garahan shook his head. "Why is it the lasses are so quick to trust the O'Malleys?"

His cousin grinned. "We aren't dark and forbidding like ye Garahans. Ma always said with our light hair and green eyes, we look like angels." He walked toward the front door, where the Watch and Burke's men stood with the prisoners.

Garahan snorted. "Angels me *arse.*"

Sally patted O'Malley's cheek. "He said a bad word."

"Bugger it," Garahan mumbled.

"That's a bad word, too," Jenny whispered in O'Malley's ear.

O'Malley's chuckle irritated Garahan, who silently swore a blue streak. The O'Malleys had always attracted attention with their blond good looks and bright green eyes. He and his brothers were nearly as broad as their O'Malley cousins, but not quite as tall, and it had been a bone of contention between the cousins for years.

He followed O'Malley outside and jolted to a stop, noticing one of King's men waiting for them. "Thompson, why are ye here?"

"King thought you might need a hand transporting the prisoners," the Runner explained.

Garahan noted there were two carriages in front of the building. O'Malley was helping the lasses into the smaller one. "Thank him for me."

"I will," Thompson replied.

Garahan turned to Burke, his men, and the watchman. "Thank ye for yer assistance, men. Thompson here will take this lot off to Bow Street. King'll be waiting for them."

The others dispersed, and Garahan walked over to stand beside his cousin, who was speaking to the lasses. He waited for O'Malley to finish speaking, then leaned inside and pitched his voice low, so the driver would not hear him. "O'Malley and I will be riding on either side of the hack protecting ye. 'Tis for yer safety, as well as that of the woman we'll be delivering ye to. I need ye to promise not to mention where we're going."

When they didn't answer right away, O'Malley added, "We won't hurt ye—we're after taking ye to safety."

The girls silently agreed and huddled in their seats, holding on to one another. Garahan straightened, approached the hack driver, and gave the address. "We'll be riding beside ye."

The driver nodded, and Garahan reached into his waistcoat pocket for coin to pay the man. "Burke's a friend," the driver said, refusing.

"He's one of mine, too," Garahan replied. "Thank ye."

O'Malley mounted his horse and waited Garahan to do the same before pitching his voice low to ask, "Do ye think Miss Michaela will be able to handle five more lasses?"

Garahan smiled. "She can handle twenty."

O'Malley's brow rose in silent question.

Garahan shook his head. "Ye'll see. If anything, the rumors about the angel of the streets do not do her justice—she's far stronger and more skilled at healing than she's been given credit for."

"Is she now?" his cousin murmured.

They took up positions on either side of the hack, as vigilant in their protection of the young women as they would be guarding the duke and his family.

CHAPTER SEVEN

GREENWOOD OPENED THE door. "Twice in one day, Garahan? Is Miss Michaela expecting you?"

"Aye, though not tonight. I've five more lasses for her. Three that were in the boarding house with Miss Anderson—and two who arrived a short while ago." Garahan's throat worked as the anger and frustration he'd controlled for the last two hours bubbled to the surface. "They cannot be more than eight or nine years old."

Greenwood's jaw clenched as anger flashed in his eyes. But Garahan was impressed to see the guard tamp it down as quickly as it appeared.

"I'm thinking it'll be best if we lead the older lasses in single file, with me in the lead, and O'Malley bringing up the rear, carrying the youngest two."

"Will the driver talk?"

"Nay," Garahan reassured him. "He works for one of me contacts who haunts the bowels of London. We can trust him."

The guard scanned the area and nodded. "Be quick about it."

Within minutes, the three young women—and two young girls—were spirited in through the door and up the stairs.

Michaela was waiting at the top of the stairs in the open doorway, her eyes wide with surprise, though her expression otherwise remained serene. Miss Anderson moved to stand beside her, blue eyes glistening with unshed tears. Staring at him, she rasped, "You kept your promise," before stepping aside to let Mary, Alice, and Beatrice into the room.

"O'Malley, would ye remind the lass that I always keep me word?"

"He always keeps his word, lass…unless he's unconscious." O'Malley locked gazes with Michaela as he walked past her, ducking to enter the room to avoid hitting his head on the doorframe.

Garahan closed the door behind them. "I would have returned to the boarding house, lass, even if I had not given me word to ye."

O'Malley asked, "Where do ye want these two little darlings?"

Garahan answered, "I'm thinking they'll feel more secure with the other lasses."

O'Malley tried to set the little ones down, but they wouldn't let go of him. "Ye need to let go, Sally. Ye too, Jenny." In answer, they tucked their heads against his neck.

Garahan was about to speak when Michaela walked toward his cousin. She seemed pleased that the little lasses were clinging to O'Malley, and amused by the helpless look on his face. Garahan had only seen it once before, and that was years ago.

"I planned to ask Gavin King to send someone back to the boarding house," Michaela said. "If you were too busy to return, Garahan. I would have asked for one of his men. I knew there would be more young women arriving at that establishment, but I am surprised at how young these two little ones holding on to O'Malley appear to be."

O'Malley cleared his throat. "Now then, lasses, Miss Michaela will be wanting a word with ye. I need to set ye down." He bent down, intending to set them on the floor, but they clung to him like a burr to a horse's hide. "I could use a hand."

Garahan swallowed his laughter. "Ye look like ye're doing just fine, boy-o."

"If me hands weren't full, I'd knock yer teeth down yer throat," O'Malley replied.

"Ah, but they are full, and the wee lasses are still afraid. Mayhap ye'll need to spend some time speaking with Miss Michaela until they're more comfortable. I'm expected elsewhere."

O'Malley nodded. "I suppose Findley can handle things for a little longer. I can sit with ye for half an hour, lasses, but I need to return to me post guarding the duke's town house."

"You know a duke?" Sally asked, her eyes bright with interest.

"A real one?" Jenny added.

"Aye, to both yer questions." O'Malley turned to face Miss Michaela. "Name's O'Malley—Emmett. I'm one of the sixteen men who guard the Duke of Wyndmere—including this *amadon*."

Garahan grinned and finished the introduction. "Miss Michaela, meet me bacon-brained cousin, O'Malley the healer."

She walked over to stand in front of his cousin and stared at him for long moments. Garahan knew she was sizing O'Malley up. She'd done the same to him earlier. He couldn't help but note the interest evident in O'Malley's gaze—and Michaela's. "I'll be leaving the lot of ye in O'Malley's care, but ye must remember he needs to return to his duties as well."

The chorus of *ayes* pleased him. He walked over to stand before Aimee. Staring into eyes the color of a summer sky, he apologized, "We were pressed for time, lass. I couldn't find yer locket."

"Rescuing these young woman is far more important than any keepsake, Garahan. Thank you."

He loathed the thought of leaving her but had no choice. "I have an important meeting to attend, lass, but will return as I still have questions for ye."

A mix of sorrow and understanding shone from eyes no longer dulled with despair. They were a bit brighter. She nodded.

"Did Miss Michaela wrap yer ribs?"

Her cheeks pinkened at the question, and he wondered, was it too personal?

"Er…yes, she did."

He didn't want to ask outright if she'd told Michaela what he suspected was weighing heavy on the lass's conscience, but he needed to know. "And did ye have a conversation as well?"

"We did. In fact, Michaela had me write down an account of what happened since I first read the advert." She hurried over to the table, snatched up a bit of foolscap, and handed it to him.

"Well now, King will be pleased. I should have thought of that. Thank ye both. If I have any further questions, I'll stop by." His eyes sought hers, sending a silent message that he hoped she understood—he'd protect her from afar until they met again. Studying her face, he committed the curve of her cheek, the shape of her eyes, and the fullness of her lips to memory, knowing full well that it wasn't wise to let the lass get a tighter hold on his heart. *Bugger it*—he wouldn't be sleeping a wink tonight. He'd be remembering this fleeting moment. "Thank ye for placing yer trust in me, lass. If ye ever have need of me, Miss Michaela knows how to get in touch."

Attraction warred with worry in the depths of her eyes, tempting him to draw her close and wrap his arms around her. The need to taste her lips, and discover her flavor, nearly drove him mad. He was close enough to touch her. Was her skin as soft as it appeared? The need to find out had him by the throat.

"Promise ye'll send for me if ye need me, lass."

"I promise."

Unable to stop himself, he brushed a lock of silken hair off her forehead and tapped his finger to the tip of her nose. "Yer freckles remind me of the lasses back home."

Her expression changed swiftly, as he'd intended. The expression in her eyes pleased him. He'd rather see the fire in her gaze than despair. "Did you break many hearts when you left Ireland?"

He shrugged. "Not too many."

"A half-dozen," O'Malley added helpfully.

"Shall I list the names of the dozen hearts *ye* broke, O'Malley?"

"Later—ye'll be late, Garahan. Ye'd best shove off."

Ignoring his cousin, Garahan lifted the lass's hand to his lips and brushed a kiss across the back of it. He bowed to Michaela and the others, then strode to the door and opened it, all the while feeling the heat of Miss Anderson's gaze as it bored into his shoulder blades. Closing the door behind him broke the spell she'd unknowingly cast upon him. He blew out a breath as he descended the stairs. Miss Aimee Anderson could convince a man to change his mind.

Though he was sorely tempted, he'd be wise not to seek the lass out until after he'd gathered the information Coventry needed regarding the threat to Summerfield and put an end to the threat.

Distance might help—and Ireland just might be far enough away.

AIMEE WATCHED GARAHAN until he closed the door behind him. Slowing letting go of the breath she'd held, she wondered what it was about the man that had her trusting him so quickly. At first, she could not see past his dark hair and eyes—so like Wolfingham's that she'd wondered if he would have a similar personality. It was unsettling, reminding her of a time she needed to forget. But his forthright manner had had her looking past his hair and eye color until she was able to discern that Garahan was a full head taller than the man who betrayed her. His shoulders were broad, and his chest deeply muscled—she'd felt his strength leaning against him when he swept her into his arms.

She sighed as the memory of being held, listening to the steady beat of his heart, filled her. She sighed again.

"I could use your help settling everyone, Aimee."

Head in the clouds, she didn't really hear Michaela—she was reliving the feel of Garahan's fingertips when he'd tenderly touched her cheek. They were rough, but not because of how he touched her—it was the texture of his hands, earned from honest work. He was a man who *worked* with his hands. She suspected Wolfingham delegated any work to an underling.

"Aimee!"

"Forgive me, I was woolgathering."

At O'Malley's snort of laughter, she stared at him and was about to ask what he found so amusing. But Michaela walked over to her and touched her arm, asking. "Do you need my help?"

Aimee rolled her eyes, eliciting another burst of laughter from O'Malley. She frowned at him. "You, sir, have a very odd sense of humor."

Michaela mumbled something beneath her breath. Aimee could not quite hear what it was, but she did hear when Michaela asked, "Mr. O'Malley, would you please bring Sally and Jenny over by the washstand?"

"Just O'Malley, if ye please."

"Yes, of course," Michaela replied. "The others have finished washing up, and I'd like these two to do the same."

Aimee watched her new friend walk toward O'Malley without a hint of hesitation or fear. He was taller than Garahan, and just as broad through the chest and shoulders. She marveled at Michaela's courage, wondering how the woman had gotten it back after what happened to her.

Aimee noticed the expression in O'Malley's eyes change, from amused to wary. He blinked, and the neutral expression she'd noticed earlier was firmly back in place. She thought she detected interest on his part, but now could not discern anything. Garahan had adopted a similar expression earlier when he'd rescued her. She wondered if it was part of their training for the duke.

Michaela placed a hand to O'Malley's elbow to steady herself, in order to brush a wisp of hair out of Jenny's eyes. "I have a lovely round of lavender soap. Would you like to wash your face and hands with it?"

Jenny nodded, and Aimee's heart lightened. She hadn't realized until that moment that she'd feared Michaela only helped young women—and not children.

"You'll have to ask Mr. O'Malley to please set you down first. Then you can step up onto the stool so you can reach the washbowl."

"It's blue and white, like Mum's was."

Aimee's heart ached at the sadness in Jenny's voice. She moved to stand next to O'Malley, and he shifted. Did he feel boxed in by Michaela and herself? He glanced at Michaela and cleared his throat, leaving Aimee to suspect it was Michaela's nearness that caused his uneasiness.

She would think about that later—right now, she wanted to distract the little one. "There's a round of rose soap, too. Miss Michaela let me try both soaps. And do you know what?"

"What?" Jenny asked.

"She did?" Sally asked at the same time.

Aimee smiled. "When I scrubbed my hands and lifted them to my nose, the lather smelled like the dried lavender my mum used to place beneath my pillow."

"What did the rose smell like?" Jenny asked.

"Like my mum's prized rosebush."

The girls were leaning away from O'Malley now. Aimee and Michaela had captured their interest.

Aimee added, "Mum's favorite was the lavender. Mine is rose."

"Did your mum die, too?" Jenny asked.

Aimee nodded. "A long time ago."

"How old were you?" Sally asked.

Aimee sighed. "Seven." She remembered that day as if it were yesterday. "My father was in the Royal Navy... His ship went down. When my mum found out...she died of a broken heart."

"I don't remember my father," Jenny admitted. "Mum said he was a soldier."

Michaela held out her hands to Jenny, who hugged O'Malley

before letting Michaela take her.

"I remember my father." Sally shivered. "He used to hit my mum, until the day she didn't get up, and I screamed and screamed."

Aimee reached for Sally but had to wait for the little girl to kiss O'Malley's cheek before letting Aimee take her. "It is so hard to be brave," she said. "Especially when you don't have your mum or father, and you don't know what's going to happen next. Where will you go? What will you do?"

O'Malley had been silent through the exchange. When she glanced at him, she noticed his expression was one of understanding. He and Garahan seemed to be compassionate and protective by nature—not just of women, but children too. They must have been raised by loving parents. "I need to take me leave of ye," he said.

Jenny was on the stool, rolling up her sleeves. She paused and looked up at him. "Do you have to?"

"Aye, lass."

"Couldn't you be just a little bit late?" Sally asked.

"Nay. I gave me word to the Duke of Wyndmere. I never break me word, nor shirk in me duty." He shifted his gaze to Michaela and said, "Never would I break a promise. Garahan and I are cut from the same cloth. Not one of the duke's guard will break their word or promise, once given."

"Thank you for saving me, Mr. O'Malley," Jenny said as she washed and dried her hands.

"Just O'Malley, if ye please."

Jenny nodded, and Sally took her place on the stool. "Thank you for saving me too, O'Malley."

He grinned at the little girls before turning back to Michaela. "Remember to send for Garahan or meself should ye have need of us, Miss Michaela."

She smiled. "Just Michaela, if you please."

Aimee noticed the fire in O'Malley's emerald eyes as he stared at her friend. "Well then, lass, Michaela it is."

A gasp of shock had Aimee turning back to the girls as Mary asked, "What happened to your arm, Sally?"

"It was an accident."

O'Malley moved like lightning to the little girl's side.

Michaela rushed over to examine the inflamed wound on Sally's arm. "How long ago did you hurt your arm?"

"I didn't hurt it—someone…"

When the little girl's voice trailed off, O'Malley stiffened. "We'll start with a poultice to bring down the swelling. Have ye the herbs we need, Michaela?"

"Yes, in the locked cabinet hanging over my worktable." Michaela rushed over to the cabinet. She opened it and retrieved a small, linen-wrapped bundle tied off with threads.

Without being asked, Aimee emptied the washbowl into the bucket by the worktable and held out a pitcher to Alice. "Please refill the ceramic bowl for me, Alice." Eyeing the neat stacks of linen squares and strips, she told Beatrice, "Please bring a handful of the squares and linen strips over to O'Malley and Michaela."

Aimee was grateful that the older girls followed the instructions quickly and quietly. She knew without asking that Sally's wound was worrisome. It needed to be cleaned, and she was worried that the infection would need to be drained.

She watched O'Malley and Michaela work together, efficiently and without speaking. A look between them was all it took for one to understand what the other needed. All Aimee knew of healing was that wounds had to be cleansed—and kept free of dirt—and that tepid to cool water was best to use when trying to bring down a fever.

When Sally whimpered, Jenny rushed over to hold her free hand. "Don't be afraid, Sally. You can cry now; no one will whip you."

O'Malley never looked away from his task when he asked, "Who dared to strike ye with a rod, lass?"

The fear in Sally's eyes went right to Aimee's heart. "You don't have to answer now, Sally," Aimee assured her. "You're being so brave, but O'Malley will need to know later."

He glanced up. "Aye, lass, ye're a brave little warrior."

Sally whispered, "You're not like my father at all."

"I should hope not, lass. I've never—and will never—raise me hand to a child or woman."

"I believe you," Sally said.

"Me too," Jenny echoed.

Aimee knew in that moment that O'Malley had forged an important bond with the two little girls, restoring their faith that not all men were evil. She realized that Garahan had done the same for her, convincing her to trust that he would never harm her.

A glance at Michaela, and Aimee thought mayhap O'Malley was well on the way to convincing her that he could be trusted too.

◇◆◇◆◇◆◇

CHAPTER EIGHT

GARAHAN FELT AT home walking through the warren of enclosed docks. Even though the decade-old system protected a majority of the goods that had been offloaded, there was still a surprising amount of theft. Moving from alleyway to alleyway, he slipped into the shadows to wait for his contact.

With an eye toward the tavern that stood across from the Thames, where he hid in the alleyway, he watched and waited. It was wise to be alert. The Pelican had long ago earned its nickname, the Devil's Tavern. When it was rebuilt nearly fifty years ago, the owners changed the name to The Prospect of Whitby, but the kept the cockfighting pit and bare-knuckle arena. Which, in large part, was why it still had the reputation for being a rough establishment where all manner of criminals could be found. Tonight, one of his contacts was in that arena, challenging all comers.

If he were not currently employed by the duke, he'd have accepted the challenge, and won—mayhap even wagered a few pounds on O'Shaughnessy's nose. But he, his brothers, and cousins no longer took part in—or wagered on—bare-knuckle fights or horses. That ended when they accepted the offer of employment from the Duke of Wyndmere's London man-of-affairs, Captain Coventry.

Cheers and jeers erupted from inside the tavern as the door

swung open and O'Shaughnessy stumbled through it onto the street. "Bugger it." If Garahan gauged the man's condition accurately, his contact would be in a bloody bad mood. Beneath the lighted lantern, the man stumbled, but not from the drink—from the blows that had split the skin on his forehead. Garahan would have to stanch the flow of blood, or else O'Shaughnessy would never make it home.

Though he wanted to rush to the man's side, he could not take the chance he would be seen leaving the narrow stairs that led to the beach. When O'Shaughnessy went down on one knee, Garahan crept closer to the mouth of the alleyway, still holding his position. Finally, the man got to his feet and made it to where Garahan waited.

"Ah, what a fight," his contact told him. "Never felt as much pleasure beating a man in my life."

"Ye won?"

O'Shaughnessy snorted and leaned heavily against Garahan, who steadied him. "Left him unconscious in the middle of the arena—couldn't take the chance he'd wake up and claim it wasn't a fair fight."

Garahan asked, "Was it?"

"In a way."

Garahan chuckled and shook his head. "A roundabout way, I'm thinking." He removed his cravat and wrapped it around the man's skull. "Ye'll need that tended to."

O'Shaughnessy shrugged, glanced around them, and pointed to the other end of the alley. "There's no windows or doors halfway down—we'll speak there."

Understanding that O'Shaughnessy did not want to be overheard, Garahan moved in front of the man, in case he keeled over, and walked the short distance. "What have ye learned?"

"There's talk on the docks about a plot involving Baron Summerfield."

Garahan kept his anger in check. "Credible?"

"Aye, payback for what your brother and cousin did."

Garahan clenched his jaw and curled his hands into tight fists. "Which ones? I've three brothers and twenty-four first cousins."

"Ryan Garahan and Killian O'Ghill, who I've heard arrived a few months ago."

Garahan nodded. "I thought the matter involving Baron and Baroness Summerfield was settled?"

"It was, but now there's talk of vengeance against the baron for ruining a man's reputation."

Garahan's blood ran cold. "What about me sister-in-law's? Is it the bloody bastard that kidnapped her? Do ye know what that bleeding member of the *ton* had planned for her?"

O'Shaughnessy nodded. "Aye. Rumors ride atop the mail coach to and from London. But it's the blackguard's cousin who seeks revenge."

"Where can I find the cousin?"

"He's a known cardsharp who's dead accurate with a pistol and frequents Scarlet Ribbons and The Scarlet Boudoir. His name's Ashbrook—Harrison Ashbrook."

"How many has he killed on the field of honor?"

"Not a one. He prefers settling disputes under the cover of night."

Garahan passed the man a few coins, but O'Shaughnessy refused them. "This is about your family. Keep it for the next time you need information."

Garahan reached into his pocket and drew out his flask. "At least take a few swigs of the Irish—it'll clear yer head."

"Now that I'll accept." O'Shaughnessy grinned as Garahan handed the flask to him. When he was finished, he passed it back. "Thank you."

Garahan asked the question plaguing him: "Why isn't the man wanting to take out his vengeance on me brother and me cousin? Why the baron?"

O'Shaughnessy shook his head, then put a hand to it. "And I'm the one who's been pummeled in the head tonight. Think, man—what does the baron have that your brother doesn't?"

"Besides his title and estate… *Bloody coin!*" Garahan blamed his lack of forethought on his anger. "I wasn't thinking clearly. Me mind was going over what I plan to do to the man when I find him."

"Not a thing, if I know you as well as I believe I do."

Garahan's shoulders slumped. "Ye have the right of it, though I enjoy planning the gruesome details that I dream I'll be carrying out."

"No crime in dreaming, Garahan."

"None at all."

The two men parted, with Garahan heading toward the beach, and O'Shaughnessy up the steps leading to the tavern.

A breeze blew through the alleyway as Garahan walked toward the water. It was ebb tide, but there was enough beach exposed that he could walk along the edge and not get his boots wet. He had never owned a pair of boots made to fit before being hired by the duke. He took pride—and as much care as possible, given his duties—in the finely tailored black uniform and boots the duke insisted they wear.

A few minutes later, he walked past Execution Dock. He stared up at the gallows, suppressing a shudder. While he believed in justice, he did not agree with the High Court of Admiralty's use of the short noose—so that pirates would be strangled to death—instead of using the longer rope designed to break the neck quickly.

An unexpected chill raced up his spine, annoying the *shite* out of him. For a moment he wondered if it was the spirit of one of the four men hanged for piracy at the dock last month. Thinking of the recent hangings reminded him of what his cousin Finn O'Malley had suffered at the hands of the crooked official in Cornwall. The man was purported to have been dealing with wreckers and smugglers. Garahan wondered if the official had intended to use a short noose on Finn. The excise man had nearly succeeded in hanging his cousin—if not for the timely interference of Darby's brother James, and two of Coventry's men,

Tremayne and Hennessey. Last he heard, Finn, his wife, and their infant daughter were all doing well.

He ignored the mist and accompanying chill settling around him and continued past the dock and the scaffold looming above his head. A wisp of a breeze from the water swirled past him, and he wondered if the family rumor was true. Was there a pirate on Ma's side of the family? 'Twas long rumored every last one of the Flanagans were crafty liars and pirates. But his ma insisted they were privateers who sailed with the express permission of the king—and not pirates who answered to no man. His ma never lied and had a bone-deep faith that she'd passed on to her sons. Mayhap he'd ask her in his next letter home.

He walked past the first few sets of steps leading up to the street, choosing one that was a good distance from the tavern where he'd left O'Shaughnessy. No one was about, which had his hackles rising. It was still a few hours before dawn. The alley should have had at least one footpad plying his trade.

A faint shuffling sound echoed behind him. He spun on the balls of his feet, blade in hand, balanced to spring in either direction to avoid the cudgel and the behemoth that held it above his head.

Garahan recognized the mountain of a man at once and sheathed his weapon. "What in the bloody hell are ye doing on the docks, Leach? O'Malley said ye were working in Covent Garden near the Dark Walk."

Leach lowered his arm, resting the cudgel on his shoulder. "Ran afoul of the Watch—but it wasn't my fault."

"What happened? Mayhap I can fix it for ye."

"Got any whiskey left in your flask?"

Garahan grinned. "I might. But ye'll have to tell me the truth. Ye know the lot of us have to keep our noses clean—that includes our contacts that walk that fine line between right and wrong."

"I was in the wrong place at the wrong time and interfered where I shouldn't have. Even a blind man could see the lass was an innocent."

Garahan's gut iced over as he thought of the angel-faced lass and the others they'd rescued. "Was she harmed?"

Leach shook his head. "Not one hair on her head, but I cannot say the same for the man intending to have his way with her."

"How does the Watch figure into this?"

"The watchman arrived as I knocked the blackguard off his feet into the street."

"Did ye tell him what happened?"

"Didn't have the time—the lass was about to keel over in a dead faint. I couldn't very well let her bash her head on the cobblestones after I saved her virtue, could I?"

"Only ye could rescue a lass and end up in a tangled web, Leach."

"Aye. Now, about that whiskey…"

Garahan handed over his flask. While he drank, Garahan promised to speak to Coventry and King—both of whom knew how valuable the contacts in and around the seamier sides of London were, as they had their own. Combined, the web of information flowing from the streets and alleyways to Grosvenor Square and Bow Street aided their goal of protecting the duke and his family. To interrupt the source would be detrimental to their ability to perform their duties.

Garahan nodded to Leach. The men parted ways, with Garahan walking toward the lone lighted lamppost to hail a hack that would drop him off a few blocks from Grosvenor Square and the duke's town house. Halfway there, he wished he'd ridden his horse, but his mount deserved a rest after the last two days.

WHEN GARAHAN ARRIVED at Grosvenor Square, O'Malley and Findley were waiting for his report. By the time he'd finished giving it, O'Malley's anger more than matched his own. "We need to speak to King immediately about Leach. He's a trusted source, but his size has been known to intimidate those who don't know the man."

"Aye, me thoughts exactly," Garahan replied. "He and

O'Shaughnessy share the same battered looks and size. If I didn't know the man, I'd have pissed meself when he came at me with that cudgel."

Findley snorted, and O'Malley glared at him. "'Tisn't a laughing matter."

"Aye," Garahan agreed. "'Tis a complication, and places Miss Michaela and the lasses in more danger than they are already in."

O'Malley stared at him. "And as far as we've been told, the man responsible for his part in kidnapping yer sister-in-law is still being held?"

"Aye. The cousin is determined to free him at any cost."

O'Malley digested the information. "When Ashbrook finds out we diverted the lasses from their final destinations at Scarlet Ribbons or The Scarlet Boudoir, we may be in for a minor war."

"We'll handle it, though we'd best send word to Coventry and King," Findley said.

"Aye," Garahan agreed. "We can put our protection plan together while we work out our plan to take care of Ashbrook." He waited for O'Malley to agree before leading the men inside.

While O'Malley roused one of the footmen to have him deliver Garahan's messages, Findley told Garahan, "Mrs. O'Toole was worried that you hadn't had time to eat. She left a few of her meat pies and a large slice of her butter cake for you."

O'Malley caught up to them and chuckled. "With strict instructions that ye weren't supposed to share a bit of the cake with either one of us."

Findley grumbled, "Her butter cake with currants melts in your mouth."

Garahan quickly finished the meat pies. Reaching for the cake, he grinned. "I know where she hides the cake at night."

O'Malley grinned back. "Do ye now?"

"Where?" Findley asked at the same time.

Garahan finished the cake in a few bites, brushed the crumbs from his waistcoat, and said, "Follow me, lads." He led the way to the room just beyond the pantry and the new wardrobe Mrs.

O'Toole had had the men carry down from one of the upstairs bedchambers, claiming she needed it for extra linens and things.

He opened the wardrobe door and reached for the covered plate on the top shelf. "Only a thin slice each, mind." O'Malley and Findley immediately started to complain, but Garahan cut them off. "If I know Mrs. O'Toole, she'll have stuffed the both of ye earlier, with as big as slice as the one she left for me." The men had to agree as Garahan carried the cake to the kitchen. "We'd best not leave a trail of crumbs."

"She'd know we've been in the cake," Findley said.

"And ban us from the kitchen," O'Malley predicted.

"I heard she only did that when she caught you and James fighting over Melinda."

"And I'd do it again," the familiar female voice said. "No one brings a fight into my kitchen!"

Garahan flinched. "Mrs. O'Toole! We didn't hear you come in."

"Is everything all right?" O'Malley asked.

"What do you need?" Findley added.

"I heard three overgrown *mice* in my kitchen," Mrs. O'Toole said, looking from one man to the next.

"Faith, if ye don't remind me of me ma! Ready to clobber us upside the head." Garahan walked over and pressed a kiss to her cheek.

"What a woman," O'Malley agreed, kissing her other cheek.

Mrs. O'Toole smiled and stared at Findley until he grinned and walked over to kiss her forehead. "Your butter cake is hard to resist, Mrs. O'Toole."

"It is a good thing I knew Garahan's big heart would feel sorry for you two—even though you both had a huge slice earlier," the cook said. "He knows where I keep one of the extra cakes I always bake."

"Do ye have other hiding places?" O'Malley asked.

Garahan grinned. "That's a challenge I may have to accept."

"I wasn't challenging you to search for it." Brushing a lock of hair out of her eyes, she crossed her arms in front of her. "You should be happy that I bake for the lot of you, even though I know you try to filch more cake after I've gone to bed!"

He opened his mouth to speak and quickly closed it. "Ye have me word not to search for yer other hiding place, Mrs. O'Toole," Garahan promised. "As long as ye keep an extra cake—or plate of scones—in the wardrobe down the hall."

"I'll think about it. Now, give me what's left of my cake and be about your business. I have to be up in a few hours to light the oven."

"Thank ye, Mrs. O'Toole." Garahan bowed to her and heard the echo of a door opening and closing. "Our man's back," he told the others. The trio walked down the hallway to the rear door.

The footman jolted in surprise. "I didn't hear you coming."

"Ye weren't supposed to," O'Malley said.

"Any message from King or Coventry about Leach?" Garahan asked.

"Aye," the young man said. "They will handle matters."

Garahan nodded. "Thank ye, lad. Ye'd best get some rest now. Ye'll be busy tomorrow." When the young man headed to the servants' staircase, Garahan elbowed O'Malley in the ribs. "I'm wide awake. I'll take the early shift."

"Findley's had the most sleep," O'Malley said. "He'll take it. Grab a few hours' sleep. If I don't see ye in four hours, I'll send him to wake ye."

Garahan sighed. "All right, but as O'Shaughnessy's me contact, I should be the one to meet with Coventry in the morning."

"And Leach is mine! I'm thinking—" O'Malley began.

Garahan interrupted his cousin, "And thinking's where ye always end up in trouble. I'll need ye to speak to Miss Michaela first thing. She needs to be prepared."

O'Malley frowned, and Garahan added, "Tell her—and the lass—that I'll stop by after me meeting. We'll be needing one of Coventry's men to help us protect her and the girls."

"Ye have the right of it," O'Malley finally agreed. "Findley, ye know where to find us."

CHAPTER NINE

A FEW DAYS later, Aimee hugged Michaela. "I cannot thank you enough for your help. I had given up hope and nearly resigned myself to a life that I could never have possibly envisioned."

"You're welcome. Now do remember that Lord and Lady Smythe-Wyatt are trusted friends and have been instrumental in lending aid whenever possible. Their housekeeper, Mrs. Plumton, trains the young women I send to her. After their training, they can choose to take a position in another household as a maid—upstairs or downstairs—or a lady's maid. Mrs. Plumton is quite thorough in her instruction."

Aimee hesitated. "Are you certain that I'm ready? I don't want Mrs. Plumton or Lord and Lady Smythe-Wyatt to think that I am not good enough."

Michaela raised a hand. "What happened was never about all that is good inside of you, Aimee. It was about control and exerting the physical strength to take what you would not freely give. Do not forget that I too have had the same worries and thoughts that you are experiencing right now. Never give in to them! That black-hearted lord took what you never offered, and he had no right to. That does not demean you—no matter what Society says! You were not a willing participant."

"But I—"

"You thought he was offering marriage and a chance at a better life," Michaela continued. "When you balked at becoming his mistress, you hurt his insufferable pride, and he took his revenge physically and left you to face the consequences of his actions alone...penniless. He deserves to be drawn and quartered."

Aimee flinched at the thought. "A traitor's death?"

"You're right," Michaela said. "That would be too good for him. Are you familiar with Greek mythology?"

Aimee smiled. "Father enjoyed myths from other lands. One of the books my cousin took from me when I arrived on his doorstep was my father's favorite book of Greek myths."

"Took it?"

"He said it was too valuable to let a child keep, so he sold it."

"I'm sorry." Michaela was silent for a moment before asking, "Do you remember the myth about Prometheus?"

Aimee shivered. "Yes. He stole fire from Olympus and gave it to humans."

"I think his punishment might be more fitting for what was done to you...and to me." Before Aimee could respond, Michaela said, "We should bind the guilty parties and chain them to a rock for all to see."

For the first time since she'd been compromised, Aimee felt as if she were regaining control of her life. "But should it be an eagle or other bird of prey that will land on him and eat his liver?"

Michaela's eyes narrowed. "Why not a flock of them?"

"Er...yes...but the torment would not last as long," Aimee murmured. "I wonder, do you think it was as painful as for his liver to grow back as it was to be pecked out?"

Michaela's eyes widened. "An excellent question. I wonder if there is an account of scholars debating that question, and if so, what their collective hypothesis was."

"I'm afraid that I have not had access to a library in years," Aimee admitted. "It would be heaven to be able to run the tips of my fingers along the spines of books, reading the titles, selecting a book to read at my leisure." She blinked and shrugged. "A dream I have often had. I know it is not realistic, though. Servants dust the spines of books in their master's library—they are not at liberty to read them."

"You would be surprised at how things are done in the Smythe-Wyatt household."

"How so?" Aimee did not want to get her hopes up. She had already cried her eyes out the night before, having missed seeing Garahan the day before when she was meeting with Mrs. Plumton about the possibility of working for the Smythe-Wyatts. Her heart sank. She had a feeling she would never see her knight in shining armor again. The knights in the stories her mother read to her all those years ago were just that—legends, myths, and stories. Real heroes did not exist.

Then what would you call Garahan? her head asked.

Wonderful, her heart replied.

"Now then, I have made a note of the address where Mary, Alice, and Beatrice will be scullery maids."

"But I thought they wanted to cook?"

"Ah," Michaela said. "They will watch and learn working under Mrs. Peachtree's tutelage."

Aimee admitted, "I remember hearing you tell them about Mrs. Peachtree, but I cannot remember the name of the employer she cooks for."

"Lord and Lady MacAfee. Do not worry about the girls. From what I have gleaned from speaking to them individually, they were beyond shocked when they were forced to observe what would be expected of them at the boarding house. Mary was the only one who mentioned missing one of the stable lads and confessed he kissed her cheek." Michaela's relief was evident when she continued, "Just as the Smythe-Wyatt household is a safe environment, the MacAfee household is a safe haven. They will do well under Mrs. Peachtree."

Aimee nodded, and Michaela continued, "Sally and Jenny are in Sussex in Squire Needham's household. Did you know he married a seamstress? The girls will learn to sew as well as help the scullery maids in the kitchen after both being all but sold to that horrid woman at the boarding house."

"Why did their orphanage allow it?"

"Apparently, one can have credentials forged quite easily," Michaela answered. "If one has connections. Unfortunately, the orphanage did not have the resources to verify those credentials."

Aimee shook her head. "I have been dealt with unkindly by my relatives since losing my parents, shuffled from home to home, until I ended up at with my cousin and his wife."

"You were fortunate not to have been sent to an orphanage."

"Was I? They never treated me as one of the family, and I was constantly reminded I was the poor relation. I scrubbed their floors and did their mending until I was strong enough to help with the family's laundry. Their servants were getting too old to haul in the water and handle the sheer amount of work without assistance. When I was four and ten, I took on the brunt of those chores, along with others."

Michaela's sympathetic expression soothed her. "While I was not allowed to do household chores, I was Father's right hand when he had patients. It was my job to set out the proper instruments, the cleansing and healing herbs and salves, boiled threads, and linen squares and strips of all lengths. I calmed his patients, and acted as his extra pair of hands when called upon. While he gave the patients the instructions for their continued care, I was the one who straightened his surgery and restocked the supplies. Not the same amount of work, but work nonetheless for a young girl who previously was taught to play the pianoforte, embroider with silk threads, and paint watercolors."

Aimee marveled at the varied extent of Michaela's instruction and experience. Head whirling with all that the woman had learned, she blurted out, "Did you have singing lessons or a dance master?"

Michaela smiled. "My poor voice instructor told Father there was no hope, as in her opinion I would never be able to carry a tune, unless it was in a bucket."

Aimee giggled. "What did your father say?"

"He offered the woman a bonus to stay on for a fortnight."

"Did she take it?"

"Sadly, she did not," Michaela admitted.

"What of the dancing master?"

"He was the most beautiful man I had ever laid eyes on. Romantic and effusive in his praise of my aptitude for dancing...but..."

Michaela's voice trailed off, prompting Aimee to ask, "What happened?"

"Father interrupted our lessons and was horrified to learn that Signore Moralto was teaching me the waltz—without Father's knowledge. He was let go on the spot." Michaela sighed. "Whirling around the upstairs ballroom was a heady experience for a young woman of six and ten."

"Had you already made your debut?" Aimee asked.

"No. Mother passed away when I was three and ten. Father was consumed with his physician's practice. When I wasn't in his surgery, he had me continue the lessons my mother had begun. She promised to hire a dance tutor the year I turned four and ten—instead, we spent that year mourning Mother. Father finally realized I had been spending too much time assisting him, instead of following my mother's plan for my future. But after the fiasco with Signore Moralto, nothing was ever mentioned about engaging another dance instructor."

"What of carriage rides in the park, or tea at Gunter's?"

Michaela shrugged. "Enough talk of the past. We were speaking of Sally and Jenny, were we not?"

Aimee wanted to know more about Michaela. To her, the woman was an enigma, a woman to emulate, and she intended to aid Michaela once she had completed her tutorship with the Smythe-Wyatts. Promising herself to prod Michaela into speaking of it again, she replied, "You were telling me how the girls were getting on."

"They are coming out of their shells now that they are once again able to spend time out-of-doors and in the stables, where they have been given the duty of feeding the squire's horses their favorite treats."

"Have you received word from the squire's wife? Are they adjusting to their lessons from Mrs. Needham and the cook?"

Michaela smiled. "Yes, quite well, as a matter of fact, especially given that I normally send older girls to them."

"I wonder, do Sally and Jenny still ask for O'Malley?"

Michaela laughed. "Indeed, they do. There is something about the men in the duke's guard that inspires trust."

"How many of them have you met?"

"Just a few. My introduction to the men who work for the duke was Garahan's brother James," Michaela answered. "His bone-deep worry for Miss Waring—one of the women I rescued, and whom he later married—was plain to see. Poor man thought he was hiding his feelings."

"He wasn't?"

Michaela sighed. "It was the intensity in his gaze, and the way he proposed to her in this very room."

Aimee glanced around. "Here?" The sparse room in the run-down building wasn't exactly a romantic setting, and mayhap why the very idea of it appealed to her. "And she accepted?"

Michaela shook her head. "I could tell that she was shocked by his declaration, and still in pain from her injuries." She locked gazes with Aimee. "What is more, she did not feel worthy because of her circumstances—her own cousin accepted coin from his tavern's customers to do whatever they wished with her."

Aimee's hand covered her mouth, but not the anguished gasp she could not contain. "Did she... Did they..."

"James saved her from that fate, too. I do not normally share what happened to the others whom I have been able to aid, but I need you to understand that your past does not have to define your future."

"Do you know, Darby Garahan mentioned something similar to me. I thought…" Aimee's voice trailed off. What could she say? That she'd hoped to see him again? He had kept his word to return, although she had not been here, as she was taking that first step toward her new life, meeting with the Smythe-Wyatts' housekeeper at the time.

"He and O'Malley constantly move about the city," Michaela reminded her. "They chase down threats and ferret out those who make them against the duke and his family. When the duke's family travels to London, they are accompanied by the members of the duke's guard."

"Have there been that many attempts on the duke's life?"

"More than I imagine they realize, if my sources are accurate, and I do believe that they are. His twins were only a few months old when there was a kidnapping attempt at his estate in the Lake District."

"Infant twins? How horrible!" Aimee could not conceive of anyone acting in such a manner—or why. "What could they possibly want with two innocent babes?"

"Triple their weight in coin, no doubt," Michaela replied.

"Does it always come down to coin?"

Michaela nodded.

"I overheard both Miss Scarlets speaking to Mrs. Underwood about the coin they would charge for the innocents from the country." Aimee shook her head. "When I heard that, I thought about confessing what had happened to me to distract them—but realized it would not matter if I were innocent, or not once they sold me to their first customer. I decided to not to let them know I was eavesdropping."

"Wise decision—neither woman is to be trusted. Besides, it was none of their affair. At least Mrs. Underwood will pay for her crimes, though I'm not certain that we will know the extent of them, as she has more than likely been involved in this scheme for years. As for the two Miss Scarlets, they have benefactors in high places—and will not receive more than a reprimand."

"That does not seem fair at all! Especially considering their part in this whole scheme. I understand luring young women who would be interested in seeking better positions in London, but Sally and Jenny are not old enough for what they intended for us!"

"With their light hair and angelic blue eyes, they were to be groomed for an elite group of customers—"

Aimee put her hands to her ears. "Don't tell me any more. I cannot bear to listen."

Michaela sighed. "You do not have to, but you need to know that such depravity exists and that those with such proclivities are willing to pay handsomely to satisfy their unholy needs. Be aware and on the lookout—you may be able to save others like those two little girls."

Aimee dropped her hands and met Michaela's gaze. "You're absolutely right. I cannot hide from it any more than I could hide from what Wolfingham intended and did to me. I promise to be vigilant and send word to you if I suspect or hear anything untoward."

The two women hugged one last time. The knock on the door was the signal that it was time for Aimee to leave. "Your future awaits, Aimee. Remember you are a survivor, and you deserve this opportunity to earn a living working in a household where you will be treated with kindness and respect, and your work ethic will be rewarded."

"I can never thank you enough."

Michaela smiled. "You already have. Remember what we spoke of and please be vigilant. Never go anywhere alone in London!"

"I promise." Aimee paused in the doorway and asked, "If Garahan should happen to stop by, will you tell him I said thank you again?"

"You have my word."

As Aimee descended the staircase, she wondered if she would ever see the handsome-as-sin Irishman again. He'd not only rescued her, he'd turned her life upside down, and inside out as well.

Settling in the carriage, she rubbed at the ache in her breast where her heart used to be. From the moment Garahan swept her into his arms, it was no longer her own.

He held it in his strong, callused hands.

CHAPTER TEN

GARAHAN LEAPT FROM his horse and jumped into the fray, pulling the first one of three thugs off Greenwood's back.

No longer weighed down, Miss Michaela's guard elbowed one in the face and the other in his gut.

Garahan grabbed the man holding his gut and flung him against the building. Satisfied he'd knocked the man out when the blackguard slid into a boneless heap, he turned to help subdue the third attacker and shook his head. "If ye were aiming for his nose, Greenwood, ye missed. I'm thinking ye broke his jaw."

"Obliged, Garahan," Greenwood said. "They jumped me when I opened the door—tried to get past me—but I blocked them."

Garahan untied his cravat and told the guard, "Hold still—yer head's bleeding like a stuck pig." He wrapped it around Greenwood's head, but it did little to stop the bleeding. "Miss Michaela's going to have to tend to that gash on yer head. What in the bloody hell did they hit ye with?"

Michaela's guard lifted his chin toward the bloodstained metal bar lying on the sidewalk.

Garahan winced. "Aye, that'd do it. Hang on." His short, sharp whistle was answered immediately by Burke and one of his men. "Have ye any spare rope on ye?"

Burke sighed. "Can't remember to bring your own?"

Garahan cuffed him on the shoulder. "I used three of them an hour ago and haven't had the time to replenish me supply."

His contact shook his head and told Greenwood, "Garahan always says that."

"'Tis the truth, Burke."

He snorted. "And he says that, too."

Greenwood smirked. "But he's a good man to have at your back in a fight."

"We'll be needing the Watch," Garahan said.

"Already sent for him," his contact replied. "You mentioned the need to keep an extra eye on things here," Burke reminded him. "I also sent word to your man, Coventry."

"Thank ye, Burke."

The watchman arrived while Garahan was tying the third man's hands behind his back. He shoved him beside the others and greeted the watchman, "Edwards, isn't it?"

"Aye, Garahan. You get around London, don't you?"

Garahan shrugged in answer and pointed to the third man. "I arrived in time to pull this one off Greenwood's back while the other two were beating the *shite* out of him."

"Never would have happened if the one holding his gut had not clocked me in the head with that iron bar," Greenwood insisted.

The watchman picked up the bar and nodded. "Surprised it didn't knock you unconscious."

"Saw stars for a few minutes, but it cleared well enough," Michaela's guard replied. "Couldn't let them get past me inside."

The watchman studied Greenwood for a moment before asking, "Guarding your family—isn't that what you said a sennight ago?"

"Aye," the man agreed. "Garahan here's a distant cousin."

Two men on horseback rode up and dismounted. Recognizing the one with the scar bisecting his face as working for Coventry, Garahan knew both men would be armed to the teeth.

"What have you done now, Garahan?" the scarred man

asked.

"Nothing me brother James would not have done. Thank ye for coming, Tremayne. Edwards is the Watch hereabouts."

The retired dragoon nodded to the man beside him. "Bayfield wanted to meet the youngest of the Garahan brothers."

The men acknowledged the introduction, and Garahan said, "I've heard yer name mentioned along with Hennessey and Masterson. Coventry speaks highly of ye."

"Coventry saved my life," Bayfield said. With a glance at the men lined up on the sidewalk, he frowned at Tremayne. "We should have hired a hack."

"There isn't always a need for one," Tremayne reminded him. "Why don't you see if you can flag one down?"

Bayfield snorted. "I doubt we'll find a hack willing to pick up a fare on this street. I'll backtrack two streets—should be able to hire one there."

Garahan noticed Burke had slipped back into the shadows but did not call attention to that fact. Burke may be his contact, but the man did not know Tremayne or Bayfield. No need for him to call attention to himself more than he already had.

"Since ye're here, Tremayne, would ye mind helping Edwards keep an eye on these three?" Garahan asked. "I'm thinking Greenwood needs that gash sewn closed."

"Not a problem." Tremayne walked over to the men, putting his hands on his hips so they could see the two pistols tucked in his belt. "I've a short knife in my left boot and a long one in my right."

The men stared up at Tremayne. Two flinched, and Garahan wanted to beat them bloody for staring at the slashing scar on Tremayne's face, but did not want to call attention to it. The former dragoon acted as if it wasn't there, so Garahan would as well. Instead, he chuckled. "Do ye always give away where ye have yer weapons stashed? I like to keep mine secret until I need them."

Tremayne shrugged. "I use my scar to my advantage—most

miscreants are too busy staring in horror at it to even hear me tell them what weapons I'm carrying and where."

Garahan didn't know how to respond to that comment, so he didn't. "After I deliver Greenwood to his family, I'll return."

As soon as he closed the door behind them, Greenwood swayed. Garahan steadied him and helped him up the stairs. He knocked on the door. "Miss Michaela, Greenwood's injured—can ye open the door?"

The door swung open, revealing the angel of the streets. Garahan noted she was alone.

The flash of worry in her eyes was quickly masked by a neutral expression. "I'll need the light. Come, sit by the lantern, Greenwood."

Garahan deposited the man in the chair and scanned the room. "I know ye said the little ones are tucked away in Sussex, but where is everyone else? I thought we'd be needing to cart them to safety."

While Michaela washed up, she answered, "It's been a fortnight since you stopped by to see Aimee—who was out at the time. Mary, Beatrice, and Alice have found positions working in an excellent household. For their safety, I cannot disclose where." She paused, then asked, "Would you mind washing up? I may need your help holding the wound closed while I sew it. That gash is deep and the edges a bit ragged."

Garahan did as she asked and returned to her side. "Ye'll be wanting to close yer eyes, Greenwood—otherwise ye'll go cross-eyed watching. Do ye have any spirits, Miss Michaela?"

"There's a flask of brandy behind the pile of linens."

Greenwood shuddered. "Never touch the stuff."

Garahan reached into his waistcoat pocket. "Well now, how does a few sips of Irish whiskey sound?"

Michaela's guard sighed. "Not as good as a tot of rum." Garahan started to put the flask away, but Greenwood stopped him. "Did I mention I have recently developed a taste for whiskey?"

Garahan could tell the man was in pain, so he didn't tease

him further. He removed the stopper and handed it over. "Take all ye need."

"A few sips only," Michaela cautioned. "The injury to his head may have other complications which do not need to be muddled by spirits." Reluctantly Greenwood returned the flask after a few large sips.

With a nod to Michaela, Garahan positioned himself where she indicated and placed his hands where she instructed. She worked quickly and efficiently, reminding him of Emmett's skill with needle and thread. When she finished, she said, "You can let go now, Garahan. Thank you." She bandaged the wound and wrapped a length of linen around her guard's head.

"Ye're welcome. I need to see what's happening downstairs."

"You should rest, Greenwood." The man mumbled beneath his breath and stood, but Miss Michaela ignored him, placing a hand to the middle of his chest. Garahan marveled that the petite woman showed no fear. "Surely whoever was out there has been subdued." She locked gazes with Garahan, who nodded.

"I'll return shortly. I need to be asking ye a few questions." He sensed Miss Michaela knew what he wanted to ask. The last time he was here, he'd asked after the lass and was told she had a meeting with a possible employer. He needed to know where in the bloody hell she was this time. How could he keep his promise to protect her if he never saw her again?

"Thank you for assisting me, Garahan, and for helping Greenwood."

"Me pleasure." Leveling a hard look at her guard, he told him, "Wait here."

He jogged down the stairs and slipped outside to find the sidewalk empty. Scanning the area, he sensed Burke was no longer there. Confident Coventry's men and the Watch had handled the situation, he retraced his steps.

Greenwood was standing, feet spread, arms crossed, while Miss Michaela was moving around the room, piling her medicinal supplies into a large satchel. "What are ye doing?" Garahan asked.

She paused to look at him, then turned back to her task. "Packing. It is no longer safe here."

"Where will ye go?"

"There are a few possibilities, though I cannot divulge them at this time. Every few months, I change locations, for safety's sake. I would never be able to remain anonymous if rumors started."

"I'm thinking more people know of ye than ye realize, Miss Michaela. Wouldn't ye agree, Greenwood?"

"We were just discussing that fact."

Michaela spun around. "*We* most certainly were not. *You* were telling me what to do!"

"I was doing the job you hired me to do," he responded. "Protecting you."

Garahan noted the same frustrated anger roiling inside of him on the other man's face. "Well then, it appears ye have no concern for yer own safety."

She glared at him. "For your information, I do not have the time, nor the resources, to chase after every person who tries to storm their way into my rooms! I would not be able to continue my work if those men had succeeded in getting past Greenwood. Anonymity is essential to my ability to help these women."

Garahan heard the edge of fear in her voice and knew he would be adding Miss Michaela to his growing list of those he protected. "Will ye tell me where ye're going?"

She extinguished the lantern on the table along the wall, grabbed her satchel, and turned to face him. "That would not be wise. I have no idea who those men were downstairs, or if they are connected with the boarding house owner, the brothels—or a host of other possibilities tied to the young women I have helped in the last six months."

With only one lantern lit, it was hard to see her expression, but he felt her unease as it swirled around her. "I cannot protect ye if I don't know where to find ye."

"Miss Michaela thinks she does not need our protection,

Garahan. Though she does. In fact, she puts up with me because of the time—"

"I'm ready to go, Greenwood," Michaela interrupted. "Please fetch the lantern."

Garahan watched with interest as the older man stared down at her for long moments before doing her bidding. Instinct demanded he toss the woman over his shoulder and cart her to the safety of the duke's town house, but fought against that to ask, "Are ye certain ye do not need me help?"

"She'll send word to you when she has established her new location," Greenwood promised.

Michaela frowned at her guard. "You know I cannot do that. It compromises the safety of those I aid."

"No matter," Garahan told him. "I'll find her," he promised, blocking the door. When she tried to go around him, he said, "I need to know where ye sent the lass."

"Why?"

"I gave me word that I'd be back to see her. Me word is me bond."

"And I told her that you stopped by and spoke with me," Michaela replied.

"'Tisn't the same, and ye know it. I won't be breaking me word to the lass. She needs to know that there is one man she can trust to keep his word. That would be me."

"I will send word in the morning. By then I will be settled in my new location."

He relented, knowing how volatile their situation would be if they stayed a moment longer. Whoever had sent the thugs may send more. "If ye don't, ye'll find me camped out on yer doorstep."

"But you don't know where I'll be," she protested.

"I have me ways of finding ye."

"Then I suggest you use them to find Miss Anderson."

"Do ye want to risk having the lass thinking all the men she meets are not trustworthy? Don't ye think she needs to learn to trust again?" When Michaela's eyes welled with tears, his suspicions about her were confirmed. "I'm thinking ye need to learn the same."

She blinked, and the tears were gone. "I trust Greenwood almost as much as I trusted Alasdair."

"Almost?" Greenwood asked.

"We need to leave. Now, Greenwood. Please?"

The man's heavy sigh was another indication that the woman was as stubborn as Emmett. Thinking of the sparks between his cousin and Michaela, Garahan had a feeling he was destined to be related to the lass.

He stepped aside and held the door open. "I can follow at a distance."

She shook her head. "Not necessary, thank you, Garahan. Greenwood, I'll follow you down." Garahan reached for her bag, but she tightened her hold on it. "I always carry my supplies with me. If I get separated from Greenwood, I will have what I need at a moment's notice."

"Do ye mean to travel on foot?"

"Every question, every minute, could bring more trouble, Garahan. Please try to understand from my point of view."

"Aye, Miss Michaela."

He paused, and she told him, "We'll wait until you leave."

Knowing he had no choice if he wanted the hardheaded woman to reach her new location safely, he acquiesced. "I'll be speaking to ye in a few days."

She reached out and touched his sleeve. "And you'll speak to Miss Anderson?"

"I will. I gave me word."

"But I haven't told you where she is—for her safety, and that of the family she is working for."

"I know. And I'm grateful for the precautions ye're taking. I'll find her."

"Then why did you bother asking where she is?"

"'Twould save time," Garahan said. "Keeping me word to the

lass is but one item on me list of duties."

He nodded to Miss Michaela and held Greenwood's gaze. The other man inclined his head, and Garahan knew the message was received. They would keep in contact with one another in their bid to keep the angel of the streets safe.

$$\diamond$$

CHAPTER ELEVEN

AIMEE BRUSHED A hand over the soft material of the new gown she wore, courtesy of Lord and Lady Smythe-Wyatt's generosity. She'd been in their household for a fortnight and had easily adapted to working alongside the other downstairs maids. When asked to help one of the upstairs maids with her duties, she performed those tasks without instruction. She'd handled all those tasks—and on occasion helped with the cooking—at the inn where she had been employed after being abandoned there.

She felt lucky to be sharing a bedchamber with two of the other maids on the third floor and was slowly accepting the fact that she was safe. Aimee was proud of the fact that she didn't think of Garahan every waking hour—as she'd feared she might. She only thought of him every *other* hour.

So many things about the handsome Irishman haunted her thoughts. It wasn't just the width of his shoulders, nor the breadth of his chest... And they were impressive. It was the lack of censure in his dark brown eyes that pulled her to him. He had every right to think badly of her, given where he'd rescued her from. But he didn't; he'd even encouraged her to let go of the past and look to the future.

Her first thought upon waking was Garahan. Not just his heroic rescue, but how he had kept his word and gone back for the other girls, delivering them from evil to Miss Michaela and a chance at a new future. When she laid her head on her pillow at night, her last thought before sleep claimed her was the warmth of his strong arms wrapped around her.

Her heart ached for the man.

As she dusted and polished the furniture, she prayed she would be able to forget him. But she kept imagining that she had seen him while accompanying Mrs. Plumton on her errands. A tall, broad-shouldered, dark-haired man in black had passed by on horseback, but when she blinked, she had lost sight of him. Twice she felt as if she were being watched and caught a glimpse of a dark-haired man out of the corner or her eye. Was it truly Garahan, or was she slowly losing her mind?

"Miss Anderson?" Mrs. Plumton gently touched her on the arm. "Are you all right?"

She reined in her imagination, certain that was behind her thinking Garahan had been close by, watching her, protecting her from a distance. "Er...yes. Forgive me, Mrs. Plumton. I was woolgathering."

The gray-haired housekeeper smiled. "Happens to me on occasion, though I noticed you seem a bit more troubled the day after you accompany me on my errands. Perhaps you should stay behind today. I could ask one of the other girls, but I thought you would enjoy the opportunity to visit some of the shops and meet the shopgirls—and shopkeepers. It will give you an idea of what positions you may wish to pursue after you've completed your instructions here. You have proven you have an excellent work ethic and are unafraid to pitch in wherever needed. I know his lordship and her ladyship will give you an excellent letter of recommendation."

Warmth filled her. "You have been so kind to me, when I don't deserve—"

"I'll stop you right there. You deserve a chance to forge a new future for yourself. It is not your fault that you were lured in by a false advert."

Her belly ached as her hands tightened around the polishing

cloth. She had made her decision to leave the kind innkeeper's wife swiftly, decisively, and it had been a big mistake…almost as huge as her decision to elope. That was the wrong choice, too. "How could I have been so easily fooled?"

The housekeeper sighed. "You are not the first young woman taken in by unscrupulous people. You were looking for a dream— a new position where you could better your life. And that, my dear, is still a possibility once you fully let go of the guilt you feel for reaching for that dream."

Tears filled Aimee's eyes, blurring Mrs. Plumton's kind face. She blinked, but it didn't stop them from falling. The soft linen handkerchief pressed into her hand helped her to regain her composure as she wiped her tears. "Thank you, Mrs. Plumton. You have treated me as if I have worth since the moment I arrived."

"Never doubt your worth, Aimee."

She shook her head. "You do not know my circumstances, and if I told you, you would show me the door."

Mrs. Plumton slipped her arm through Aimee's and led her over to the small settee by the window of the rear parlor.

"Oh, but I cannot sit!"

"You can," the housekeeper insisted. "Now please do."

Aimee sat and folded her trembling hands in her lap.

"Years ago, I worked in one of the finest estates in Sussex. I was a few years younger than you at the time, and aspired to rise from the position of downstairs maid to lady's maid. I did not heed the warning from the other maids to steer clear of his lordship and her ladyship's youngest son, believing I could handle myself in all circumstances."

"What happened?" Aimee rasped.

"I was cornered in the library one night after returning one of her ladyship's novels."

Aimee's heart beat faster. "Cornered?"

The housekeeper nodded. "By his lordship's youngest son. He had often made suggestive comments to me, and I rebuffed him successfully…or so I thought. I never believed the tales of the other maids—until that moment when he pinned me against the ladder."

Fear scraped Aimee's belly raw. "Did he take liberties or force…" She could not continue, as her shame and fear returned, and she was once again in the close confines of Wolfingham's carriage.

"Look at me, Aimee."

Unaware that she'd covered her mouth with her hands to keep her own horror inside of her, she obeyed.

"I did not encourage his advances and was not believed. I was let go without references and had nowhere to go, no one to turn to. Is that what happened to you?"

"I had someone to turn to—not my cousin. He would never take me in after I ran away to elope. The man promised to take me away from my life of drudgery to live the life he convinced me I deserved. We were nearly to Gretna Green when he forced himself on me." Gathering her courage, she told Mrs. Plumton how he had laughed when she mentioned marriage. "You see, he never planned to marry me. He was going to set me up as one of his mistresses."

"Then what happened?"

"I gathered what was left of my pride around me and refused. He stopped at the next inn and left me there with the clothes on my back—he refused to give me my reticule or my portmanteau."

The housekeeper reached for her hand and held it. "I was far more fortunate," Mrs. Plumton told her. "The housekeeper got wind of what happened from one of the maids. While I gathered my things, she penned a letter of recommendation—despite being told I was to be turned out without one. Then she handed me a small bag of coins."

"To pay your fare on the mail coach?"

Mrs. Plumton softly smiled. "No. She also gave me a letter of introduction to her sister who worked in a household near

Mayfair."

"She saved you as the innkeeper's wife saved me," Aimee said. "I hadn't realized that I had fallen to my knees as the coach drove away. The hostler helped me to my feet and brought me to Mrs. Potts. She never asked what happened. While she plied me with whiskey-laced tea, she told me I was not the first young woman to be dropped off unceremoniously at the inn." She met Mrs. Plumton's understanding gaze and added, "The inn was just a few miles from Gretna Green."

"You are far more resilient than you realize, my dear. Your Mrs. Potts was concerned when she did not receive the letter you promised to send upon arrival. She was instrumental in finding you. Once her message reached one of the inns just outside of London, word spread quickly. That was how the angel of the streets was able to ascertain your whereabouts."

"I can never repay her or M—" She bit the inside of her cheek—she'd almost murmured Michaela's name. "—or the angel."

"Ah, but you are wrong. Every day you embrace your new position here at Lord Smythe-Wyatt's home, earning an honest day's wages, you pay her back. That you asked Garahan to go back for the other girls cemented your ties to the angel he delivered you to."

"You know about Garahan?" Should she ask if Mrs. Plumton had ever met the man? Would she be able to identify him on sight and confirm Aimee had indeed seen him?

"I have had not had the pleasure of meeting the man, but I know of his connection to Mr. King of the Bow Street Runners, and that he is one of the sixteen men in His Grace's personal guard."

"Would you think I had attics to let if I confessed I thought I caught a glimpse of Garahan recently?"

Mrs. Plumton's smile widened. "Not at all—the man is honorable and would of course wish to see for himself that you are safe and well."

"He did say he would protect me, whether I wanted him to or not."

The housekeeper laughed softly. "Then I have no doubt that you have seen him." She rose to her feet, and Aimee did the same. "Now then, if you have finished with the drawing room, you may borrow a book from the servants' library. I find that reading is a wonderful way to relax."

Aimee thanked Mrs. Plumton before rushing to the door to the servants' side of the town house. Her mood light, her heart full, she slipped into the small, book-lined room and drew in a deep breath. She touched one spine and then another, reading the titles, until she found what she was looking for—a tale of brave knights by Sir Thomas Mallory. Hugging the book to her chest, she closed her eyes and made a wish that someday, she would have a small collection of books that she would lend to those in need of escape from their trials and troubles.

Rather than return to her shared bedchamber on the third floor, she sat on the stool on one side of the doorway. She opened the book and was immediately swept away with tales of the bold, brave, honest knights who served King Arthur.

"Have ye spoken to the lass?"

Garahan stared at his cousin. "Which lass?"

O'Malley snorted with laughter. "The one that has had yer temper on edge for more than a fortnight."

Garahan shrugged. He had no intention of admitting the lass had been much on his mind—and his heart. Although the boarding house owner and her thugs had been carted off to Bow Street, he was concerned that the owners of the two brothels would try to find the lass...and the others they'd liberated.

"Coventry mentioned there's an empty apartment in his building. It is on the ground floor." O'Malley cleared his throat.

"'Twould be a fine place to live…if one had a wife."

Garahan shoved his cousin aside with his shoulder and walked out the rear door. "Bugger it! How in the bloody hell does me *eedjit* cousin know what I'm thinking? I've barely said a word to him—or Coventry, for that matter."

The short, sharp whistle had him spinning around, braced for attack. But there was no sign of an intruder lurking in the shadows…only Emmett grinning from ear to ear. "We all know what ye're thinking, boy-o. 'Tis plain as the nose on yer ugly mug."

Garahan curled his hands into tight fists and mentally imagined how satisfying it would be to rearrange O'Malley face. When he could all but see his cousin's mouth and nose bleeding, he relaxed his hands at his sides. "Ye aren't worth the trouble."

"While ye're out on yer rounds, checking with yer contacts to see if there's any word about the imminent attack on Summerfield, ye might stop by Madame Beaudoine's shop."

"Why in the bloody hell would I? 'Tis ye O'Malleys who have the close connection with the modiste and her seamstress, not the Garahans."

O'Malley nodded. "Aye, which is why I happen to know that a certain lass will be accompanying Smythe-Wyatt's housekeeper to the shop before teatime."

Garahan grinned. "Well now, I may be able to squeeze in a quick stop to see how Her Grace's favorite modiste is doing."

O'Malley chuckled. "Don't dawdle. I need to check in with me contacts when it's me shift to do so."

Garahan was already halfway to the stables when O'Malley called out, "And stop in to speak to Coventry about the apartment."

"*Feck* me," Garahan mumbled, not bothering to answer his cousin. That O'Malley knew what he was thinking did not surprise him—but it irritated the bloody hell out of him.

He strode into the stables and drew in a deep breath. The scent of hay and horse reminded him of home and immediately eased the knot of tension at the base of his skull. "Why in the bloody hell do yer relations always think they know best?" he asked the gelding. When the horse shook his head, Garahan answered his own question. "To irritate the ever-living *shite* out of us, that's why!" He scratched behind the animal's ears. "We'll be gone for a few hours—to the docks, the stews, and the modiste's shop—before we work our way to the corner of Hart and Lumley."

The horse whinnied.

"Now don't ye start in on me, laddie—or no carrots!"

He mounted his now-silent horse and rode toward his first destination—the docks. O'Shaughnessy had nothing new to report.

Burke was waiting for him at the usual place in the stews, a bad sign. Normally, Garahan sought out his contact who hung in the shadows.

Garahan read the man's posture and prepared for bad news. He dismounted and approached. "Miss Michaela?" Burke shook his head, and Garahan's gut iced over. "Miss Anderson?"

This time his contact nodded. "They know where she is—and plan to snatch her back."

"Which brothel?" Garahan asked.

"Rumor is both, Scarlet Ribbons and The Scarlet Boudoir."

"They'll have to get past me!" Garahan vowed. "I was on my way to Madame Beaudoine's shop—O'Malley said she'd be there."

"Then that's where they'll try to grab her," Burke said. "Do you need my help?"

Garahan hesitated. "I may, if I meet with opposition."

Burke nodded. "You don't have much time."

"I'm in yer debt, Burke."

"As I'm in yours."

Garahan mounted and urged his horse forward. "We've got to save her, laddie. Ye know these roads as well as I do. As soon as it's safe, I'll be giving ye yer head!"

When traffic was light, the gelding increased his speed—when carriages and other horses blocked the way, his horse slowed down.

Garahan leapt from his horse and tied off the reins as a loud crash resounded from within Madame Beaudoine's shop. He put his shoulder to the door, forcing it open, attracting attention from passersby.

The duke's guard were recognizable by some because of their black uniforms—but not by all. A hulk of a man rushed into the modiste's shop after Garahan. "'Ere now! I'll fetch the constable if you don't leave at once!"

Garahan waited until he sensed the man was close enough and, without turning around, rammed his elbow into the man's gut. The loud *oomph* told him he'd hit his mark. Rushing from the front room through the shop, he stopped in the doorway to one of the back rooms. Madame Beaudoine threw a brass urn at a man attempting to push Miss Anderson through the window, while the Smythe-Wyatts' housekeeper and Mademoiselle Augustin wielded bolts of material, battering the man.

Garahan whistled through his teeth—and the three women froze. He stepped into the fray, yanked the man by the back of his coat, and tossed him into the wall. Miss Anderson was still moving... There had to be another man pulling from the alleyway!

"Hang on to the lass! I'll take care of the bloody bastard!" He barreled through the store and, with a flying leap, tackled the man in the alley, who let go of the lass. The quickest way to subdue the man and see to Miss Anderson was to clock him in the jaw. Not as satisfying as cracking his head on the pavement, but he couldn't take the chance he'd break the man's head and have to answer to the duke.

He heard a low moan. Fearing for the lass, he tossed the man over his shoulder. "Hold on—don't move!"

She lifted her head, and their eyes met. The pain he saw there sliced him to the bone. He would do anything to ease her pain.

Needed to be the one to protect her for the rest of her life. A dozen plans raced through his brain, but only three words popped out of his mouth: "Marry me, lass."

Her eyes were round with shock. Was it from the pain or his question?

"Ye don't have to answer now. Wait there. 'Tis easier to go back in than for me to pull ye out."

Inside the shop, he rushed to the back room and the women waiting for him. Without missing a beat, he tossed the man he'd carted from the alley on top of his partner on the floor. "Thank ye for holding her still, ladies. I'm not certain if she's injured her ribs hanging there. From the way the bloody bastard was tugging on her arms, the poor lass may have separated a shoulder."

"*Oui*, Monsieur Garahan. I fear that as well," Madame Beaudoine remarked.

"Thank goodness they didn't break the window—she would have suffered from lacerations as well as bumps and bruises," the housekeeper added.

"Or broken ribs," Mademoiselle Augustin whispered.

The women stepped back as he moved the table out of the way and braced a shoulder against the wall to steady himself as he placed his hands about Miss Anderson's waist. "I'm going to ease ye back inside." When she didn't answer, he worried that she'd fainted. "Lass, are ye all right?"

"Yes."

"Did ye hear what I said?"

"I may have dreamed what you said."

"Ye didn't. But if ye doubt me, I can ask ye again—after ye're safe in me arms. Now then, brace yerself, and I'll do me best not to injure ye further."

Mindful of the windowsill, and the fact that she'd been stretched between two thugs as if she were on a Medieval instrument of torture, he whispered, "'Tis all right if ye cry. No one will think less of ye." He carefully extracted her from the window and cradled her in his arms. Brushing loose strands of golden hair out of her eyes, he wondered if the lass would agree to his offer. But now was not the time to repeat the question. The scrapes on her face and the bruise on her jaw needed tending—not to mention possible injuries he could not see. Resisting the urge to pummel the two men lying unconscious on the floor behind them for inflicting the wounds on her, he asked, "Which one hit ye, lass?"

She stared at him as tears welled in her blue eyes, magnifying the emotions rioting through her.

"Ye're safe now. Do ye not remember me promise to protect ye, whether ye wanted me to or not?"

She rasped, "I remember. Thank you, Garahan. Those men said…" Her voice trailed off.

"Ye can tell me on the way to the duke's town house."

"Oh, but I cannot go there!"

He sighed. "Ye must. I cannot leave ye unprotected. I'm due to report in for me next shift."

He heard the heavy footsteps and turned to face the man he'd elbowed standing in the doorway. "I'd be obliged if ye'd fetch the constable to collect these two."

"Who are you?" the man demanded.

"His name is Garahan," Madame Beaudoine replied. "He is one of the Duke of Wyndmere's personal guard."

"You know this man?"

"Not personally," the modiste remarked. "However, I know his brother James and a few of his O'Malley cousins."

The big man nodded. "Name's Fiske. A mutual friend sent me."

Garahan shifted his hold on the lass so her head rested against his heart. "After ye fetch the constable, you can find me—"

"I know where you're headed if I need you," Fiske said as he retraced his steps.

Mrs. Plumton walked over to Garahan. "It all happened so fast. One moment we were admiring a lovely bit of cloth—"

"*Oui!* Those two *diables* rushed into the shop and grabbed hold of Mademoiselle Anderson," Mademoiselle Augustin explained.

Madame tucked in a loose hairpin and folded her hands at her waist. "I am not certain Mademoiselle Anderson should be moved. I shall send for the lieutenant."

"'Tis best if I spirit her away from here, though I thank ye for the offer. No doubt yer lieutenant will be able to protect ye ladies."

Madame Beaudoine sighed. "Lieutenant Sampson is a physician with connections on Bow Street."

"Sampson? Well now, that name is well known to those of us in the duke's guard. Between himself, me cousin Emmett, and Dr. McIntyre, they saved our cousin Sean's arm."

"*Oui*," the modiste said. "A frightening time for Mignonette and Monsieur Sean, no?"

"Aye."

"How did you know where to find us?" the housekeeper asked.

"I have me ways, Mrs. Plumton. I've been keeping an eye on Miss Anderson and yerself."

"Monsieur O'Malley stopped in earlier," Madame Beaudoine said. "He warned that trouble may be coming to our door again."

Garahan was not surprised by the news. "The O'Malleys are fine men to have at yer back." He was starting to worry that the lass hadn't spoken again, but knew that shock could be the reason. With his anger under control, he did not look at the scrapes and bruises again, or else he'd be laying hands on the men at his feet. Gritting his teeth, he glanced down and saw that her eyes were closed, and she was breathing quietly. Was the lass asleep? She must truly trust him if she fell asleep in his arms amidst all the danger.

"I'll be taking me leave of ye. If ye have need of meself or O'Malley, send word and we'll go wherever ye are."

"*Merci*, Monsieur Garahan," Madame Beaudoine replied.

"*Merci*," Mademoiselle Augustin echoed.

"Will you let us know how our Aimee is doing?" Mrs. Plumton asked.

"Ye have me word."

A few moments later, he was astride his horse with a groggy lass on his lap. Worry shot through him. He wondered if she had suffered more than the blow to the cheek. The rumors and threats surrounding the baron had heightened in the last few days, but it was the news that the blackguards from the brothel were after Miss Anderson that nearly stopped his heart. He had to protect her and get her to safety! Marriage was the only answer.

"Ye'll be right as rain as soon as me cousin has a look at ye, lass."

He prayed he was right.

CHAPTER TWELVE

"Bring her in here, Garahan." The duke's cook motioned him into one of the rooms between the kitchen and the pantry. "Lay her on the cot. Gently, now."

Reluctantly, Garahan did as Mrs. O'Toole asked. Unable to resist, he brushed the tip of his finger along the curve of Miss Anderson's uninjured cheek.

"Who have you brought us, Garahan?"

"'Tis the lass I rescued a fortnight ago. To speak of the circumstances could put her the other young women in jeopardy. I cannot risk telling ye more."

"I'll mix up a soothing herbal for her," Mrs. O'Toole said. "What is her name?"

"Aimee, er…Miss Anderson. She recently arrived from the country."

"I'll be right back." The cook paused in the doorway and nodded when footsteps approached. "That will be Mrs. Wigglesworth. She'll sit with you while you wait for O'Malley. He and Jenkins were discussing which footman will stand guard in his place while he sees to our guest."

Guest. The word ate a hole in Garahan's stomach. "Miss Anderson was on an errand with Mrs. Plumton on Bond Street. 'Tis getting so that London isn't safe for any woman."

"The poor young woman," the duke's housekeeper said,

entering the room. "Reminds me of the young woman your brother James brought to us."

"Miss Anderson is currently working for the Smythe-Wyatts. Mrs.—"

"Plumton," Mrs. Wigglesworth interrupted him. "I have known Edith for a number of years. The duke's father always spoke highly of Lord and Lady Smythe-Wyatt. How was Miss Anderson injured?"

"As I just said to Mrs. O'Toole, I cannot speak of the circumstances. I did alert O'Malley and Findley to let them know to be on guard. O'Malley sent word to Captain Coventry."

"And Mr. King as well?" the housekeeper asked.

"Aye. I'm afraid I've placed yerself and Mrs. O'Toole in danger."

Mrs. Wigglesworth smiled, and warmth flowed over Garahan's shoulders, easing the tension there. "We are used to danger coming to our door, Garahan. Especially during the previous duke's tenure—though that was an entirely different sort of danger. Mrs. O'Toole and I have proven our ability to handle ourselves in an emergency many times over the years."

"'Tis good to know, but the fact remains that I did not mean to bring trouble to yer door. This poor lass didn't ask for any of it." Garahan brushed a lock of silken, sun-kissed hair off the lass's face. "Ye're safe now. Mrs. Wigglesworth and Mrs. O'Toole will be taking care of ye." Her dark lashes fluttered. "There's a lass. Open yer eyes and see that ye're safe within the walls of the Duke of Wyndmere's town house."

She opened her eyes and blinked rapidly—her expression changing from surprise to concern. "I do not belong here... I cannot stay here."

"Of course you can, my dear. I'm Mrs. Wigglesworth, the duke's London housekeeper."

"Does he have more than one?"

Garahan chuckled at how quickly the lass's curiosity made itself known. "Aye. His Grace has an estate in the Lake District, the family manor in Sussex, and a crumbling—Well, it's been restored, so 'tis no longer a crumbling tower on the coast of Cornwall."

Miss Anderson seemed unnerved by the prospect of staying at the duke's town house. He noticed her struggling to sit up and slid his arm around her back to aid her, while Mrs. Wigglesworth placed another pillow beneath her head and said, "A good portion of the duke's staff has been with the family for a number of years. Jenkins, Mrs. O'Toole, and I were hired by the fourth duke."

"How many dukes have there been?" the lass asked.

Garahan's lips twitched, but he didn't smile for fear she would think he was laughing at her. "His Grace is the sixth duke. He and Captain Coventry were instrumental in forming His Grace's personal guard, consisting of meself and three brothers, eight O'Malley cousins, and four Flaherty cousins."

"I remember you speaking of them briefly." She shifted, sucked in a breath, and closed her eyes.

"Easy, lass," he warned. "I'm thinking ye may have reinjured yer ribs."

"Would you rather sit in the chair," Mrs. Wigglesworth asked, "or lie on the cot, Miss Anderson?"

"Sit, if you don't mind."

"Not at all. Garahan, please help Miss Anderson into the chair. Carefully," the older servant added.

Garahan stared at Miss Anderson for a moment, trying to decide which would cause her less pain: helping her to her feet, or scooping her into his arms. He reasoned that a quick scoop would get it done quickly, with the least amount of discomfort.

Before either woman could ask what he intended to do, he'd lifted her off the cot and deposited her in the chair. "I'm thinking a pillow behind ye, and a blanket across yer lap."

The lass's eyes met his, and he nearly lost himself in their depths. So many emotions swirled in the endless, clear blue, but there was only one he searched for: hope.

He'd been holding out hope that she'd say yes to his earlier question. True, they'd only met a short while ago and hadn't had more than a few short conversations—but bloody hell, he knew in his heart that he wanted to be the one to shield her with his body, protect her with his strength, and love her with every fiber of his being for the rest of their lives.

The starch simply leached from his legs. *Love?* He had to call on his ironclad control to not keel over. The realization that his desire to protect the lass was equal to his desire to wake up beside her for the next fifty years robbed him of speech.

"Garahan, are you all right?"

He glanced over his shoulder at the duke's cook standing in the doorway with a steaming mug. The worry on her face snapped him out of it. "Aye, Mrs. O'Toole. Was thinking the lass may have reinjured her already cracked ribs. The bruise on her jaw is coming up, and who knows how many bruises she has that we cannot see?"

"Really, Garahan," the housekeeper admonished him. "You should not speak so familiarly of Miss Anderson."

"If it's any consolation," the lass rasped, "I think he's right."

"Who's right?" a deep voice boomed from the open doorway.

"O'Malley! What kept ye?" Garahan asked.

"Had to arrange for coverage. Has something else happened to Miss Anderson?"

"Aside from what happened at the modiste's shop, nay," Garahan replied. "But I believe she's been hiding how much pain she's in from us."

"Has she now?" O'Malley remarked. "Ye'd tell us if ye were in pain, wouldn't ye, lass?"

"Ye should address her as Miss Anderson," Garahan grumbled, watching his cousin like a hawk. "Miss Anderson, ye remember me *eedjit* cousin, Emmett the healer."

"Of course I do. You have a wonderful way with children, O'Malley. Sally and Jenny were quite taken with you. Thank you again for your aid. I will be forever in your debt for helping the others."

Emmett smiled. "'Twas me pleasure."

"Just O'Malley's debt?" Garahan asked, unable to believe he'd blurted the question out.

She swung her gaze back to meet his. "I will always be in your debt, Garahan. You saved me."

O'Malley swallowed a chuckle, and Garahan knew the bugger sensed how he felt about the lass. He imagined knocking O'Malley's teeth down his throat before reminding him, "We cannot discuss what happened until Mrs. O'Toole and Mrs. Wigglesworth leave the room—'tisn't safe."

His cousin nodded. "If ye don't mind—"

"Of course we mind! Have you forgotten how many times we have been on hand when you have brought others to the duke's household for protection?" Mrs. Wigglesworth asked.

"And healing?" Mrs. O'Toole added.

"Nay, but—" O'Malley began, only to be cut off by the cook.

"The sooner we examine this poor young woman, the sooner we can help her heal," Mrs. O'Toole said. "If you two gentlemen would kindly leave, Mrs. Wigglesworth and I will examine Miss Anderson to see where else she is injured."

"But what of her ribs?" Garahan demanded.

"Once we bathe her bruises and cuts, we will call O'Malley back in to wrap her ribs—if need be," Mrs. O'Toole informed them.

"And not before." Mrs. Wigglesworth stood beside Mrs. O'Toole. Both were frowning at Garahan and his cousin.

"What do ye think?"

O'Malley shook his head. "We'd best be agreeing. The sooner they find out where else the lass is injured, the sooner I can immobilize her ribs. From the black looks we're getting, we have just been reminded that we aren't thinking of Miss Anderson's reputation."

Garahan shook his head. "'Tis the truth—I was only thinking of easing her pain. Forgive us for not thinking of yer reputation, lass." He did not want his cousin to know that he'd already asked

Miss Anderson to marry him. He needed to hear her answer before telling anyone—especially O'Malley.

He lifted her hand to his lips. Waiting for her eyes to meet his, he pressed a kiss to the back of her hand, inordinately pleased with the dazed look she could not hide. "I'll take me leave of ye for now. Know that I'll be waiting on the other side of that door if ye have need of me, or if ye have anything ye'd like to say to me."

She opened her mouth to speak, but quickly closed it. Her look of adoration was there for anyone to see.

His heart soared. The lass was not immune to him. He hoped he could convince her to marry him in the next few days—any longer, and he was afraid she would be the target of another abduction. God help any man who tried to take her from him!

He and O'Malley left the room and closed the door behind them. "Tell me what happened."

Garahan described the scene when he arrived at Madame Beaudoine's shop. "Though I've sent a missive to Coventry, I need to speak with him about another urgent matter. I cannot risk anyone overhearing our conversation—or getting hold of a message."

His cousin frowned. "What matter would that be?"

"I'll be marrying the lass as soon as she agrees."

"But ye just met her!" O'Malley replied.

"Nay, I met her nearly three weeks ago, when I rescued her from the boarding house."

"Ye cannot just ask a lass to marry her because ye feel responsible for her."

"The lot ye know about it. 'Tisn't the only reason I asked her to marry me."

O'Malley's eyes nearly popped out of his head. "Ye already asked her?"

"Aye. Ye don't know what the lass has suffered. I cannot allow her to suffer more."

"So ye've proposed marriage to her, and she'll live the rest of her life with a man who needs to protect her from the world, but has no other feelings for her."

Garahan's fist shot out, connecting with O'Malley's face. "*Feck* yerself, Emmett!" He spun on his heel and returned to stand right outside the door. He didn't need his cousin's permission to ask for the lass's hand, and he sure as bloody hell did not intend to listen to any of the bugger's *fecking* wisdom.

The door opened, and Mrs. O'Toole peeked out. "Are you and O'Malley fighting?"

"Nay, we were having a discussion," he assured her.

"We thought we heard what sounded like a groan and shuffling of feet."

Garahan's lips twitched. "Me poor cousin has developed a bit of a headache and may need to swallow a bit of his own herbal— or yours."

The cook shook her head. "We need just a few minutes more." She eased back inside and closed the door.

O'Malley rubbed the side of his head as he walked toward Garahan. "I let ye take that shot for free—the next one'll cost ye."

"Fine."

"Fine," O'Malley echoed. "What did Mrs. O'Toole have to say?"

"They're nearly finished. It cannot be as bad as I thought. I didn't notice any broken glass when I was helping the lass from the window, but I was distracted by the sight of Madame Beaudoine hurling a brass urn at the intruder, while Mademoiselle Augustin and Mrs. Plumton battered him with bolts of material... I may have missed it."

O'Malley grinned. "Sean's wife has mentioned in the past how brave her friend Yvette and Madame Beaudoine were. 'Tis a relief that Mrs. Plumton is too, especially if word gets out that there are three other lasses from the boarding house working at one of the more prominent houses in Mayfair."

"Aye, me thoughts exactly," Garahan said. "I was going to speak to Coventry about that, too."

"After I examine her injuries—which, Lord willing, won't

need us to summon Lieutenant Sampson or Dr. McIntyre for assistance—I can speak to Coventry on yer behalf about the other matter while ye guard the lass."

"I'll be needing to send me request via special messenger to His Grace first," Garahan said.

"Best compose the message now, while we're waiting. Mrs. O'Toole keeps writing supplies in the pantry for just that reason."

Pleased that his cousin was no longer trying to talk him out of his plans to marry Miss Anderson, he said, "'Tis much the same at Wyndmere Hall. Merry and Constance are just as efficient as Mrs. O'Toole and Mrs. Wigglesworth…though less strict about certain protocols."

"Just the way Her Grace prefers things, I'm thinking," O'Malley remarked.

"Ye'd be right about that," Garahan replied.

The door opened, and Mrs. Wigglesworth motioned to them. "You may come in now, gentlemen."

"Faith, haven't we mentioned more than once," Garahan said, "we're not gentlemen. We're farmers who crossed the Irish Sea to find work and send the coin home to our families."

"We were in the right place at the right time when the duke was forming his personal guard, and that doesn't make us anything more than what we are," O'Malley added.

"Let's agree to disagree," Mrs. Wigglesworth said with conviction. "It will save time."

The two men stepped into the room, and Garahan was immediately aware that the lass had been crying. Rushing to her side, he brushed the tips of his fingers beneath her eyes, capturing her tears. "What's happened? Where are ye hurt?"

She shook her head. "It's nothing, really."

"O'Malley, we'll need you to wrap her ribs firmly," Mrs. O'Toole said. "Garahan is correct. I believe one is cracked, another broken. But her breathing isn't labored, and that is a good sign."

Garahan knelt beside her chair, reaching for Miss Anderson's hand. He pitched his voice low, asking, "Are ye ready to say yes? Ye'll never have to suffer at the hands of malcontents and thugs again if ye marry me. I'll guard ye with me life, lass."

"Marry?" Mrs. O'Toole asked while Mrs. Wigglesworth covered her mouth with both hands but couldn't contain her gasp of surprise.

Garahan didn't bother to turn around or answer. O'Malley answered for him, "Aye. Me cousin's mind is made up. He's going to send a missive to His Grace, and I'm going to speak with Coventry on his behalf while he sits with the lass, after I tend to her injuries."

"Well, I suppose that's that," Mrs. O'Toole murmured.

"Aye," Garahan agreed, never tearing his gaze from Miss Anderson's. "Well, lass, will ye marry me?"

She beckoned him closer. He moved so their lips were a breath apart. Was she wanting a kiss, then, to seal their pledge?

"For protection…in name only," she whispered.

"Are those yer conditions, then?"

Eyes wide, tears magnifying the endless blue, she nodded.

"I accept yer conditions. We'll wed as soon as the special license arrives." He lined up their lips, anticipating their first kiss.

Her eyes never left his until the last moment, when she turned so he kissed her cheek instead of her mouth.

He wanted a true marriage with the lass, but he had accepted her terms and given his word. He would marry her, but 'twould be in name only…until he could fully earn her trust and her heart.

He could be patient…

✦✦◆◆✦✦

CHAPTER THIRTEEN

"WHAT HAS YOU smiling, my darling?" the Duchess of Wyndmere asked.

The duke folded the urgent missive he'd received a few moments earlier and slipped it into his waistcoat pocket. "I thought you agreed to wait for me to come to you in the nursery."

"Our babes are napping, and I grew impatient."

He sighed. "I have come to expect that you refuse to follow instructions."

She held out her hand to him and smiled. "I'm so pleased that you have ceased telling me to stay put. Could you not do the same and cease insisting that I follow instructions?"

The duke took her hand and pulled her into his embrace. Tilting her chin, he pressed his lips to hers. "I'm afraid I cannot. Your safety—and that of our children—is paramount." When she tried to ease out of his arms, he tightened his hold around her. "You are my life, as are Richard and Abigail. Try to remember that when I vex you with instructions that are only given to keep you out of harm's way."

"There are times in life when we have no choice but to walk through fire to save the ones we love, Jared."

Knowing the back-and-forth would only delay his response to the missive, he lowered his lips to hers. He kissed his wife gently, persuasively, until she melted against him. "I trust that will hold you until later."

"You are a beast to use my desire for you to get your way."

He traced the curve of her cheek with the tip of his finger. "But you love me in spite of that fact."

Her sigh was audible. "You know me too well, my darling duke."

"Indeed. It is good of you to admit. In case you were wondering, and because you did not demand an answer from me, the missive is a request for a special license." Persephone's smile was a balm that never failed to soothe him. "It seems to be a pattern with the men in my personal guard," he added.

"They are so dedicated to serving you, protecting our family, that they spend all day, every day, working. It must be quite a blow—between the eyes—when they meet the other half of their heart. Do you blame them for wanting to act quickly, decisively, and follow in your footsteps?"

"By accepting a title they never wanted?"

She frowned at him. "Offering marriage to protect a woman they are attracted to and feel responsible for."

"My darling duchess, that was not the only reason I offered for your hand."

"Perhaps," she agreed. "But it was the most urgent of your reasons."

"Have I given you reason to regret your decision?"

PERSEPHONE CUPPED THE side of his face, marveling at the strength her husband held in check. "Quite the opposite, Jared—you have given me two reasons to love you more each day."

He frowned for a brief moment, then slowly smiled. "Ah…Richard and Abigail."

"By the way," she said. "There is something I have been meaning to speak to you about."

"Can it keep? I need to pen my request to the archbishop and send the messenger on his way."

She knew he would realize her condition in another few weeks. For now she would hold her discovery close to her heart and pray for another healthy babe. She lifted to her toes and brushed a kiss to the strong line of his jaw. "Absolutely. Do not let me keep you from arranging the marriage for another of your guard."

"Do you have any idea how very much I adore you, Persephone?"

She laid her head to his heart, and the steady beat of it comforted her. "At least as much as I adore you, my love."

He kissed her once more and eased her out of his embrace. "I'm wondering which one of my men will fall next—one of the O'Malleys or one of the Flahertys?"

"Shall we wager on it?"

"Minx!"

She laughed. "I'll take that as a no."

He snorted with laughter as they parted. Watching the man she loved more than life itself stride purposefully toward the servants' staircase—the fastest route to where the messenger waited for a reply—she placed her hand on her still-flat belly. "Your father is in for a surprise."

CHAPTER FOURTEEN

W HEN GARAHAN WAS not visiting with the lass—soon to become his wife—he spent his time ensuring the owners of both brothels were closely watched. He feared they would attempt another abduction and spirit his wife-to-be away.

While her ribs healed, she badgered Mrs. O'Toole and Mrs. Wigglesworth to give her a chore—any chore—as her way to thank them for their care and generosity. He'd been laid up with an injury a few years earlier and knew how difficult it was to sit still and be patient. When the women discovered she was adept with a needle and thread, they let her help with the mending.

"Are ye certain ye don't mind mending me clothes or O'Malley's, lass?"

Looking up from the long slash in the sleeve of one of his frockcoats, she tilted her head to one side. "Not at all—in fact, it opened my eyes to the realization of how much danger you and O'Malley are in on a daily basis."

"What makes ye say that?"

She held up the sleeve. "This slice is perfectly straight. If it wasn't made with a pair of shears, then my guess would be it was caused by the blade of a knife."

Garahan thought of the deep slash to his biceps that his cousin had stitched closed two nights ago...and his words of warning to take it easy and let it heal. "Well now, I'm thinking yer imagination is running away with ye, lass. I caught me sleeve on a nail in the stables."

She narrowed her eyes and stared at him for long moments without saying a word. When he saw the hurt replacing the frustration she could not hide, he was sorry for the lie, but it was necessary in his line of work. To continue to protect the duke and his family, he had to conceal more than he could reveal. He may need to have that conversation with her… He hoped she would become accustomed to it.

"The head of a nail would not cause such a tear."

"Well now, ye'd be right—'twas the point of a nail on an exposed board."

Her expression changed to one of resignation and acceptance. "Please be careful on your rounds today, Garahan."

"I will. Be certain not to overdo or lift anything heavier than yer smile, lass." He bowed and walked to the door, wondering when the duke would answer his missive. Garahan could not wait much longer to kiss the lass when they exchanged promises and their vows.

Unless he could convince her otherwise, it would be some time before she allowed him to kiss her again. He didn't fault her for asking for a marriage in name only—it only confirmed his suspicion that she'd been taken against her will. But he was not deterred. He planned to earn her trust—one kiss at a time.

He had just mounted his gelding when Captain Coventry arrived at Grosvenor Square. Relief filled Garahan. It wasn't that he'd doubted the duke would grant his request—it was the fact that, as far as he knew, none of the other married members of the guard had asked the duke. Viscount Chattsworth and Earl Lippincott had sent requests to the duke in the past, and the duke himself had requested a special license after receiving reports from Coventry. Garahan was the first of the guard to send a request directly to the duke.

When the captain reined in next to him, Garahan asked, "Well?"

Coventry grinned. "You're the first to realize you were in over your head where a woman is concerned—and to request a special license from the duke. Apparently, His Grace was intrigued by the reasons you set forth in your missive."

Garahan shrugged. What could he say? He'd pleaded his case to the best of his ability then prayed the duke would agree. He shifted in the saddle and finally blurted out, "Are ye here to deliver bad news, or good?"

The captain reached inside his waistcoat pocket, withdrew a folded, sealed document, and handed it to Garahan. "There is a note that accompanies the document. Would you care to read it first?"

Garahan was only half listening and had already broken the wax seal and read the names on the special license—twice. "We can be married immediately." He met Coventry's gaze and rasped, "She'll be safe."

The captain handed Garahan the sealed note from the duke. "You may want to open the note, just to ensure His Grace doesn't have any extra instructions for you."

Garahan broke the wax seal and skimmed the note. "He's congratulating me. Said to ask ye to tell me when it was His Grace decided to offer for Her Grace's hand."

Coventry smiled. "I'd be happy to, but it can wait until you return from your rounds."

"I was going to speak with me contact at White's. Care to join me?"

"One of the waiters?"

"Aye."

Coventry's solemn expression had Garahan wondering what the point of the questions were. Before he could ask, the captain posed yet another question: "Are you meeting him in the alley alongside White's?"

"What is it ye're trying to warn me about?"

"Watch your back. Summerfield and I were ambushed there a year or so ago. When I awoke, I was alone—bound and gagged.

It was the first time I'd been caught unawares."

"Thank ye for the warning, captain. Ye're welcome to join me."

"Welcome or not, that was my intention. I take it Miss Anderson is healing as expected and on the road to recovery?"

Garahan hesitated, trying to decide whether or not to share his worry.

They'd ridden a few moments before Coventry spoke again. "Sometimes an outside opinion can be invaluable."

"The lass is improving daily, though her ribs will take longer to heal than the scrapes and bruises. O'Malley mentioned a vacant apartment in yer building. Is it still available?"

The captain kept pace beside him. "Aye. Given Miss Anderson's circumstances, I would encourage you to let the apartment."

"I know she's uncomfortable staying at the duke's town house, but at least O'Malley and Findley are there to guard her—as well as the additional footmen we recruit to fill our posts from time to time."

Coventry nodded. "A guard is essential when our loved ones could be in constant danger because of our position working for His Grace."

"Then ye understand why I did not give ye me answer about the apartment when O'Malley returned with the news that ye'd be saving it for me a few days ago. I wanted to be certain His Grace would grant me request. We'll marry immediately. She deserves to be coddled and protected. I can see the pain in her eyes. I want to be the man responsible for easing her pain and gaining her trust. I've the time and the patience."

"Miss Anderson will be safe," Coventry said. "She'll be surrounded by His Grace's newest guard."

Garahan stared at the captain. "Is the duke after replacing us?"

"Not at all," Coventry replied, slowing down to accommodate the slower carriages in front of them. "These four men have been essential in a number of situations and are well known to those of you in the guard."

"Are ye at liberty to tell me more?"

"His Grace will apprise you and the others shortly. As with the sixteen of you when the duke's private guard was formed, no formal announcement will be made. Their function is more clandestine than your protection detail. We do not want anything to impede their success, as much hinges on it."

"Well then, I'll not be asking what jobs they'll be doing, but as you mentioned the men are well known to us, I'm thinking Tremayne and Bayfield are among them."

"Aye."

"Me brother James mentioned working with Hennessey and Masterson in Cornwall as well. Are there others in the new guard?"

"Just the four at the moment. I trust these men with my life and have known them for years because of our common background, serving in His Majesty's forces—and having to leave that service due to injuries sustained in battle. Though in no way will their injuries affect their ability to perform their duties."

Garahan nodded. "I never thought it would. I've seen ye in action and agree with James—those that meet ye for the first time won't underestimate ye a second time."

Coventry chuckled. "James said that?"

"Aye." Garahan nodded at the tangle of carriages ahead of them and asked, "Can ye tell me when His Grace proposed?"

The captain smiled. "A series of events occurred after Her Grace fell backward into His Grace's arms."

"I've heard the tale. 'Twas the borrowed spectacles that caused her to lose her footing, wasn't it?"

"In part. Rumors were rife after that moment, especially given Her Grace's penchant at the time for wearing bilious colored gowns."

Garahan chuckled. "Her Grace's beauty would shine no matter what color gown she wore."

Coventry agreed. "Those rumors were founded in supposition and innuendo—not fact."

"They never are." The carriages ahead of them sorted themselves out, and they were able to proceed.

"His Grace was captivated from that first moment and felt the unfounded rumors that continued to circulate around Her Grace were due to his interest and interactions with her."

Garahan absorbed the information. "He felt responsible to protect her."

"Aye. He admitted he formed a *tendre* for Lady Persephone, and protecting her and her mother was paramount to him. He knew being seen with her would have the whole of Society spreading gossip that he was about to propose. If he did not come up to scratch, they would label her as being a social climber, only after his title."

"I see." And he did. Garahan's need to protect Miss Anderson was equal to his need to convince her she could trust him with her heart...and more.

"I suggested he offer for her hand."

"And she accepted immediately," Garahan said.

"Er...actually, she refused at first, then accepted."

"I'm thinking it sounds just like something Her Grace would do. She is the duke's equal in so many ways. Thank ye for telling me."

They rode at a snail's pace, but at least they were moving closer to their destination. "Me brother mentioned ye were teaching yer stepson how to defend himself. How is Michael's training going?" Garahan asked.

The captain grinned. "He's grown into a fine young man, though Miranda worries about his future. I believe she has finally come to the realization that she cannot put him off much longer—he wants to join the Royal Navy."

Garahan slowed his horse as they approached a cross street near the gentlemen's club. "He's had two fine role models who served in the navy—his da and yerself, captain. Ye must be busting yer buttons with pride."

The pair dismounted and tied their reins to the hitching post outside. "I am immensely proud of him. I wish I could ease his mother's worry. There is no more honorable, nor dangerous, way to serve king and country than defending it—whether on land or at sea. She counts on our son more than he realizes with her duties seeing to the tenants in the building. Our daughter is at an age where she's into everything, and as of late, Miranda tires more easily."

Garahan smiled at the way Coventry referred to his stepson and daughter as "our" and had to ask, "Me cousin Michael seemed to accept his stepson Bart easily—was it the same for ye?"

Coventry nodded. "I met him when he was a week old and was awed that something so tiny could grab hold of your heart so quickly." He fell silent, staring ahead of them. "His father and I were in the Battle of Trafalgar. His father, the best of friends, gave the ultimate sacrifice. I gave my eye and most of the use of one arm."

Garahan turned to study the captain. "What of Miranda and little Michael?"

"She was one of the first visitors I recall when I came out of the delirium from the infection and fever."

Garahan had heard about their connection from his brother. "James said she was a constant in that hospital, bringing cheer with her smile and reading letters to the injured."

Coventry nodded. "She saved me and gave me a reason to want to carry on. I'd made a promise to my friend that should he fall in battle, I would look after his wife and son."

"Ye've always been a man of yer word."

"I never intended to fall in love with them," Coventry confided. "It happened over time, and so slowly, I didn't realize how deeply embedded Miranda and Michael were in my heart, until it hit me one day. When she was injured..." He let his words trail off.

"Ye felt as if yer sole purpose in this world was to protect her and see that she never came to harm again," Garahan finished for him.

Coventry nodded.

Sensing the man had not intended to share so much of what was in his heart, Garahan changed the subject. "James confessed he fell in love with your little Emma the night ye let him hold her. He said she was crying in pain from teething."

"Tremayne and I saw a new side to your brother that night, though I would venture to say he would have preferred if we hadn't."

Garahan motioned toward the rear of the building. "'Tis a far different thing for an enemy to know yer weakness—they'll exploit it at every turn. Having yer comrades know of it, well now, that will make ye stronger. Ye'll know what part of yer impenetrable wall needs to be braced in case of attack."

"One of the wisest decisions His Grace ever made was forming his personal guard. I count myself fortunate that he granted me the duty of searching London to locate Patrick O'Malley's brothers and cousins and offering them positions."

"Faith, I won't be arguing with ye on that score! Me contact should be taking his break shortly. If not, I can ask one of the lads to fetch him. I usually meet him at the rear door."

Scanning the alleyway and the area surrounding it, the pair made their way to the back door. It opened as they approached, and a broad man walked outside and lit a cigar. "That's him," Garahan said. Instead of calling to the man, he whistled through his teeth.

The man spun around. "You're late."

"Couldn't be helped," Garahan replied. When the man stared at Coventry—and didn't react to the captain's black eyepatch or matching sling—he introduced them. "Captain Coventry, meet Cocker—we worked together for a time when I first arrived in London." The two men acknowledged one another before Garahan added, "I trust the captain with me life."

Cocker nodded, glanced around them, and moved closer. "I recently learned the name of the man vowing to exact revenge on

Baron Summerfield. Harrison Ashbrook."

Garahan's gut clenched. They had more than enough proof that Ashbrook was behind the threats. King needed this information.

Coventry nodded. "Was anything more said?"

"Aye," Cocker said. "He boasted of being an excellent shot."

Garahan sighed. "A man bragging about his skill with a weapon isn't against the law, or enough to bring the man in for questioning."

"I disagree," Coventry said. "Given that the threat of exacting revenge was stated first, the additional boasting that he was an excellent shot will be enough for King to have him brought in for questioning."

"Do ye remember who was with Ashbrook last night?"

"Cocker, back to your shift!" a gray-haired man wearing an apron called from the back door.

Cocker put out his cigar and answered, "Coming!" Turning back to Garahan and Coventry, he told them, "Lord Robertson and the Honorable Mr. Farrell."

"I owe ye," Garahan murmured.

"Aye, you do," the other man agreed before sprinting up the back steps and disappearing inside White's.

Garahan saw movement out of the corner of his eye. "Behind ye, captain."

Coventry had already spun around and slipped his arm out of the sling, brandishing a wicked-looking blade.

The footpad held up both hands and backed away. "Thought you were someone else—my mistake."

Coventry slipped his arm and the blade back in his sling. They left the alley and walked over to where their horses were tethered and mounted. "Where are you headed now?"

Garahan wanted to follow the thug but had an appointment to keep. "I've a meeting near Scarlet Ribbons."

"Watch your back."

"Ye as well, captain."

Winding his way through the streets to the stews, Garahan wondered what the lass would have to say when he showed her the special license. He hoped she would be pleased, despite his worry that she would go back on her word. The tenuous trust between them had formed the night he rescued her from the boarding house.

The bond would hold strong—it had to. It would be the foundation he planned to build their lives upon.

But first he had to marry the lass.

CHAPTER FIFTEEN

THE TWITCH BETWEEN his shoulder blades had Garahan on
alert. His ma had always told him he had guardian angels
watching over him. From the number of times he had been
injured over the years, he doubted they were as diligent as he was
in watching over his intended.

Before he could show the lass the special license, he had to
meet Burke. It was essential to find out if there were any new
rumblings on the street after what occurred at the modiste's shop.

He felt the air behind him change and leapt from his horse.
Feet spread, balanced on the balls of his feet, he faced his attacker.
Deflecting the cudgel aimed at his head, he absorbed the blow to
his shoulder. He fought with a single-minded thought—he had to
emerge the victor in order to marry Miss Anderson. She would
not have the full protection of his name until they were wed!

He disarmed the thug, then kicked the side of the man's knee.
The sound, and the groan of agony, as his leg collapsed beneath
him told Garahan the man would not be leaving the alleyway
without help. Satisfaction speared through him, but it was short
lived. Four other men jumped him from behind. Two of them
held his arms, while the other two rained blow after blow to his
ribs, his gut, and his face.

With a will of iron, he took the blows. Timing it carefully, he
kicked his right foot back—surprising the man pummeling him

from behind—then swung it forward, planting his foot in the other man's bollocks, dropping him to the ground.

His fear for the lass gave him the added strength he needed to pull the men holding his arms closer. His body ached, his mouth and nose were bleeding, and one eye was swollen shut, but he would never give up! He sensed the moment the men realized that he was not going to go down alone. Using their hesitation, he grunted with the effort needed and knocked their heads together.

Freed, he stood over the men, struggling to catch his breath. As he wiped the blood from his face with his sleeve, his vision began to gray at the edges. He'd be a dead man if he lost consciousness now. With the lass's name on his lips, and a prayer in his heart, he put one foot in front of the other and stumbled toward his mount.

Dizzy from the blows to the head, he wrapped an arm around his gelding's strong neck to steady himself before heaving himself onto the animal's back. "Take me home, laddie."

He knew the animal would follow his nose to the stable—and the extra scoop of oats that would be waiting for him. The gelding slowed down when Garahan slumped forward, and sped up when Garahan groggily straightened. "Good lad. Nearly there."

The sharp whistle cut through the pain in his head and was music to his ears. Strong hands grabbed hold of him before he fell off his mount. "Brought me home—promised him extra oats when he did." His vision impaired, and with the use of only one eye, he saw double! He blinked, and his blurry gaze revealed O'Malley and Findley. Relief washed over him—he had made it to the duke's townhouse. "Tell the lass…I have the license."

"Ye're an *eedjit*, and ye can tell her yerself after we put yer face back together," Emmett told him. "I'll support him on the left, Findley. Brace him up on the right."

Pain shot through Garahan as his broken ribs shifted, and his world went black.

THE MUSICAL SOUND of water, and the blessedly cool cloth to his aching face, brought him around. He felt a weight on his eye that had swollen shut and reached out to touch it, but a small, soft hand stopped him.

"O'Malley warned that the bandage on your eye had to stay in place until Lieutenant Sampson arrives."

"Lass?" He struggled to open his good eye, relieved that he could still see out of one.

"Please don't try to move, Garahan. O'Malley and Mrs. O'Toole are afraid your broken ribs are not the worst of it."

"I've had worse, lass." He cataloged the aches and pains as familiar. Nothing felt off. He'd been beaten before. The time he went three rounds against the bare-knuckle champ that outweighed him by half came to mind. "Ye have no reason to worry. It takes more than a few blows to keep a Garahan down."

He started to sit up, felt a world of pain shoot through his midsection, and decided to wait before attempting it again. "Did O'Malley give ye me message?"

Tears welled in her eyes but didn't fall. "He did."

He reached out and brushed the tip of his finger along the curve of her cheek, ignoring the pain blossoming everywhere at once. He did not need the lass to know the truth of how he felt. She did not need to worry about him. Though he was loath to admit it, he was more than a bit concerned by the message behind the beating…and the source. He had no doubt that it all stemmed back to his rescuing the lass from the boarding house. "Would ye ask O'Malley to send for the vicar? I'll be on me feet and right as rain before he arrives."

"Ye'll likely keel over just like that time Murphy beat the ever-living *shite* out of ye a decade ago."

His good eye met O'Malley's. "My mistake for greeting the lass he was courting with a smile." When his cousin flinched, Garahan knew the pain spearing through him wouldn't be leaving in an hour—more likely in a day or so. "'Twasn't even a fair fight," he reminded his cousin. "Murphy jumped me from behind—even if your brothers and mine tried to wade into the fray to stop it."

"But yer pride got in the way, and you refused help. Pride will be yer downfall every time, Darby."

He ignored O'Malley's wise words. It wasn't the first time he'd heard that warning. Faith, it wouldn't be the last. "Could ye send for the vicar?"

"As soon as Lieutenant Sampson clears ye." O'Malley paused, glanced at Aimee, and told her, "The lieutenant is a trained surgeon who served in His Majesty's Dragoons for ten years."

Garahan noticed a flicker of fear flash in her expression, but it was quickly replaced with her smile.

"Ye'll have me bride-to-be worried for nothing when the lieutenant pronounces me fit to return to me duties—which I know he will. But even more importantly, he'll proclaim me fit to marry the lass tonight!"

"Lieutenant Sampson is here," Mrs. O'Toole announced, stepping aside for the physician to enter the small room off the kitchen.

"What's this about getting married?" the lieutenant asked.

"Thank ye for coming so quickly," O'Malley said, before turning to ask the cook, "Would ye mind taking the lass with ye to the kitchen? I need a private word with the lieutenant and me cousin."

"I'd rather stay," Miss Anderson said. "That is, if you don't mind."

Garahan watched the lass straighten in the chair next to him and saw the spark of temper flare in her eyes. *Well now,* he thought, *as the temper is on my behalf, 'tis a step in the right direction toward me goal.* "Me cousin and the lieutenant are only thinking of yer delicate sensibilities."

"It is best that you know before we marry," she warned him, "I left those sensibilities, and my life as a poor relation, behind before I journeyed to London."

"Lass—" Garahan only got one word out before she shot to

her feet, her eyes flashing a deep blue fire.

"Do not think to protect me from the difficult and darker side of life. I am well acquainted with it."

He watched in amazement as the shy woman he'd rescued changed before his eyes into a warrior queen. "I'm not trying to shield ye, lass. I'm thinking to protect ye—the treatment they're going to discuss may leave yer belly unsettled."

She crossed her arms beneath her breasts and glared at him.

He grinned, though it had the split in his lip bleeding again. "What a woman I've found to wed. Eh, O'Malley?"

Her expression did not change as she turned to glare at O'Malley. "I am not weak."

Garahan asked his cousin, "Who does she remind ye of?"

"Me ma—and yers."

"Well then, Lieutenant Sampson, it seems as if me bride-to-be will be staying."

She nodded and returned to her seat.

"In that case, I must insist that if you feel even the slightest bit nauseated, Miss Anderson, that you will quietly leave the room," Sampson said. "I cannot be worried about you fainting at my feet and striking your head while I'm examining Garahan and ascertaining the extent of his injuries."

"I will not leave," she told him. "And I won't swoon."

The lieutenant held her gaze. "I have heard those words many times before. Unfortunately, the last time, I was not close enough to the woman who said them to catch her when she fainted."

"I'll take that chance," the lass said.

Garahan nearly burst his buttons—if they hadn't already been torn from his waistcoat during the altercation in the alley. "As will I, lass."

When she beamed at him, he crooked his finger at her. She leaned close to him, and he whispered, "If me lip wasn't split and swollen, I'd kiss the breath out of ye." Her face flushed a becoming pink, and he felt another tiny victory at her reaction.

"Ye're as lovely as the roses in me ma's garden back home. Thank ye for wanting to stand beside me—no matter the circumstances. We'll do well together, lass. Ye'll see."

She reached for his hand and hesitated before squeezing it. He wondered at her hesitation, glanced at his hand, and saw the reason. His knuckles were battered and bruised. "There are times when our duties require us to use our fists when trouble jumps out of the dark."

The lieutenant glanced at Garahan's hands and face. "Just how many men jumped you, Garahan?"

"One man—"

"Only one?" O'Malley asked. "Did he whack ye upside the head and rattle yer brains?"

"Ye didn't let me finish. There was one at first. After I took care of him...four others"—he glanced at Miss Anderson and cleared his throat, deciding not to share the full version of what happened—"converged upon me." Garahan didn't want the lass to worry any more than she already was. He ignored his cousin when O'Malley rolled his eyes.

"Miss Anderson, would you mind helping Mrs. O'Toole?" the lieutenant asked. "I believe the poultice she prepared, along with the boiled threads and extra lengths of linen for bandaging, is ready."

She leaned close to Garahan and whispered, "I'll be right back. Do not let them do anything until I return."

"I see ye found yer grit, lass," he replied. "I'm thinking I like it."

She sighed and rose to his feet. "There may come a time when you will be vexed with me for interfering."

"Obviously yer ma wasn't Irish," Garahan said.

She shook her head and hurried after the cook.

"Now then, lieutenant," O'Malley said, "ye need to look at Garahan's eye. I'm thinking we may need to drain the swelling above it to be able to open his eye to see the full extent of the damage. 'Twill take too long using cold compresses to bring the swelling down."

"Exactly what I was thinking," the lieutenant replied, rolling up his sleeves.

While Sampson washed his hands, Garahan glanced at the doctor's back and then at O'Malley, who sat on the chair beside the cot. His cousin tensed. "What didn't ye want the lass to know?"

Knowing O'Malley would tell him the unvarnished truth, Garahan said, "After ye drain the swelling, I need ye to tell if me if me eye looks cloudy to ye."

O'Malley studied him for a few moments, the expression on his face neutral. "Ye have me word, though I'm wondering why ye're asking. Was yer vision blurred before yer eye swelled shut?"

"Aye." Garahan had never feared an injury before. He accepted them as part of his duty, knowing he would heal without question. He'd been shot, stabbed, and clubbed over the head, but nothing came close to what he was facing at this moment. Losing his sight scared the ever-loving *shite* out of him. "Ye were there when Sean's arm was flayed open to the bone. Did he seem worried that he might lose his arm to the infection?"

"Aye, and he spoke of it to Mignonette."

Garahan needed to know: "How did she react to the possibility that he could lose his arm? Did she refuse to marry him?"

"She did all that she could to aid me when the fever took hold, and later, when we had to drain the infection, and wait to see if gangrene would set in. Mignonette stood fast, would not change her mind—whether Sean came through with one arm or two."

"It took three healers to save your cousin's arm," Sampson said. "And the strong woman of faith who loved him." Meeting Garahan's gaze, he asked, "What did you neglect to tell me when Miss Anderson was in the room?"

"Me vision was blurry before me eye swelled shut."

"The swelling may have had an effect on your sight," Sampson advised. "I need to manipulate your eyelid before I proceed with anything else."

The physician's silence as he studied Garahan's eye unnerved Garahan. Finally, the lieutenant said, "There is a prodigious amount of blood marring the sclera near the iris."

"What in the bloody hell is the sclera?"

"The white of yer eye," his cousin replied before the lieutenant could.

"Ah. So, when the swelling goes down, will the blood in the white of me eye be absorbed into it? Will I see clearly again?"

"The chances are very good that you will," Sampson said, "although I cannot make any promises at this time. Eyes do not heal at the same rate as other injuries."

Garahan's heart stopped, then began to beat again. "Chances?"

"We won't know the full extent of the injury until the swelling goes down and you begin to heal."

He silently prayed his sight would return when the injury healed. Until then, he would not speak of it. "Don't be telling the lass."

The lieutenant hesitated. "She has already shown remarkable resilience by refusing to leave your side, unless it was to retrieve something to help in your treatment. I believe it is best to tell her, as it will aid in your recovery."

"I'll tell her meself," Garahan insisted. Turning to his cousin, he said, "I'll have yer word now, Emmett, that ye won't say anything."

"Ye have it, Darby."

"Lieutenant, do I have yers?"

"She'd best have been told by the time I return tomorrow, or I will tell her myself."

"Agreed," Garahan replied.

"Now then, Garahan," the lieutenant said, "hold still."

"Aye." Garahan wasn't worried about a little thing like draining a wound—he'd suffered through that particular treatment more than once over the years. It was the worry of going blind in one eye, and not telling the lass right away of the possibility, that weighed heavy on his mind. How could he serve in the duke's guard with an injury like that? Needing to take his mind off his worry, he confessed, "I'm actually more worried about one of me ribs poking through a lung."

"I wrapped them, didn't I?" O'Malley grumbled.

"That ye did, but I'm thinking the lieutenant will be unwrapping them to see me colorful bruises for himself."

"You would be right in that regard, Garahan."

The physician worked quickly and efficiently and was in the process of cleaning the mix of fluid and blood from Garahan's face when Mrs. O'Toole bustled into the room with Miss Anderson hot on her heels. Both women jolted to a stop at the sight of Garahan's face—but neither one made a sound.

The lieutenant looked up. "Ah, Mrs. O'Toole, the wound has been drained. I'll need those threads. Miss Anderson, after I close the incision, we'll need that poultice."

Garahan had felt immediate relief when the pressure above his eye was gone. He wasn't too proud to admit his stomach was a bit uneasy when he felt the warmth of his blood begin to flow freely. He needed a connection with the lass but hadn't been told that he could move his head yet. He held out his hand, hoping she would take hold of it. When she did, he squeezed. When he felt her answering squeeze, his stomach leveled, and his world stopped spinning.

He detested needles and hated the stitching of any wound. And if asked, he'd rather have a blade slice his arm again—or better yet, have a hot blade sear the wound closed. The pain and scent of burning flesh was preferable to needles piercing his skin.

"Thank you for your assistance, ladies," the lieutenant said after he'd placed a bandage over Garahan's eye. "I'll need to examine Garahan thoroughly now that we have taken care of the most pressing wound. Mrs. O'Toole, please escort Miss Anderson from the room. We cannot have her reputation damaged if word gets out that she was present when I removed his clothes to examine him."

"If you knew—" the lass began.

Garahan interrupted her, "If ye don't mind. Ye'll be helping me change me bandages after we wed later tonight, and ye'll have ample time to ogle all of me if ye wish."

Her sharp intake of breath was followed by O'Malley's snort of laughter. "Only an *amadon* like yerself would say such to a gentle lass like Miss Anderson before ye were wed." He turned to her and said, "Ye'll have to forgive me cousin—he's a bit out of his head in pain at the moment."

Her eyes widened as she turned to stare at Garahan. "You never said you were in pain."

The lieutenant spoke up, "Ladies, time is of the essence. You can continue this conversation when you return…after I have finished my examination."

"Of course, Lieutenant Sampson," Mrs. O'Toole said. "Come along, Aimee." When the lass hesitated, the cook linked arms with her, pulling her to the door.

Miss Anderson looked over her shoulder and said, "I'll be right outside if you need me."

"Ah, lass. I'll always need ye." Garahan waited until the door closed behind them before reminding his cousin, "Ye need to send word to the vicar. I'll be marrying her tonight!"

"Aye," O'Malley agreed, "as soon as the lieutenant and I confer about the rest of yer injuries."

"Thank ye. Will ye stand beside me as me witness, Emmett?"

O'Malley nodded. "'Twould be an honor, Darby. Now then, lieutenant, shall we start with his legs and work our way up?"

"Any reason to start there?" Sampson asked.

"Aye," Garahan said. "I expect the lass to be knocking at the door demanding her right to be with me, as we're to be married in a few hours."

"Very well, let's have a look at your legs, then your back. It may be uncomfortable when I check for broken bones."

"Not as uncomfortable as when the bloody buggers jumped

me from behind and grabbed me arms to hold me, while the other two tried to beat the *shite* out of me."

"I'd say they succeeded," the lieutenant remarked.

Garahan grinned. "Ye should have seen the thugs I left unconscious and bleeding in the alley."

CHAPTER SIXTEEN

"WILL HE BE all right, Mrs. O'Toole?"

The cook patted Aimee's hand. "Garahan is a strong man—better still, he is strong *willed*. He will heal as expected, you'll see."

But Aimee needed reassurance now. What if something unexpected happened preventing them from marrying? A rib could poke through something important inside of Garahan! An infection could set in. "I need to be in there with him. Would you please ask the lieutenant if I may be permitted to return?"

"Now, Miss Anderson. Your concern for Garahan does you credit, though your insistence on being in the same room with him while his chest and back are exposed—"

Desperate to be by Garahan's side, Aimee interrupted, "You don't understand. I have no reputation left to be damaged. Though I agreed to run away to Gretna Green…I did not agree to what happened before we arrived."

Understanding filled Mrs. O'Toole's gaze. "There are many times in our lives when circumstances are beyond our control. How we rally from those circumstances and move forward reveals the true character of a person. Garahan said you answered an advert to work in a shop offering better wages. I'd say you are a brave young woman who sought to take back control of your life. I am proud of you and will speak to Lieutenant Sampson.

Wait here."

"Thank you, Mrs. O'Toole." Aimee watched the cook turn around and knock on the door, then opening it when bade to enter. Although she could not hear the short conversation between the cook and the physician, the smile on the cook's face when she looked over her shoulder gave Aimee hope.

"Lieutenant Sampson agreed that you may return, now that Garahan's chest, face, and head are all that remains to be examined."

Aimee hugged the woman and waited for her to open the door. Garahan looked up at her with a knowing look in his eye. "Ah, there ye are, lass. I told the lieutenant ye wouldn't be caring what was proper. We're to be wed tonight, and anyone who takes exception to that—or speaks ill of ye—will have to answer to me."

"And me," O'Malley added. "Ye're family now—or at least will be shortly. O'Malleys and Garahans protect their own."

"Don't be forgetting the Flahertys," Garahan reminded him.

"They're just as fierce as the rest of us protecting our families," O'Malley said.

"You may sit on Garahan's left," the physician instructed her. "Mrs. O'Toole, would you bring that length of linen with you? I will need it after I check his ribs."

"Of course, lieutenant."

Aimee noticed the deep bruising, and for a moment watched the physician, before returning her gaze to the man who'd vowed to marry her and protect her for the rest of her life. He was badly beaten, but he claimed not to feel a thing. She wondered about the damage to his face—especially his eye, which had been bandaged more heavily than she expected. She did not bother to ask him about it, knowing he would brush it off as minor.

He flinched when the physician pressed on his ribs. Helpless to alleviate his pain, she blurted out, "Mrs. O'Toole mentioned that you were considering moving to an apartment nearby. Am I the reason you would leave the duke's town house?"

He answered, "The men stationed here have rooms above the stables—a room where we sleep between our shifts. We can come and go as our duties dictate without disturbing the duke's household. We have room to store our weapons, and the rest of our belongings, until we're assigned to another of the duke's residences."

"I didn't realize you were not permanently stationed in London. How often do you stay in one place?"

"Up until recently, when me third brother married, we spent four months at a time. As every one of us has had the opportunity to become acquainted with the duke's properties—the villages and outlying land surrounding them—and seven members of the guard have now married, the duke has decreed that we're all to remain where we are currently stationed."

"I see."

"Will that be a problem, lass?"

"Not at all. I was hoping to be able to stay in London."

His frown was fierce. "Even after what happened when ye arrived?"

"Yes," she answered. "How could I not, when that is where I met you? I would not change that for all the world, Garahan."

"Darby—call me Darby, lass."

"Aye, Darby, and you can call me Aimee."

"That I will, lass."

The lieutenant finished his examination and said, "Only two broken ribs. Your kidneys are a concern, due to the heavy bruising. There is some damage to the ligaments and tendons in the shoulder where you said you were hit by a cudgel—"

"Cudgel?" Aimee rasped.

"'Twas a glancing blow, lass. The bloody bugger was aiming for me head."

Sampson cleared his throat. "If I may continue?"

"Of course, Lieutenant Sampson," Aimee said.

"The rest of your injuries are minor compared to the ribs, shoulder, and your eye."

"What about his eye?" Aimee asked.

"It's a bit of a bother at the moment—not to worry," Garahan answered. "Have ye ever taken a fist in the eye, lass?"

She shook her head. "But I can imagine it is painful."

"Well then," Garahan said, "there ye have it. I'll be fully healed in no time."

"Until that time," the lieutenant said, "you will not return to your duties until I have cleared you to do so."

"I disagree with ye. I've no problem ignoring bruises and such while I work. Broken ribs have never kept me from performing me duties before, and they won't now."

"I will return midmorning," the lieutenant said. "I need to check the incision above your eye, and the rest of the swelling there, before I agree that you are fit to return to your duties. Another blow to the head—particularly that eye—could be detrimental to your health, and your sight."

Garahan frowned at the physician and turned to his cousin. "I could use yer help convincing the lieutenant."

O'Malley put his hands behind his back and wiped the expression from his face before answering, "I side with Sampson on this, Garahan. Take a few days. Yer bride-to-be may appreciate the time to get to know ye better—" He paused and shook his head. "Faith, forget what I just said. The last thing ye need is for the lass to know too much about ye. She may be changing her mind!"

Garahan did not laugh, as his cousin intended. Truth was, he ached to level him with an uppercut. He'd managed to knock O'Malley off his feet once, and he could do it again—mayhap in another day or so.

"I'm not fragile, nor am I frail in heart or mind, O'Malley." Meeting the challenge in his gaze, Aimee added, "I hope I only have to say this once: I will never change my mind and will be honored to marry Darby as soon as the vicar arrives."

"Just like me ma," Garahan rasped. "I'm a fortunate man, lass. Know this: 'tis a good thing ye won't be changing yer mind, because even if ye did…I'll never let ye go."

"Now then about your treatment, Garahan," Sampson interjected. "I suggest hot compresses and a poultice on the worst of the bruising. Alert me at once if there is blood in your urine—which could indicate a more serious injury to your kidneys."

"Is that all?" Garahan asked.

"If you experience any difficulty breathing—or feel a heaviness in your chest—it could be indicative of fluid in your lungs. You are at risk for developing pneumonia, as you will be on bed rest. Wrapping your ribs is essential to keep them from shifting when you move, but it also restricts your breathing deeply...hence the buildup of fluid."

Aimee lifted her gaze to meet the physician's. "Thank you, Lieutenant Sampson."

"One more thing," the lieutenant added. "Be vigilant and pay close attention to the wound above his eye. Redness around the area, swelling—"

"And putrid *shite* coming from the wound that smells like death," Garahan bit out. "We experienced it before and know what to look for. Thank ye, lieutenant."

"If the infection worsens on one of your limbs, you could lose them. Infection on your face, so close to your brain, has more dire consequences and is not something to treat lightly, Garahan."

"With O'Malley and Mrs. O'Toole to guide me, I know I can take care of Darby," Aimee insisted.

"I prescribe bed rest and an invalid's diet until I return tomorrow and reassess the situation." The physician told Garahan, "May I advise exercising extreme caution? As your physician, I must speak plainly and suggest that you put off sealing your vows this evening—at least until we see what tomorrow brings."

Aimee ignored the embarrassment the lieutenant's words caused her and held Garahan's hand to her heart. "You have my word that Darby will not do anything strenuous tonight. He will rest whether he argues against it or not."

"Well then, Garahan," O'Malley drawled, "I'd say ye picked the perfect woman to butt heads with for the rest of yer life. Ye're a fine addition to the family, Aimee. Ye have me support—no matter if it goes against what me cousin wants or not. Ye can count on me!"

"Thank you, O'Malley." Turning to the physician, she asked, "Is there anything else I should be aware of other than fever?"

"I wouldn't move him tonight," the lieutenant replied.

O'Malley grinned. "Faith, it won't be the first marriage performed in this room, Sampson."

Mrs. O'Toole shook her head. "And may not be the last. I'll show you out, Lieutenant Sampson. Oh, and Garahan?"

"Aye, Mrs. O'Toole?"

"Do not leave that cot!"

"But I—"

"Or I shall have O'Malley and Findley tie you to it. Is that understood?"

"Now ye sound just like me ma."

"Heaven help me," the cook murmured. "Your word, Garahan."

"Aye, Mrs. O'Toole, but I'll be needing a change of clothes. I can't be marrying the lass wearing a sheet!"

"One of the footmen will bring a change of clothes to you. Before you ask, Aimee, you will not help him dress—until after you are married. O'Malley will handle that. Understood?"

"Yes, Mrs. O'Toole," Aimee replied.

"That's better. I'll send Mrs. Wigglesworth in shortly—until then, I need to prepare a wedding supper."

"Don't go to any trouble on me account," Garahan told her. "A plate of scones will do for me."

"I believe I can manage more than that," the cook replied, following the lieutenant and O'Malley out of the room.

"You are so lucky to have so many people who care about you, Darby."

He pressed his lips to the back of Aimee's hand. "Do ye not realize, as me wife, these same people will add ye to those they care about? Wait until ye meet Their Graces and the others.

They'll be just as accepting of ye as they have been with the women me O'Malley cousins have married: Gwendolyn, Patrick's wife; Mignonette, Sean's wife; Harry—"

"Harry?"

"Aye, short for Harriet—Michael's wife; Mollie, Finn's wife."

"They have accepted them without reservation?"

"Aye, lass, as they have accepted me brothers' wives. Melinda, James's wife; Emily, Aiden's wife; and Prudence, Ryan's wife. Ye're in fine company and have sisters-in-law and cousins-in-law to keep ye company."

She met his single-eyed gaze and could not hold back the feelings bombarding her. "Darby?"

"Aye, lass?"

"Thank you."

"For?"

"Offering marriage to protect me."

"'Tisn't the only reason, lass."

Confusion mixed with hope as she asked, "Isn't it?"

"Nay, ye stole me heart the night I rescued ye, with yer angel's face and concern for others."

Confessing what was in her heart, she whispered, "I cannot promise when I will be ready to seal our vows—but I do know it is important, or else we won't be man and wife legally."

"I will not rush ye, lass, but I will be doing me best to convince ye to let me show ye how much I love ye with me lips, me hands, and me body."

Her head went light at his words. "I haven't slept in the dark since the night—"

He pressed the tips of his fingers to her lips. "I understand, lass. We can leave a lantern burning all night for as many nights as it takes for ye to trust that I'll never hurt ye. I will I ever force ye to do anything ye don't want to do."

Hope filled her heart and warmed it as his fingertips traced the line of her jaw. "Even if it takes months?"

"Aye. Ye have me word. Before ye speak, know that I have

never broken me word. I won't rush ye, while I teach ye you can trust me."

Heart full, hands trembling, she leaned close and pressed her lips to his uninjured cheek. "When the split in your lip heals, I'd like you to teach me how to kiss you properly."

"It would be an honor…and me pleasure, lass."

Chapter Seventeen

"Are ye certain ye know what ye're doing, Garahan?"

He sucked in a breath as O'Malley helped him into his spare cambric shirt and waistcoat. "How can ye ask me that when I've already told ye how I feel about the lass?"

"Easily. Ye're injured, ye've taken a few good knocks to yer brainbox, and ye won't be able to stand on yer feet for more than a quarter of an hour—twenty minutes, tops. Ye can say yer vows just as easily lying on that cot."

Garahan drew in one deep breath and then another. "If the bandage around me ribs wasn't so constricting—and the one around me head tight enough to add to the pain in it—I'd knock ye on yer *arse* with me fists. Did our cousin Sean lie down while exchanging his vows?"

O'Malley shrugged.

"Ah, so he didn't!"

"Our cousin's situation was different—'twas his arm—"

"I don't care if it was his *arse*! I'll be standing on me feet with me bride-to-be at me side when I make me promises to her before God, the vicar, and witnesses."

O'Malley glared at him and was about to speak, but the knock on the door had him scrubbing his hand over his face. "'Tis open."

Captain Coventry stood in the doorway with a neutral expression on his face. "Is this a family argument, or can anyone weigh in?"

Garahan ignored the question. "Thank ye for coming, Coventry."

The duke's man-of-affairs nodded and walked over to where Garahan had dropped onto the cot. "A wise man accepts when he needs to allow his body to heal. It wasn't easy for me lying in that hospital bed after my intended sent word that she could not marry me. But I healed, thanks to the fourth Duke of Wyndmere and his son, the sixth duke. If I can find happiness, marrying the woman I have loved for years, even though I knew she deserved better, then you can bring yourself to obey orders and spend the next few days healing."

Chastised as if he were in short pants, Garahan shrugged. "I've haven't been confined to a bed in years. 'Tisn't comfortable."

"'Tis because ye're not in a bed, but on a cot," O'Malley said. "And alone..."

"Not another word," Garahan warned.

"What is all the shouting about?" a familiar, deep voice boomed from the hallway.

"Yer lordship?" Garahan was surprised to see Viscount Chattsworth standing in the doorway. "Is there trouble? What brings ye to London?"

"Apparently there is trouble between yourself and O'Malley."

Garahan grumbled, "He's a self-important *arse* like the rest of the O'Malleys. Nothing I can't handle on me own."

The viscount studied Garahan for a few moments before replying, "Well, that is a relief. I'm here at the duke's request to act as witness to your marriage to Miss Anderson."

"I...I'm honored. Thank ye, yer lordship."

"By the by, the vicar has arrived and is waiting for Miss Anderson to come downstairs."

"She's a bit on the shy side meeting new people, yer lordship. Please do not think she's being standoffish if she's quiet."

"Do you not remember how shy my darling wife was before we wed? I understand completely. Now then." The viscount glanced at O'Malley and then back at Garahan. "What seems to be the trouble?"

"Aside from being ordered not to get off that bloody cot for more than the time it takes to piss in the chamber pot behind the screen in the corner?"

The viscount's lips twitched.

O'Malley snorted with laughter.

Garahan hung his head, waiting for the viscount to ring a peal over his head for speaking so plainly. "Forgive me, yer lordship."

The viscount chuckled. "I could not have said it better myself. I was in a similar situation when I saw the barrel of a rifle aimed at my wife's uncle at Chalk Farm. I took a lead ball meant for his back. You are suffering from a beating acquired in the line of duty." He studied Garahan closely. "It appears as if your eye will take some time to heal. It would be best not to rush things. How are your ribs?"

At ease after the viscount's words, Garahan answered readily, "As expected. They'll heal."

"And your shoulder?"

"I won't be wearing a sling, if that's what ye're asking," Garahan grumbled.

"Ye will, if I have to enlist Findley's help tying it around yer blasted neck," O'Malley said.

"It would take more than the two of ye to hold me down."

The viscount sighed. "I believe a softly spoken plea from the woman you love would do the trick. Am I right, Garahan?"

How had the viscount guessed that he loved the lass? Loving her made him vulnerable—and potentially put her in harm's way. Why wouldn't everyone just accept his word that he was marrying her to protect her? "What makes ye say that?"

"Because I have seen the expression on your face before...in the looking glass the moment it hit me that I loved Calliope."

"I've seen it as well," Coventry added. "I realized that I could no longer hold out against Miranda when she and Michael reminded me that they had both seen me without my eyepatch. They nursed me back to health after I'd been beaten and left for dead in an alleyway on the docks."

"The captain and I are lucky men to have met and married the loves of our lives," the viscount said. "Do not be afraid to give Miss Anderson your heart when she offers hers."

"You will never regret it," the captain added. "Unless you withhold yours from her."

Garahan listened to the two men whom he admired and had worked closely with during his tenure with the duke's guard. "Thank ye for yer advice." He couldn't share what he suspected, and what the lass had hinted at earlier with her fear of the dark. "I'll take yer suggestions as they were meant, in friendship."

Findley knocked on the doorframe. "Mrs. Wigglesworth sent word… Miss Anderson is ready to get married. Are you?"

"Aye." Garahan struggled to stand. "I'm bloody well not getting married on me *arse!*"

"We O'Malleys have as much pride as you Garahans!" his cousin said. "Did ye think I'd let me favorite cousin sit on his *arse*, when I could steady him on his feet as I stood next to him as witness?"

"While I do the same," the viscount announced.

"Faith, I'm a lucky man," Garahan murmured.

"Quit blathering, and answer Findley!" O'Malley ordered him.

"Aye, I'm ready to marry the lass."

"Ye heard him, Findley," O'Malley said. "Go and fetch me cousin-in-law-to-be!"

Garahan hoped he would be able to stand without swaying. The bulky bandage covering his eye had his balance off. He looked at the captain, who was studying him intently. Mayhap he should speak to the man about how he'd learned to navigate life with one eye. "Captain, may I have a word with ye?"

"Of course. Miranda and Michael mentioned that the apartment is ready for you and Miss Anderson to move in—tonight if you wish."

"I wish we could, but I've been told to stay put until the lieutenant has seen me tomorrow."

"I trust Sampson implicitly—best to wait for him to release you. Was there anything else?"

Garahan noticed O'Malley and Findley were speaking to the viscount. Lowering his voice, so as not to be overheard, he said, "I'm having a bit of difficulty seeing—and it may not clear anytime soon. I'm thinking I need to learn how to balance with one good eye."

The captain didn't hesitate. "The first thing I would suggest is to wear an eyepatch after Sampson removes the bandages. If your vision is blurry in one eye, it will throw your balance off—the same as having only one eye did to me. I'd be happy to help you. Send word when you are ready to move into our building, and we will begin your training."

"Thank ye, captain. Ye'll never know how much it means to me."

"I believe I do."

Chapter Eighteen

Garahan was on his feet when the vicar entered the room. His head felt light and his stomach uneasy, but he would not give in to weakness—he was about to marry the woman who'd captured his heart with one glance.

The vicar cleared his throat and said, "Everything is in order, Garahan. Do you have any questions before I begin?"

"Nay. I'm ready to marry the lass."

The vicar studied him intently but did not ask about his injuries. No doubt someone had filled him in ahead of time so he would not be shocked by Garahan's appearance. Should he have asked O'Malley for a looking glass to see how much damage had been done to his face? Well, 'twas too late now.

"Ah, Miss Anderson." The vicar beamed. "Please stand on Garahan's left and we will begin."

The vicar's voice rose and fell as he read the words that would bind Garahan and the lass together in front of the viscount, the captain, O'Malley, and the others. His mind kept coming back to the problem he would be facing—keeping his lips and his hands to himself tonight...and until the lass was ready to trust him with more than his promise to protect her with his life. Hadn't he already done that when he was knifed rescuing her from the boarding house—and again when he was jumped in the alley? Burke had sent word, confirming their suspicions—the thugs had been hired by the owners of the brothels connected with the boarding house, and the scheme luring young women to London from the countryside.

"Is there any objection as to why this couple should not be wed?"

The vicar paused too long to suit O'Malley, who spoke up. "Ye won't get an argument from anyone here, vicar."

The soft laughter that followed his cousin's pronouncement relieved the tension in Garahan's shoulders. He should have been focused completely on the vicar and his words—and not thinking about those that needed to be rounded up, convicted, and put behind bars. He leaned close to the woman standing beside him. "Lass, I—"

"I now pronounce you man and wife. You may kiss the bride."

He turned, wobbled, and was steadied by O'Malley from behind and the viscount on his right. "Better make it quick, lass— I need to sit down." Concern filled her gaze, and he said, "Not to worry. I'll be kissing ye first."

Hope replaced the worry in her eyes. She leaned toward him as he slipped his arm around her waist and drew her closer. *"Mo chroí,"* he rasped. "Me heart." Their mouths a breath apart, he murmured, *"Mo ghrá*—me love," before pressing his lips to hers in a kiss as soft as the brush of a faerie's wings.

The viscount was the first to offer his congratulations, then the captain added his. Garahan hated to ask for help, but his strength was waning. O'Malley must have been watching him closely, as he placed his arm beneath Garahan's. "Best have a seat now, boy-o."

Garahan nodded and let his cousin help him sit without jarring his ribs or shoulder overmuch. "Thank ye."

"Me pleasure." O'Malley grinned and turned to the bride. "Now then, Cousin Aimee." He offered his arm and helped her to the chair beside Garahan. "We'll be raising a glass to toast yer marriage and then will be leaving the two of ye alone."

"When was this decided?" Garahan asked.

"When ye were busy arguing with me. Mrs. O'Toole thought it more expedient to toast yer marriage and then feed the others in the dining room while yerself and yer bride enjoy sharing yer first meal together as man and wife."

Aimee reached for Garahan's hand. "Thank you, O'Malley."

"Call me Emmett, if ye don't mind."

"Thank you, Emmett. You have been more than kind to me from the moment we met."

"'Tis just to remind ye that the O'Malleys aren't as easily goaded into losing their tempers as the man you married—or the rest of the Garahans."

Her laughter lightened Garahan's heart.

O'Malley straightened, accepted a glass from Mrs. O'Toole, and raised it high. "To Darby and Aimee. May they always be as happy as they are at this moment"—he grinned at Garahan and added—"and have a dozen children with eyes the same soft blue of his bride...and tempers to match the groom!"

Garahan felt his wife tremble and bent his head to assure her, "I'm in no hurry, but would settle for a babe as pretty as her ma, with a temperament to match."

He saw the uncertainty in her eyes and sighed. "I'm a patient man, lass." Nodding to her glass, he urged, "Have a sip, I'm thinking Mrs. O'Toole will have something wonderful prepared for us to eat."

The others laughingly repeated O'Malley's toast, offered their own well wishes, and followed Mrs. O'Toole from the room.

The concern was back in his bride's eyes, and he wanted to erase it. "I thought they'd never leave." When she remained silent, he added, "Ye've been given a reprieve from what I know is at the root of yer worries from the lieutenant, in the form of an order not to share me bed tonight. Is me word not to rush ye enough to calm yer fears, lass?"

"It isn't that," she whispered. She lifted her chin and met his one-eyed gaze. "You could have married someone worthy of you,

Darby. You did not have to saddle yourself with a woman with no prospects and a reputation damaged beyond redemption."

"I can see it's going to take more than a few days to convince ye that I meant what I said. Ye have me heart whether ye believe me or not. Once given, I cannot accept it back. Though ye may not love me—and wish to leave me—know that ye'll be carrying me heart with ye wherever ye go."

Tears welled in her eyes. "My heart refused to listen to my head when you swept me into your arms and away from Purgatory. You hold my heart too. If you decide I am not worth the wait—"

His gentle kiss interrupted her. He was encouraged when her lips softened beneath his. Careful not to reopen the split on his lip, he ended the kiss, watching her eyelashes flutter as she opened her eyes. "Accept that ye have me love now and always. I may not be easy to live with while I heal, but never doubt me heart again, lass."

"I won't. I know how important it is not to put off sealing our union. As soon as you are well enough—"

"Lass… Do ye not realize that I'm fully capable of bedding ye right now?"

Her eyes widened as she shook her head. "But you're severely injured, and the doctor said—"

"That part of me did not suffer any damage and is ready, willing, and able—but I gave me word to the lieutenant, as ye did. We'll wait. I'll have a full night's sleep, then will no doubt be receiving his blessing."

⋙⋘

AIMEE'S HEART FELT as if it were firmly lodged in her throat. She pressed her hand there, relieved when the tension eased. "Is there anything I can do to make you more comfortable tonight?"

Garahan's dark eye gleamed and his lips twitched. "Aye, but

as I'll be keeping me word tonight, we'd best not speak of it."

Intrigued by the heat in his gaze and the warmth of his hand as it caressed her cheek, she sighed. "I have a feeling there is more to the act than what was forced upon me."

His expression darkened. "Ye'd be right. Know this, lass—I'll never force ye to do anything against yer will. If it takes the rest of our lives to convince ye of that, so be it."

The conviction in his voice and the promise in his eye had her fears easing their grip on her heart. "You really mean that, don't you?"

"I always mean what I say, lass. 'Tis time for ye to accept that I'm not yer equal in Society, and it may raise concerns when others find out. I was born and raised on a farm in Ireland. Me parents still work that same farm. I send home most of what I earn working for His Grace, but that will have to change a bit now that I'm a married man. Ye're used to toffs from the *ton*— gentlemen—but I'm a self-made man, elevated by me position within the duke's guard. That's all. I use me fists, me strength, and talent with weapons to do me duty to the duke and his family. I'll not be apologizing for it."

His words wrapped around her like a hug. "I am a poor relation—with no fortune and only a distant cousin to claim as family. I only met one member of the *ton*, and he was no gentleman. He lied to me from the start, and never acted the part of a gentleman once he got me in that carriage—" She paused and shook her head. "Forgive me for bringing it up. I promise not to discuss it again, but you need to know that in my eyes, you are far more of a gentleman than you realize, Darby, and have treated me as if I matter. You have never treated me like I am invisible. My cousin did for years. For that alone, I will always be grateful."

Brushing a silken lock of gold from her forehead, he rasped, "Never doubt that ye matter, lass. I'll treasure ye for however many days the good Lord grants us. I love ye, lass."

Her heart stopped, then started beating again. "I'm not sure what love is, but I do know that I would never have agreed to marry you if I didn't feel something for you."

"Tell me what ye feel."

She looked into his eye—past the injuries on his face—to the man within. "My heart skips a beat when you look at me like you are right now."

"Does it now?" he drawled. "Tell me more."

Breathless, she added, "My stomach flutters when you lean close, like you are now. It tempts me to ask you to kiss me again."

He slowly smiled. "Is that yer way of asking me to kiss ye, lass?"

She felt her face heat but ignored her embarrassment to whisper, "Would you kiss me again, Darby?"

"I confess, it's been hard for me to resist kissing ye." He leaned close and pressed his lips to hers. Softly, reverently. "If me lip wasn't injured, I'd be kissing the breath out of ye."

"Is that possible?" Aimee wondered what that would feel like. Her belly was fluttering again. She held her hand against it, hoping the feeling would go away, but it didn't.

"I'm thinking ye've described feelings that others would call love, lass. Do ye want to love me?"

"Oh yes, Darby. I do."

"Then I can die a happy man."

She shoved out of his arms. "Don't ever say that again! You will not die! Do you hear me?" The shocked expression on his face had her regretting her outburst. "Forgive me. I didn't mean to raise my voice."

"Well now, lass, I'd say that ye feel more than gratitude to me. Never worry about raising yer voice or telling me how ye feel. I'll be doing the same. Agreed?"

"Agreed. Darby?"

"Aye?"

"I think I might love you."

Their lips met in a kiss that held the promise of a love that would carry them through hard times—and good. Easy times—and bad.

"I think ye might, too."

$$\diamond\!\!\!-\!\!\!\diamond\!\!\!-\!\!\!\diamond\!\!\!-\!\!\!\diamond$$

CHAPTER NINETEEN

GARAHAN STIRRED BUT could not move—he was pinned down! He fought against the ties that bound him. Reaching out, he grabbed hold and woke instantly when his callused fingertips encountered soft, smooth skin.

"Lass?"

"Mmm?"

Her sleepy response had him wishing they were sharing a bed. Instead, he was on a cot, and his wife was kneeling on the floor with her arm holding him in place while he slept. Had she spent the whole of the night that way?

"Wake up."

"Tired," she murmured, and he had no doubt that she was.

Trying a different tack, he touched her shoulder and rasped, "Lass, I need ye!"

She jolted upright and brushed the tangle of blonde hair from her face. "What is it? What's happened?"

Emotions, too many to name, swamped him as he stared into eyes the pure blue of a midsummer sky. He reached out and caressed her angel's face with the tips of his fingers. "How long have ye been kneeling beside me?"

She blinked. "I'm not sure."

"Best get off yer knees before Mrs. O'Toole or Mrs. Wigglesworth come in and chastise ye for tiring yerself out while caring for a man like me."

She narrowed her eyes and tossed her head. "I'll kneel next to your cot for as long as I wish. Did we not exchange vows yesterday?"

He noted the irritation snapping in the depths of her eyes and fought not to smile. "Aye."

"And did we not both promise to care for one another in sickness and health?"

His lips twitched, but he dared not smile. "That we did, lass."

"Thank you."

"Ye've lost me. What in God's name are ye thanking me for?"

"Agreeing with me," she replied. "I am honoring my vows by taking care of you."

He marveled that the woman had become fiercely protective of him overnight. While it humbled him, it also annoyed the hell out of him. *He* was the one to protect her—not the other way around. His voice still gruff from sleep, he ordered her, "Ye'll not be doing such again, lass."

She laughed. *Laughed!* "I beg to disagree."

"Married not even half a day and ye're arguing with me already?"

"Faith, she's got to have a bit of Irish flowing through her veins!" O'Malley said from where he stood in the open doorway, arms crossed, grinning. "Morning, Aimee."

"Good morning, Emmett."

"No greeting for yer favorite cousin?"

O'Malley shook his head. "That was yesterday."

"What was yesterday?" Garahan asked.

"That ye were me favorite cousin. Today, I'm thinking Sean might be, as he's sent word that he asked the earl a favor on yer behalf."

Garahan frowned. "What might that be?"

"To send a carriage to escort the pair of ye to Lippincott Manor for a brief stay at Sean's cottage."

Garahan didn't bother to hide his ire at the suggestion. Affronted by the very idea of not manning his post at the duke's town house or attending to his duties in London, he demanded, "Have ye forgotten I have duties to the duke?"

"Not in this lifetime, being as we share those duties," O'Malley answered. "Do ye not wish to see me nephew? Mignonette writes that little Iain's hair is finally growing in and 'tis as blond as Sean's—with green eyes to boot."

"Another sainted O'Malley to contend with," Garahan grumbled. "Does he at least share his mother's sweet temperament?"

"He's still a babe—it's too soon to tell."

Aimee pushed to her feet, brushing her skirts to smooth them. "Does my opinion count for anything?"

"Certainly," O'Malley replied.

"Depends," Garahan mumbled.

"Ye'd best watch yer tone, Darby, or I'll be reminding ye of yer manners with the back of me hand."

"Why not yer fist?" he taunted his cousin, easing himself to a sitting position.

"Because he and your brother James have been warned not to fight in my kitchen," Mrs. O'Toole announced from the hallway. "This room is an extension of my kitchen." On that pronouncement, the cook swept into the room with a tray laden with what Garahan knew would be more invalid's food. "That makes no sense."

"It makes perfect sense to those of us who haven't had their brainbox rattled in the last few hours," O'Malley replied. "'Tis one of Mrs. O'Toole's rules that I won't be breaking again, as I've no wish to be banished from her kitchen."

"Fighting in my domain is not allowed. Injured or not, Garahan, I'll ban you from the kitchen if I hear another threat against O'Malley. Is that clear?"

"As glass," Garahan answered.

"Let me help you with that tray," Aimee offered.

"I'll take it, Mrs. O'Toole."

"Thank you, O'Malley. Just set it down on the table beneath

the shelves—if you don't mind."

After he did as Mrs. O'Toole bade him, O'Malley turned around and glared at Garahan. "Ye'll apologize to yer bride and accept Sean and his lordship's generosity, or I'll be sending a missive off to the duke explaining how ye ignored the earl's kind offer."

Ashamed of his burst of temper, Garahan swallowed his injured pride, along with the knowledge that he was not up to fighting form yet. "Forgive me, lass. Me temper is fierce when me ability to do me duty is called into question. Add it to the fact that ye have yet to answer me question and tell me how long ye spent beside me cot to keep me from rolling onto the floor."

The hurt in her eyes trebled the shame filling his gut. On the defensive, he added, "I warned ye that me injuries would put me in a foul mood."

"Yes," she replied. "You did. I did not realize how disagreeable you would be. Lieutenant Sampson warned that another blow to your head or eye could be devastating. I will not be responsible for you losing your sight when it is within my power to do something!"

Bile rushed up his throat at the reminder, but he sent it back to his roiling gut with a will of iron.

O'Malley must have noticed Garahan's throat working to keep from puking up his guts. His cousin motioned Mrs. O'Toole and the lass toward the door. "I believe Garahan requires me assistance with personal needs. If ye'd give us a few moments of privacy?"

"Of course," Aimee answered, following Mrs. O'Toole into the hallway.

O'Malley grabbed the bucket near the cot and held it while Garahan relieved the contents of his stomach. When he collapsed on the cot, O'Malley walked over to the pitcher of water, dampened a cloth, and handed it to him. "Wipe yer face and mouth and tell me what has yer guts erupting."

"Me head aches, and there's pressure in me eye—it must still be swollen. I woke, pinned to the cot, and for a moment did not know where I was. All I knew was I had to get free. When I realized it was the lass—and she was asleep on her knees beside me cot—I felt as if I'd failed her."

"But she's yer wife. Ye both made promises to be there in sickness and health."

"'Twas the reason she spouted back at me when I questioned her."

"What is the real problem? Have ye changed yer mind? Are ye sorry that ye married the lass?"

"Nay! I wouldn't change that for the world."

O'Malley frowned. "Tell me what's got in yer craw, before the women decide ye've had enough time to use the chamber pot and burst through the door."

"What if I lose the sight in me eye entirely? What manner of man would I be then? How will I be able to perform me duties to His Grace or protect me wife?"

"Did ye lose what little brains God granted ye at birth?"

"What in the bloody hell do ye mean by that?" Garahan demanded.

O'Malley swore a blue streak before answering, "Captain Coventry has been fighting alongside of us protecting the duke and his family—as well as his own family. He not only lost the sight in one eye, but the whole *fecking* eye! And ye're blathering on about only losing sight in yer eye. Faith, but ye're a horse's *arse!*"

Garahan knew his cousin had the right of it, but he was still angry enough not to agree…yet. It was the principle of the thing. "Sure and ye'd be knowing that as ye are yerself."

"If ye weren't injured, I'd be beating the ever-living *shite* out of ye, Darby!"

"Problem, gentlemen?" a familiar, deep voice asked.

O'Malley flinched. "Yer lordship."

"We didn't hear ye knock, yer lordship," Garahan rasped.

"How could you, while the two of you were hurling insults at one another?" the viscount replied. "I trust you have resolved whatever the matter is."

Garahan and O'Malley nodded at the same time.

"Excellent. I came to bid you goodbye and to wish you a happy marriage, Garahan. I'll explain to Lippincott and Sean that plans have changed, and you'll be staying in London. Take the time alone with your bride. Marriage is a partnership, Garahan, and more easily navigated while you adjust to sharing *all* aspects of your life."

"All?" Garahan nearly choked on the word.

Chattsworth slowly smiled. "Aye, all."

"But what about me duties?"

"They will wait, and there are others who can cover for you until then."

"But—" Garahan began, only to fall silent at the direct look from the viscount. "Aye, yer lordship."

O'Malley glared at Garahan. "I think me cousin meant to thank ye."

"Forgive me, yer lordship. Thank ye for yer generosity."

The viscount nodded. "I understand from Coventry that there is a vacant apartment in his building. Take him up on it and stay put for three bloody days, or I shall send an urgent missive to His Grace. I know Jared will agree with me."

Knowing when to retreat, Garahan inclined his head. "We'll be going to the apartment after I'm cleared by Lieutenant Sampson. Thank ye for everything, yer lordship."

Chattsworth's frown smoothed out. "Thank you, Garahan, for your service to those of us who owe our lives to you."

"I'm honored, yer lordship. Lieutenant Sampson should be arriving shortly. I gave me word not to leave me cot until he deems me fit enough."

The viscount inclined his head. "Judging from the argument I overheard, and the way you appear at the moment, I have no doubt he will allow—and, in fact, encourage—it. I believe I shall ask Mrs. O'Toole if the batch of scones she was putting in the oven is ready yet. Use the time before Sampson arrives to rest."

"Aye, yer lordship." When the viscount left, Garahan turned to O'Malley and whispered, "Scones?"

O'Malley shook his head. "Ye'll not get one bite until the lieutenant agrees. The more ye put in yer gut, the more likely ye'll puke it up. Ye should wait till ye're settled in yer apartment."

"Always one to add joy to me life," Garahan muttered.

O'Malley grinned. "'Tis me pleasure."

Garahan wondered when he and Aimee would be able to consummate their marriage. Deciding that was dangerous ground, he shoved that thought to the back of his mind and pushed off the cot, but his cousin stopped him.

"Don't move," O'Malley ordered him. "I don't need ye painting the walls or floor with yer bile while I'm gone. I'll ask one of the footmen to empty the bucket."

Frustration filled Garahan because he had no choice. At least O'Malley had been the only one present when his stomach rebelled. "Any other bits of wisdom for me?"

His cousin passed off the bucket to the footman and looked over his shoulder. "If I think of any, I'll let ye know."

"*Fecking eedjit,*" Garahan grumbled.

As if his cousin did not trust him to obey the dictate, O'Malley left the door open while he spoke to the footman stationed outside.

Alone, Garahan allowed himself to wallow in self-pity. He'd never been severely injured before. Mentally cataloguing the number of times he had been injured, he reasoned through the results. When he had been shot, the lead ball grazed his arm—a few stitches, and he was good as new. The knife wound to his side missed vital organs—again, it was easily taken care of. His ribs had been cracked and broken—and healed without piercing a lung. All in all, he'd been even luckier than Sean, who survived the serious infection and did not lose his arm.

Musing over the number of injuries he and his brothers, and cousins, had incurred in the line of duty, he marveled that there had only been one or two close calls among them. He slowly smiled. The Irish were used to working hard, pitting themselves against the elements and their oppressors. Every blessed member of the duke's guard had been knocked unconscious a time or two, but praise God, were no worse for the wear. The Garahans had the hardest heads of the bunch, followed by the O'Malleys…then the Flahertys.

His ma whispered her oft-used phrase in his mind: *Be thankful for the gifts in yer lives and don't forget to talk to God now and again.*

"I may not say thank ye often, Lord, but I'm thanking ye now for me wife—and me life. Give me the strength to protect her with it."

The knock on the doorframe had him lifting his head and smiling. "I'm ready for ye to tell me I can return to me post, lieutenant."

Sampson's lips twitched as he entered the room. "I am quite certain that you are. Shall we conduct a brief examination first?"

Since there was no way out of it, Garahan agreed.

The physician manipulated Garahan's shoulder, noting the hiss of air he expelled. "Having suffered a dislocated shoulder myself, I know how uncomfortable it can be. If I managed to suffer through the remedy, I am sure you will be able to." Sampson retrieved the cloth he'd brought with him and fashioned a sling.

Garahan balked. "I won't be needing that. Me shoulder's fine."

Testing that theory, the lieutenant rotated Garahan's arm and watched the color fade from his face. "What were you saying about the sling?"

Beads of sweat formed at his temples and the back of his neck. "I'll wear it—if it'll help heal me faster."

"It will. The ligaments and tendons were severely strained when the bone was knocked out of the socket." The lieutenant eased Garahan's arm into the sling. "Give it a chance to heal. A few days of rest with the proper diet should be sufficient. Let's have a look at your ribs."

While Sampson prodded and poked, Garahan clenched his muscles to keep from giving away the fact that it hurt like bloody hell. "Take a deep breath." When he complied, the physician had him fill his lungs and expel the air a few more times before he was satisfied. "Excellent—your lungs are clear."

Sampson sat on the chair next to the cot, his direct gaze pinned to Garahan. "Now then, how does your eye feel?"

Garahan shrugged.

The physician unwrapped the bandage around Garahan's head and then carefully removed the thicker bandage covering his eye to study it carefully. "The same, or has it worsened?"

Garahan wanted to confide in the lieutenant, but if he did, would the physician demand that he rest for more than a few days?

"If you believe that you can hide the truth from me, you are mistaken. I know that you do not wish to rest. You are not unlike any other member of the duke's guard who balks at being told to do so. The difference this time is the damage is to your eye. All of you have suffered cracked and broken ribs before and are aware of the chances of a fractured rib puncturing a lung."

"I've been socked in the eye before and never suffered more than a bit of swelling."

"Garahan, I can assure you this time it will take longer to heal once the swelling is completely gone."

"Ye can?"

"I have treated this type of injury before. Rest is essential, as is not getting hit in the eye again before it's completely healed."

"How much rest?"

"It is different for everyone. As the swelling has gone down, I suggest you keep the additional folded bandage over your eye, but instead of wrapping your head with linen, I suggest an eyepatch. I brought one with me."

Garahan tried to bargain with the lieutenant. "What if I covered it at night? Can I forgo wearing the eyepatch during the day?"

"Too much of a risk. I'll stop by to see you the day after to-morrow, unless you send for me." The physician folded the linen to the appropriate size to cover Garahan's eye, and helped him affix the eyepatch to hold it in place. "You may need your wife's help replacing the bandage and putting the eyepatch on."

Garahan lifted his hand to his face and brushed the tip of his fingers over the covering. "Aye."

"If you leave your cot—or bed—use a cane," the physician told him. "Not only will it keep you from walking into chairs—or walls—it will aid your ability to balance until your eye heals and the eyepatch is no longer necessary."

Garahan did not agree or disagree about using a cane. Flexing his hands, he curled them into tight fists. "Will me sight continue to get worse before it clears?"

"As I said, everyone heals differently. Have you been hit in that eye before?"

Garahan snorted with laughter. "Have ye not heard that I was the youngest bare-knuckle champion in the Garahan family?"

Sampson shook his head. "I'll take that as a yes. And in that case, time will tell. I wish I could offer you more than that, but I never give false hope to my patients. I did not on the battlefield, when I served with the King's Dragoons, and I refuse to do so now."

Garahan offered his hand to the physician. "Thank ye for yer honesty, lieutenant. I'm grateful."

"Grateful enough to follow my instructions in order to heal?"

"As of last night, 'tisn't just meself that will be privy to yer instructions."

"Ah, should I mention that Mrs. Garahan asked me to leave instructions with her after I examined you?"

Garahan grinned. "The lass is fierce in her determination to see me well."

"Count your blessings, Garahan. You have married a fine woman. Congratulations."

"Thank ye, lieutenant. How long do ye think I'll be needing to wear the blasted eyepatch?"

To Garahan's relief, the physician did not become irritated at the repeated question. "I'll decide when I reexamine your eye. If I am pleased with the progress, I will reevaluate your condition and treatment."

The lieutenant rose to his feet and had retrieved his bag by the time Garahan remembered to ask, "Can ye tell me darling bride that I'll not be needing any more of Mrs. O'Toole's calves' foot jelly?"

Sampson smiled. "Absolutely." He had a hand on the doorframe when he glanced over his shoulder to add, "Any other questions for me?"

Garahan mentally crossed his fingers. "Aye, about last night…"

The lieutenant nodded. "If I didn't think it was imperative that you forgo having relations, I would not have insisted upon it."

"What about tonight?" Garahan asked hopefully.

"Mrs. Garahan already asked about that."

"Did she now?" Garahan's heart rejoiced. He was looking forward to teaching his bride there was pleasure to be had in the marriage bed.

"I told her there were no restrictions. I wish you and Mrs. Garahan my best."

"Thank ye, lieutenant. Since I'm well enough for that, sure and ye can change yer mind about the invalid's diet."

"Absolutely."

Garahan grinned.

"In three days' time." Sampson smiled. "Rest."

"Aye, lieutenant." Garahan knew when he'd been bested. *"Bollocks!"*

O'Malley walked back into the room. Staring at the eyepatch and sling, he asked. "Well? Has the lieutenant agreed ye can go back to yer duties?"

"I can take me wife to our new lodgings but have been ordered to rest for three days. No duties."

O'Malley nodded at Garahan's head. "Did ye ask Sampson how long to expect before yer eye heals?"

"Aye, but he claims people heal at a different rate." Garahan rose to his feet and promptly hit his shin on the chair leg.

"'Tis what I would have said, had ye asked me before the lieutenant. Best be telling yer bride. Ye'll be needing her help navigating for a bit until ye get used to your new field of vision."

"Coventry's expecting us today. I'll have to pack me things."

"Why don't I send word to the captain and let him know you're cleared to leave but have been ordered to rest for a few days? Given the number of times we've plowed our fists into one another's faces sharpening our bare-knuckle skills, it is within the realm of possibility we'd miss and punch one another in the *fecking* eyeball."

"I'll ask the lass to take notes when the captain explains how he regained his balance."

"And ye're not afraid to have her on hand when Coventry speaks to ye?"

Garahan realized he was not. "Nay. We're a team now…for better or worse. Faith, it's grand to start out with the worse."

O'Malley stared at him. "Is it now?"

"Aye, our luck and lives will only improve from this day forward."

"Always looking on the bright side, Darby. Faith, I love that about ye."

"I owe ye more than I can say. Thank ye, Emmett."

O'Malley grinned. "I have a few ideas of how ye can pay me back, boy-o. Never fear."

"Will it worry me wife?"

O'Malley shrugged. "Nay—besides, yer darling bride has a backbone of steel and a heart of gold."

"And the face of an angel," Garahan reminded him.

"That she does, Darby. Ye're a lucky man."

"Blessed is what I am," Garahan rasped. "I hope she won't be dismayed by me present condition."

"Backbone of steel," O'Malley repeated.

"Aye," Garahan agreed. "And a heart of gold."

✦

CHAPTER TWENTY

I T TOOK LITTLE time to pack his belongings. He had three uniforms—one to wear, one to wash, and one to have the slashes and holes from knives and lead balls mended. The lass had the three gowns her employer provided and then insisted she keep as a gift, her nightrail, and precious little else. For the time being, she would not be returning to the Smythe-Wyatt household.

What took the most time was arguing with O'Malley over how many weapons to take. They decided to leave half at the duke's town house—for his temporary replacement to use—and take half to Garahan's new lodgings.

The lass eyed the rifle and sword lying on the seat across from them. "Do you need to bring those with you?"

"Aye. I may have been ordered to rest for three days, but I'll be prepared for trouble when it comes calling."

She paled, and he wished he could call back the words. "You expect trouble?"

He pulled her against his side. "I could lie to ye, but I'll not do that. Ye deserve to know the truth. Until we round up the individuals responsible for luring young women to London under false pretenses, I'll be on guard—as ye should be. Don't be going anywhere without meself or one of Coventry's men."

"Will I meet them soon?"

Pleased that she did not argue with him and seemed interested in meeting the captain's men, he answered, "I'm thinking they'll be on hand when we arrive. Coventry will want his men to meet ye for yer sake, as well as theirs."

The ride to the captain's building on the corner of Hart and Lumley was short—too long for Garahan to walk, according to the lieutenant, until he'd been cleared to return to his duties.

When Tremayne opened the door, Garahan knew they'd been watching for the carriage. Bloody hell, he should have warned his wife about the former dragoon's scar ahead of time.

"Tremayne, at your service. Allow me to assist you, Mrs. Garahan."

He watched with pride as his wife smiled at Tremayne and reached for his hand—ignoring the wicked scar. "Thank you, Mr. Tremayne."

"Just Tremayne, Mrs. Garahan."

Garahan remembered to move slower than normal, and with care. He stepped down from the carriage to join the lass and Tremayne on the sidewalk.

"The captain asked that I bring you to his lodgings straight away," Tremayne said. He turned to the coachman. "Wait here. I'll return in a moment for their bags."

"And weapons," Garahan added.

Tremayne opened the door to the building and ushered them inside. "All of them?"

"Nay, O'Malley thought it better to leave half of them in Grosvenor Square for my replacement to use."

Tremayne led them down the hallway and knocked on the last door. While they waited for it to be answered, he reminded Garahan, "You aren't being replaced. Remember that when you speak to Coventry about how he recovered."

Aimee looked worried. "Ye'll be safe here, lass. Tremayne and the others have far more experience defending than meself or me brothers."

"Not more," Tremayne added. "Different."

The door swung open, and the captain greeted them. "Good to see you on your feet, Garahan. Mrs. Garahan, Tremayne, come in."

The warmth of the room enveloped them, but it was something else entirely that captured Garahan's attention when the captain's daughter squealed with delight and toddled over to him, arms lifted as she babbled in a language he did not understand until she said, "Up."

The captain's wife beamed. "Emma's never taken to a stranger so quickly."

"She's not as fragile as she looks, Garahan," the captain told him.

He bent and lifted the little girl in his arms. "Has yer da been feeding ye, lass?" He frowned at the captain. "She cannot weigh more than a handful of feathers!" The captain and Tremayne snorted with laughter, easing some of the tension between Garahan's shoulder blades. "Are ye one of the *fae*, lass? All that's missing is yer wings."

Emma put her hands on the sides of Garahan's face and frowned.

"Do ye think me eyepatch is scaring her?"

Coventry chuckled. "Mine doesn't. Why should yours?"

"He's not used to wearing it yet," Aimee answered. Turning to the captain's wife, she said, "You have a beautiful daughter and a lovely home."

The door burst open, and a tall young man grinned. "Darby! You're here!"

Garahan grinned back. "Michael? Ye've grown half a foot since I saw ye last. How are ye, lad?"

"Fine. I see Emma's wrapped another man around her little finger."

As if she understood, the little one in Garahan's arms laid her head on his shoulder, completely melting his heart. Unable to resist, he brushed the tips of his fingers on her baby-fine hair. "Ye've a beautiful sister, lad. I hope ye are up to the task of protecting her until she gives her heart to a man worthy of her love."

The captain cleared his throat. "That won't be happening until years from now, Garahan."

Mrs. Coventry smiled. "At least four and ten years from now."

Coventry frowned and stomped over to Garahan. Reaching for his daughter, he grumbled, "Not if I have any say in the matter."

Garahan had felt a similar need to protect the two little girls he'd recently rescued. "Here now, lass, go to yer da."

Instead of immediately going to her father's arms, she patted Garahan's cheek before pressing a kiss beneath his eyepatch.

Touched by the sweetness and warmth of her tiny lips, he fought to keep his emotions in check. "If ye ever have need of me, lass, yer da knows where to find me."

"At last count, captain, that's six of us who've fallen under Emma's spell," Tremayne said.

"Six?" Garahan asked.

"Aye, myself, Bayfield, Hennessey, Masterson, James Garahan...and you, Darby."

Garahan didn't bother to deny it.

"I'll grab your things and send the duke's coachman on his way."

"Please thank him for us," Aimee said.

"I will, Mrs. Garahan," Tremayne promised before saying to Michael, "I could use a hand."

"I looked inside the carriage," the boy admitted. "Can I carry the weapons?"

"No!" his mother answered. "Tremayne will carry whatever weapons Garahan brought with him."

"I'll be practicing with me rifle and pistol later today, lad, if ye'd like to join me," Garahan said.

"Lieutenant Sampson ordered you to rest," Aimee reminded him.

"Nothing more restful than aiming at a target that doesn't move, lass."

"Mayhap a bit later," the captain said. "Miranda baked a loaf of gingerbread in anticipation of your arrival. Tremayne, join us. Afterward, we can show the Garahans to their new home."

"Will do, thank you." Tremayne motioned for Michael to follow and closed the door behind them.

"Thank ye, captain," Garahan said. "I need to keep me skills sharp."

"Later," Coventry told him. "While Miranda helps your wife settle in, we'll be meeting with the rest of the men upstairs in my office."

Garahan knew something had occurred. Anxious to find out but knowing not to ask questions with the women present, he nodded. "Aye, captain."

As if she sensed that her husband and Garahan needed to discuss something of import, Miranda slipped her arm through Aimee's and steered her toward the kitchen table. "I hope you like gingerbread. It's one of Gordon's favorites."

"I haven't had it in an age. Why don't I serve the gingerbread while you pour the tea?"

"I'd appreciate the help. Thank you, Aimee."

When Emma squirmed to get down, Coventry set her on her feet. She wavered for a moment, then scooted right over to the table, babbling and pointing to the gingerbread. "Emma loves Miranda's gingerbread almost as much as I do."

As he watched the women and Coventry's daughter, Garahan's gut twisted at the thought of anything happening to Aimee. He had to know if their meeting had to do with his wife or the baron.

Pitching his voice low so the women would not hear, he asked, "If whatever happened involved yer wife, would ye be able to wait a few hours to find out?"

Coventry frowned and admitted, "Nay. It is not about Summerfield."

Garahan's control snapped into place. "When do ye expect trouble to arrive at yer door?"

The captain met and held Garahan's gaze. "Tonight."

Garahan nodded. "We've plenty of time to form a plan."

"Tea's ready!" Miranda announced.

"Be right there, my love," the captain answered.

MICHAEL AND TREMAYNE returned as Miranda was pouring tea. "Come and join us," she said.

While the men devoured the moist and delicious treat, Aimee took her time and savored every bite. "Miranda, this is delicious!"

"I'd be happy to share the recipe with you if you'd like."

"I would, thank you." It all seemed so normal, Aimee realized, seated at the large oak table in the warmth of the captain's lodgings. No servants were waiting on them, and one of the captain's men joined them. She wondered if it was a regular occurrence, and supposed she would find out soon enough.

Not really paying attention to the conversation, she was surprised when Miranda said, "Will you keep me in the dark, Gordon, or are you planning to advise me on the latest round of trouble coming our way?"

The captain set down his teacup and frowned at his wife. "It is my job to protect you, Miranda."

She reached for his hand and held tight. "And you have been doing an admirable job of it since Michael was two years old." Holding up her scarred hands, she asked, "Have I not proven I can take care of myself?"

Instead of the harsh words Aimee expected to hear, the captain pressed his lips to his wife's hands. "Ah, lass, if I could turn back time…"

"You cannot."

"If I had been there—"

Miranda interrupted, "It would not have happened."

"She's right, Father," Michael added. "He'd been keeping to himself, waiting for the chance to catch her alone."

Aimee's heart trembled, but she strove not to let it show. This beautiful woman with the sunset hair and scarred hands had been attacked too? Somehow the knowledge loosened another knot inside of her. Miss Michaela, Mrs. Plumton, and Miranda Coventry had all been victims and yet seemed to survive—and thrive.

What if Miranda did not know of anyone else who'd been in a similar situation? Aimee needed to let her know that she was not alone…that she understood. "I know from experience that it takes courage to defend yourself against someone stronger and determined to harm you."

Miranda looked at her. "Did you wonder if you somehow encouraged the attack?"

Did Aimee dare answer? How could she not? Throat tight, unable to speak, she nodded.

Coventry and Garahan rose at the same time. Both men pulled their wives into their arms and held them…just held them.

"Put that thought out of your head, Miranda," Coventry said.

"But I—"

"Listen to him, Mum," Michael interjected. "You never encouraged him. I watched him."

"Why?"

Michael shrugged. "Never trusted him."

"Our son has good instincts," Coventry murmured.

"I'm sorry to have brought it up, but you need to trust that I can take care of myself, Gordon."

"I'm humbled by your courage, while at the same time hope that you would understand my need to protect you, love."

Garahan brushed a lock of hair out of Aimee's eyes. "Strike that thought from yer mind, lass. Never think it again."

"But—"

"Later, love," he rasped, pressing his lips to her forehead.

"Mum, Father's need to provide and protect you is a part of who he is," Michael continued.

"Well said," Tremayne remarked.

"And a part of meself, as well as me brothers and cousins," Garahan chimed in.

Michael turned his teacup upside down and frowned, and Emma did the same with her sturdy cup. "Is there any more tea, Mum?"

"More tea!" Emma cried.

"We emptied the pot," Miranda replied.

"I'll put the kettle on for you, Mum."

"Thank you, Michael." Turning to Aimee and Garahan, Miranda said, "You're probably exhausted. I'll show you the apartment so you can settle in. Darling, would you please put Emma down for her nap?"

Coventry swept his daughter off her chair and into his arms. "Time to close your pretty eyes." Emma batted her eyelashes at him and giggled.

"She doesn't look tired," Garahan whispered to Aimee.

"She's adorable," she whispered back.

They stared at one another, and for a moment Aimee wondered what it would be like if they had a daughter with dark brown hair and warm brown eyes.

"Michael, would you fetch the key?" Miranda said.

"Aye, Mum."

"It's just across the hall," the captain's wife said.

"Thank ye for the delicious tea and the gingerbread," Garahan said. "I'll just grab our bags and we'll follow you."

Tremayne picked up the weapons. "Best not to leave these lying around."

Michael unlocked the door and pushed it open.

Aimee stood on the threshold, her gaze sweeping the room. "It's furnished!"

"Is there something ye wish to change, lass?" Garahan asked.

She shook her head. "Not a thing. I thought we may be sleeping on the floor tonight."

He chuckled. "I didn't think that far ahead. I'm happy to realize the captain and Mrs. Coventry have."

"It's perfect," Aimee said as she walked around the room, straightening the looking glass on the wall and pushing one of the chairs under the kitchen table.

"There are fresh linens on the bed and in the wardrobe. If you need anything, just let me know."

Garahan thanked Miranda again, then asked, "How soon do you think the captain will need to meet with me?"

"Emma may take some convincing before she closes her eyes. Half an hour, maybe longer. I can have Michael knock on your door when it's time. Gordon usually likes to go over his reports and things beforehand."

"That will give Garahan time to rest—"

"I'm standing right here, wife, and have not said I'm tired."

Aimee was smiling when she told Miranda, "It may take some convincing before he agrees to rest."

When Michael snorted with laughter, Garahan frowned at him. The lad shrugged and said, "You should have seen how long it took to convince my father to close his eyes after the time they found him half dead in the alley."

"Oh?" Garahan said. "How long?"

Michael backed toward the open door. "Ten minutes…maybe less. I'll straighten up for you, Mum." He was laughing as he sprinted across the hall.

Garahan's lips twitched. "A sense of humor is a good thing to have, Miranda."

Hand on the doorknob, she admitted, "He keeps me on my toes. If you aren't too tired, Aimee, come over when Garahan goes upstairs to the meeting."

"Thank you. I will."

When the door closed behind the captain's wife, Garahan pulled Aimee into his embrace and breathed deeply. "Thank ye for opening up to Miranda. She's never met Miss Michaela, and

I'm thinking she might not have known anyone else who'd been through what she has."

"The same thought occurred to me. And before you ask, I do wonder if agreeing to run away to Gretna Green was all the encouragement he—"

Garahan's lips silenced her, coaxed her to sink deeper into the kiss until she'd all but forgotten her name as his lips and teeth and tongue moved to the line of her jaw, the nape of her neck.

"Ye taste of heaven, lass. I'll be wanting another taste after the meeting." Taking her by the hand, he led them to the small bedroom off the kitchen. "Lie down with me, lass. I want to hold ye in me arms."

Aimee's eyes went immediately to the bed with the pale butter-colored quilt and pillows, charmed by the warmth it added to the tiny bedchamber. She felt Darby's arm tighten around her, and for a brief moment, she faltered in her earlier decision to ask him to seal their vows later tonight. Digging deep, she found the fortitude to endure the painful joining that would need to take place before they were legally wed.

"Now then, wife of mine, what is weighing so heavy on yer mind?"

She flushed to the roots of her hair but ignored the heat to answer honestly, "I was thinking of tonight."

He turned her in his arms so they were face to face. "As it happens, so was I." Tipping her chin up, he said, "We do not have to consummate our marriage tonight, lass. It can wait a few days until ye're more comfortable doing so. But for yer safety, I would not recommend putting it off more than a sennight."

When she couldn't think of a reply, he added, "I'm not ex-pecting ye to be ready to do more than fulfill our vows to make it official in the eyes of the law, the church…and the Lord."

She nodded, bit her bottom lip, and could not help but notice his eye was riveted to her mouth. Nerves had her licking her lips. As she did, she saw desire swirling in the depths of his dark brown eye.

"Lass, ye have no idea what ye're doing to me."

"I don't mean to, Darby."

He pulled her against him until she could feel the pounding of his heart. Did he suffer from nerves as well? "Are you concerned about our… Er… That is… When we—"

"When I make love to ye, claiming me bride as me wife?"

She had difficulty forming the words to answer, so she nodded again.

"Nay. I promised not to ever cause ye pain, and I have never broken a promise, lass. I'll treat ye with care and teach ye the way a man and a woman can share what is in their hearts with their lips, tongues, hands…and their bodies."

She shivered as the depth of his voice, and his words, seeped into her soul. "I trust you, Darby."

"If I didn't have to meet with Coventry, I'd begin your first lesson this moment."

Aimee got lost in the promise of passion and desire swirling in the depths of his one-eyed gaze. Inexorably drawn to him, she whispered, "Would you kiss me, Darby? Please?"

"With pleasure, lass."

The kiss was endless. Lips parted, tongues delved, and bodies quivered before it ended. He dropped his forehead to hers and sighed. "Though it pains me to stop kissing ye, if I don't, we'll begin yer lessons now—and I'll be late for the meeting and risk the captain pounding on our door."

She laughed at the idea until she realized Darby had stiffened and gone quiet. "I did not mean to offend you, Darby. I thought you were jesting with me about the captain."

"I never disobey an order from Coventry, though I suppose the idea of him beating on our door could be amusing. And just so ye know, I'm looking forward to teaching ye how to make love."

He pressed his lips to hers again. Softly. Tenderly. "Lie down with me—just for a wee bit. Then we'll both be rested—me for the meeting and yerself to visit with Miranda."

He slipped the sling over his head and tossed it on the bedside table. He unbuttoned his frockcoat and waistcoat while she watched, all the while wondering how he could appear as if he hadn't been beaten severely.

Darby turned to her and asked, "Would ye like me to help ye off with yer gown? 'Twould save it from wrinkling while ye rest."

Panic iced the blood in her veins, as her past threatened to overwhelm her. Firm hands grasped her upper arms and gently pulled her into his embrace. His sigh didn't sound exasperated, as she worried it might—it sounded sad. Why would that be? Before she could stop herself, the words slipped out.

Darby rested his chin on her head and said, "Ah, lass, 'tis the truth—when I'm not mad enough to search out the blackguard who compromised ye, I ache for what ye went through. What we'll share between us as husband and wife should be a joyful experience. Pleasure to be given, to be received. 'Tis mortal sorry I am that ye expect only pain, lass."

She felt her breath hitch in her breast as emotions swamped her. Fear and hope tangled in a knot that she would have to accept and deal with. Mayhap if she shared what she felt with her husband, he would know how to unravel the knot, so that only hope remained.

Darby eased back and locked gazes with her. "Lass, the fear in yer eyes unmans me, but the hope… Well now, that lifts me heart. We'd best remove our boots. The last thing we need is Coventry or his wife ringing a peal over me head for damaging the quilt."

She couldn't help but smile at his thoughtfulness. "You are a kind man, Darby."

He helped her remove her half boots and then his own. With a wicked grin, he swept her off her feet and onto the bed. "I'll be lying next to ye, lass, but that's not all."

A sliver of worry slithered through her. "It isn't?"

"Nay, lass—I'm wanting to hold ye while we rest."

Tears welled up, and one slipped past her guard. Darby captured it on the tip of his finger and pressed his lips to her cheek. "I'm thinking it won't be easy to earn yer trust with words alone, lass. I need to show ye. Consider this me first test."

She nodded as he slid onto the bed and pulled her into his arms. "What about your shoulder? I don't want to add to your pain."

"It doesn't bother me at all. I'm leaning on me other shoulder. I have two, ye know."

The twinkle in his eye had her lips lifting into a smile, and she realized that with this man, she was beginning to find a part of herself she thought she'd lost.

"There's a lass." He pressed his lips to her forehead. "Close yer angel eyes."

"What if I fall asleep?"

He traced the line of her jaw before smoothing the fingertip across her bottom lip. "Any other worries, lass?"

She shook her head. "Darby?"

"Aye?"

"Thank you."

"Aimee?"

At the sound of her name, she wondered if she'd said something wrong. He had only used her name a few times and preferred to call her "lass." She liked the way it rolled off his tongue. "Yes?"

"Close yer eyes."

She did.

"Lass?"

She heard his voice a short while later but wasn't ready to stop the sweet dream—lying in a meadow with the sun warming her all the way to her bones.

"Lass? Ye need to open yer eyes."

"But you told me to close them," she grumbled.

"Aye, but that was forty minutes ago."

Her eyes shot open. "It was?"

He chuckled. "Michael knocked on our door already."

"Why didn't you wake me?"

He snorted with laughter. "I tried, but ye kept mumbling to let ye be."

"Forgive me." She sat up. "I'll be ready in a trice."

He moved to let her off the bed and put his boots on while she washed quickly. When it was his turn to wash, she put her half boots on and watched him unabashedly. Before he could reach for it, she grabbed his waistcoat. "Is it proper for a wife to help her husband dress?"

"I'd rather ye were undressing me, but aye, 'tis proper."

She reached for his frockcoat while he buttoned his waistcoat. He donned it, buttoned it, and frowned at her when she held out the sling and waited. "You should wear this."

"Are ye planning to tell me what to do now, lass?"

"Are you going to ignore the physician's orders?"

He swore beneath his breath as he took the proffered sling and slipped it over his head. Before he could adjust it, Aimee took care of the chore.

"Thank you," she said. "I know it is hard for you to accept that your injuries need time to heal."

"I'm fine."

She tilted her head at him and nodded. "I'm certain that you think you are, but would you please allow me to take care of you?"

He brushed a strand of hair off her forehead and pressed his lips to hers. "If ye do me a favor in return."

"Of course. What do you need?"

"I need you to promise ye'll not go anywhere without one of Coventry's men or meself as yer guard."

"Won't I be taking them away from their duties?"

"Nay, lass. Until me current assignment is over and until we dismantle the ring of blackguards behind luring young lasses to London, Coventry's men will be protecting ye as part of their duties."

She hadn't considered that aspect of being married to Darby. "I see."

"Well?"

Aimee knew she would have to agree with him—otherwise, they'd spend the next quarter hour staring at one another until she capitulated. "Fine."

"Fine?" His intense stare clued her in to the fact that he was waiting to hear her repeat the words.

"I agree not go anywhere alone."

"It may take some time to get used to the way it needs to be, now that ye're me wife. But I will not take any chances where the matter of yer safety and well-being are concerned."

She cupped the side of his face and, lifting to her toes, pressed her lips to his. "I will do my best not to antagonize you."

"Thank ye. We'd best be on our way."

"Darby?"

"Aye, lass?"

"Thank you for marrying me."

He chuckled. "Ye'll be praising God before the night's over."

She frowned. "Oh, will I?"

He pulled her flush against his heavily muscled chest, and she gasped, feeling the pulse of his desire where it pressed low against her belly. "Aye, lass, that ye will." He sealed his promise with a mind-numbing kiss.

GARAHAN KNOCKED ON the door to the Coventrys' lodgings and ushered her inside when Michael opened it. "Do ye promise to stay here until I come back for ye?"

"I just promised that I wouldn't leave without a guard," she huffed.

"Give me the words, lass, or I'll be late for me meeting with the captain and Tremayne."

"I will be right here until you return."

Garahan kissed the top of her head, bade Miranda goodbye, and motioned for Michael to follow him outside. Leaning close, he rasped, "Me wife isn't used to being under anyone's protection. Can I count on ye to guard me wife as well as yer ma and yer sister?"

Michael squared his shoulders. "You can count on me, Garahan."

"Good, lad. Ye have me thanks."

"I won't let you down."

With one hand on the railing, Garahan took the stairs two at a time and knocked on the door to the captain's office.

"Enter."

He crossed the threshold and jolted to a stop. As one, four men turned around.

"Men, meet Darby Garahan. Darby, you already know Tremayne and Bayfield. Hennessey and Masterson are part of the guard I spoke to you about."

"I've heard about what you men did for me cousin, Finn O'Malley. I'm in yer debt. Whatever ye need, whenever ye need it, ye've but to ask."

The men murmured their thanks, and Coventry said, "Hennessey delivered a missive from King. I know you are supposed to rest, Garahan, but I do not want to leave my wife and family alone tonight with the rumored threat hanging over our heads."

"I told Sampson I was ready to return to duty," Garahan reminded the captain.

"He's worried about your eyesight."

"Ye can count on me, captain. Who is going with ye to meet King?"

"No one. I'm leaving the five of you here to guard my heart and yours."

Garahan gave a brief nod. "Ye can count on me. What have ye told the women?"

Coventry shifted from foot to foot. "Not a bloody thing."

"Don't ye think ye should?"

"I normally tell my wife I have a meeting, and she knows not to answer the door unless it's myself or one of the men."

Garahan frowned. "I doubt the lass would be as understanding as yer wife, captain. She already knows to expect trouble tonight and is with Miranda right now. I've asked Michael to add me wife to those he protects—his ma and his sister."

"You can trust Michael. He's grown into a fine young man."

"He learned from the best," Garahan replied.

Coventry nodded, accepting the compliment. "Now then, men, the usual stations tonight. One man guarding the rear door to the building, one guarding the front, one by the side alley, and two men inside." His gaze met Garahan's. "Tremayne and you will be inside. Try to avoid any blows to the face or head."

"Aye, captain."

The men followed Coventry downstairs. While he bade his wife goodbye, three men went outside to take their positions, while Garahan and Tremayne would guard their charges from the inside.

✦ ⬥ ✦

CHAPTER TWENTY-ONE

"I DO NOT care how long it takes! I want my cousin's name cleared of any connection with the abduction of that harpy, Prudence Barstow."

"But sir—"

Harrison Ashbrook pounded his hand on the desk. "The next time we meet, I expect you to bring the news that Baron Summerfield is dead." He glared at the dockworker wringing his cap in his hands. "Understood?"

"Aye, sir."

When the man turned to go, Ashbrook added, "I have connections throughout London. If the job is not handled to my satisfaction, there is nowhere you can hide where I won't find you and kill you myself."

The man nodded and rushed out of Ashbrook's study as if he feared a lead ball in his back.

"How do you know you can trust him?"

Ashbrook frowned at Robertson. "I don't, though I had to make the lackwit believe I trusted him to do the job, didn't I?"

Robertson sighed. "I cannot believe Farrell has defected. We trusted him and thought we could count on him to follow this through to the end."

Ashbrook snickered. "He hasn't the stomach for killing."

"Not certain I do," Robertson admitted, "unless it is on the field of honor."

"Are you suggesting my plan to eliminate the baron is not honorable?"

The two men locked gazes. After a charged moment of silence, Robertson capitulated. "You misunderstood, Ashbrook."

"Just so," Ashbrook murmured. "Now then, my plan includes another man to step up if Harriman is unable to complete his assignment."

"Eliminating Summerfield?"

Ashbrook slowly smiled and held up a crystal decanter. "Brandy?"

⇶✖⇷

GAVIN KING CLUTCHED the missive in his hand and lifted his gaze to Captain Coventry's. "Have you sent word to His Grace and Baron Summerfield?"

"Aye. The duke and the baron should be receiving their urgent missives in a few hours' time. O'Malley and Findley are stationed at Grosvenor Square. Darby is standing guard on the inside of our apartment building with Tremayne. Bayfield, Hennessey, and Masterson are standing guard outside."

King grumbled, "Of all times for one of the women a member of the duke's guard rescued to overlap with one of our cases..." Meeting Coventry's gaze, he sighed. "I'm glad you were able to convince His Grace to add to his London guard the last time he was in town. We'll have enough men to handle both situations. The threats against Garahan's bride and the ones against Summerfield."

"It was essential. Besides, if you add O'Malley and Garahan's contacts in and around London, there are a half-dozen more men we can count on."

King nodded. "Are you worried about Garahan's weakness tonight?"

Coventry answered immediately, "Even with his balance a bit off, he is as agile as a cat. You can count on Garahan. I plan to begin working with him tomorrow on compensating for his lack of vision."

"He's lucky to have you working with him, Coventry," King said. "And for the record, *I* wouldn't want to meet you in a dark alley."

"I can guarantee Garahan will outdo me in no time."

"As to the threats against Summerfield, my men have determined they are credible."

"I agree. More than three of my sources have confirmed the threat and names," Coventry said.

"Apparently, Ashbrook idolizes his cousin," King said. "Robertson would do anything for Ashbrook. They are thick as thieves."

"I trust your men have also verified the information about Mr. Farrell?" Coventry asked.

"A few hours ago. The Honorable Mr. Farrell—a very close friend to Ashbrook and Robertson—spilled his guts about their plans, then promptly demanded round-the-clock protection from them."

Coventry sighed. "I would not want to be in his shoes when Ashbrook and Robertson find out they've been betrayed from within."

"The information on Ashbrook is minimal—not so Lord Robertson. He has been involved in half a dozen duels in the last handful of years," King said. "Although illegal, challenges are still made—and accepted."

"At either Chalk Farm or the park at dawn," Coventry added. "I've heard he is an excellent shot."

"From his record of six duels fought," King said, "and six opponents buried, I would not want to cross the man either."

"We'll rely on our sources on the docks and in the stews," Coventry said. "Shall I send word to Chattsworth and Lippincott? They will need to be prepared, in the event the attempt on

Summerfield's life takes place. They too could be considered targets."

King got up to pace in front of his desk. "All things considered, it would be best to have their lordships remain in Sussex."

"Aye, especially if their ladyships hold true to form," Coventry added, "and wait until their lordships leave before following after them."

"That is a risk we dare not take," King said.

"Agreed."

"We'll send five of the duke's London guard along with four of my men to Wyndmere Hall," King suggested.

"His Grace hasn't met his new guard, as I advised him they would be scouring parts of London the duke would never venture to—and he should not be seen with the men for the sake of his title."

King smiled. "Always wise to have eyes and ears in as many places as possible. How soon can you get the word out and have the men report to me?"

"A few hours."

"I'll send Thompson, Franklin, Jackson, and Greeves to Wyndmere Hall," King said. "The duke is accustomed to working with them."

"Aye," Coventry agreed, "and depended upon them during the attack on the duke and his family at Wyndmere Hall."

"Advise your men that they'll be accompanying mine to the Lake District from here," King told him.

Coventry nodded. "Consider it done."

━━━━◆━◇◆◇━◆━━━━

CHAPTER TWENTY-TWO

FOUR HOURS LATER, Masterson had his hands full with two thugs who'd thought to slip by him and enter through the rear door.

Hennessey battled with three more who thought he would turn tail and run when they rushed him to get to the front door.

Bayfield silently took out one man attempting to sneak into the alley with a chokehold. After dropping him to the ground, he was able get behind the second man and sweep his legs out from under him.

Alerted to the trouble by Bayfield's short, sharp whistle, Garahan slipped inside the downstairs apartment, motioning for Michael and his mother to be quiet. "Where's the lass?"

"Telling Emma a story," Miranda replied. "What is it? What's wrong?"

"A minor situation outside. Coventry is upstairs in his office, and Tremayne is guarding yer door. Don't worry, no one will get through me, though I'd appreciate it if ye'd join me wife and little Emma." He hesitated as a dark thought occurred. "Are there any windows in Emma's room?"

The fear in Miranda's eyes was his answer.

"Michael, guard yer ma!"

Garahan's heart was in his throat as he approached the bed-chamber. By God, they would not take his wife or little Emma!

"Aimee-lass, are ye ready to go home?"

The door was open a crack, and he gently opened it further. Aimee had her back to the corner, protecting little Emma, who was curled in a ball behind her. God love his wife—she had a ceramic chamber pot raised above her head and flung it at someone as Garahan stepped into the room.

"Ye bloody wench! Ye knocked Ambrose out!"

Garahan stuck out his leg, tripped the man rushing toward Aimee, and placed his knee in the middle of the blackguard's back. "Ye've a fine arm on ye, lass. I'll have this one tied up in a moment. Why don't ye take little Emma into the kitchen? Michael's guarding his ma. Likely by now Tremayne has joined Michael and Miranda."

Fire flashing in the depths of her eyes, Aimee reached behind her. "Take my hand, Emma—we're going to find your mum and Michael."

Garahan nodded when Aimee's searching gaze met his. "Go on now—I need ye and Emma safe." When he heard Miranda and Michael's excited voices, he knew they were safe. He reached into his frockcoat pocket, pulled out a hank of rope, and tied the man's hands behind his back. He got to his feet and nudged the man his wife had beaned with the chamber pot.

"He's not moving... She killed Ambrose!"

Garahan squatted down beside the fallen man and watched the steady rise and fall of his chest. "Nay, but she knocked him clean off his feet. Must have knocked himself out when the back of his head hit the floor."

"But she—"

"*My wife* was defending the captain's daughter and herself. If you two hadn't climbed in the window hoping to snatch her, ye could have been raising a glass with yer friend here."

"He's not my friend—he's my cousin."

"What's yer name?"

The man glared at him.

"Gavin King has ways of convincing prisoners to talk."

"King?"

"Aye, of the Bow Street Runners. Good man, friend of me employer. Ye may have heard of him—the Duke of Wyndmere."

"Duke?"

"Aye," Garahan replied, using another bit of rope to tie the unconscious man's hands in front of him. "'Tisn't the best choice, but if I roll him over, it will make a mess on little Emma's floor. We can't have that, can we?"

"Can't you stop the bleeding?"

"I could, yes. But why would I?"

"What if I tell you my name?"

"Will ye now? Well, that would change things." Garahan watched the man and noticed an expression of fear and sincerity on his face. "Tell me yer name, and I'll wrap me cravat around his head. 'Tis clean."

"My name's Merriman. Thank you."

Garahan tied the makeshift bandage around Ambrose's head and pushed to his feet. "Now then—"

The sound of something heavy catapulting down the stairway in the hall had him sprinting toward the door. "Stay here!" he ordered Merriman as he stepped into the hallway.

Tremayne had a man in a headlock, while at the top of the stairs, Coventry delivered a right cross that sent a second man down the stairs.

Garahan shook his head. "How many bloody buggers are up there?"

"None," Coventry said, coming down the steps and stepping over the two men at the bottom. "How many outside?"

"Last count, seven. The three who thought to break in from the front, two who tried their luck in the alley, and two who tried to get inside using the rear door," Tremayne answered. "Hennessey and Masterson are loading them up in the wagon."

"Wagon?" Garahan asked.

"Aye, there's times when it's easier to haul prisoners off all at once," Tremayne replied. "The watchman is a good man and agreed to cart them off to Bow Street for the captain."

Garahan shook his head. "Two men climbed through Emma's window—"

Coventry leapt over the two men at the foot of the stairs and shoved Tremayne aside. "Emma!"

"She's fine, Tremayne," Garahan said. "Ye should have seen the way me wife lobbed a chamber pot at the one thug's head. Knocked him clean off his feet. Hit his head on the floor and was still unconscious when I came to see what the racket was."

"I take it you tied them both up."

"Aye. I only have one bit of rope left, or else I'd be tying those two by the stairs for ye. Do ye have any spare?"

Tremayne handed him a length of rope from his frockcoat pocket. "Whoever wanted to abduct your wife must want her very badly to send ten men to distract us."

"Irritate us, is what they did," Garahan replied, pushing to his feet after tying up one of the men. "Do ye need me to help cart these three outside?"

"I've got this," Tremayne said, tying the last man's hands behind his back. "I'm thinking your wife may need reassurance that you are not lying on the floor bleeding. That was a hell of a racket when the second man fell down the stairs."

"Bloody excellent right cross Coventry leveled him with, wasn't it?"

"The captain is fierce in a fight," Tremayne said. "Lethal when his family is threatened."

"Thank ye, Tremayne. Give a shout if ye need me."

Tremayne nodded, then dragged the prisoners to the front door.

Garahan's hand was on the doorknob when it opened, and he suddenly had an armful of rose-scented woman.

"Darby! I was so worried that you were hurt. What was that awful racket?"

"Well now, I may be telling ye, if ye'd give a man the chance."

She pressed her lips together and nodded.

"Coventry's right cross—a thing of beauty—had one of the intruders flying backward down the stairs."

Aimee placed her hands on either side of his face, searching for any new signs of injury. "You're not hurt."

"Nay, lass. I'm fit and fine."

She laid her head on his chest and burst into tears.

"That's the way, lass—get it all out."

Coventry and Michael had Miranda and Emma sandwiched between them. The anguished look on the captain's face spoke volumes.

"Everyone all right, captain?"

"Aye, Garahan. Thanks to you and your valiant wife."

Garahan rubbed Aimee's back and smiled. "Saw it for meself—she's dead accurate with a chamber pot."

"Will you sit with my family while I speak to the Watch?"

"Aye. Before ye go, ye should commend Michael for keeping his head and protecting his ma."

"But I didn't think anyone would try to get in through Emma's window," Michael rasped.

"Me wife was with Emma, so ye had no reason to even think of it. Ye did a fine job, and I'll not hear another word otherwise."

"Aye, Garahan."

"That's more like it. I'm thinking a shot of whiskey in a cup of tea would be just the thing."

Coventry paused in the open doorway. "I only have rum in the house."

"'Tis a good thing young Emma isn't teething. Whiskey's the only thing that eases a babe's sore gums."

Coventry chuckled. "James said the same thing the night he met Emma. She stopped crying the moment he rubbed whiskey on her gums."

"James has always had a way with infants. Come have a seat next Miranda and Emma, lass," Garahan urged. "Michael and I will make a pot of tea and ye can serve it."

Miranda cuddled her daughter in her arms while absently rubbing soothing circles on Emma's back. "How can I ever thank you for protecting our daughter, Aimee?"

"It was because of me that those blackguards climbed in her window…they were after me."

"If I were to tell you the number of times we've had trouble come to our door that we had nothing to do with, you would be amazed."

"Now, Mum, I think the number of times trouble came looking for Father outnumbers the other times," Michael added.

Miranda shook her head at her son. "The kettle's ready. Would you make the tea, Michael?"

He jumped up and grinned at Garahan. "Twice as many thugs have come looking for my father."

"Have they now? Recently?"

Michael shook his head. "It all started the year Mum accepted the job as housekeeper for the building and we moved in."

The door was still open, and Coventry leaned in to say, "I believe trouble came looking for you and your mum, lad."

Miranda started laughing and a moment later was crying. "I've never been so scared in my life."

Aimee got up from her seat and wrapped her arms around Miranda and Emma. "Neither have I."

The captain's gaze locked on the women. "We've been blessed, Garahan."

"That we have, Coventry," Garahan replied. "Don't forget the pair of intruders in Emma's room."

"I was coming to escort them out. Would you and Michael mind forming a wall, so the women don't have to see the prisoners?"

Garahan and Michael stood shoulder to shoulder, effectively blocking the sight of the two men being led from Emma's bedroom. Once Coventry had the men in the hallway, Garahan pressed a kiss to his wife's forehead. "I need to ask the prisoners a few questions. Will ye be all right here with the others?"

"Aye, Darby. I'm going to enjoy my tea, though it would taste better with a splash of whiskey in it."

He reached into his waistcoat pocket. "Share what's in me flask with the others."

She smiled, and he just had to have a taste of her sweet lips.

"Stay here, lass."

"As long as there is whiskey-laced tea, I'm not moving."

◇◈◇◈◇◈◇

CHAPTER TWENTY-THREE

GARAHAN WALKED OUTSIDE and finally let his anger show. "Where're Merriman and Ambrose? I have a few questions for them."

Tremayne nodded toward the wagon. "About to be loaded in there."

Garahan strode over to the wagon where Hennessey and Masterson had taken control of the prisoners. "Merriman, if ye want King to go easy on ye, ye'll tell me why ye sent so many men to capture one woman."

"I didn't send them, but it's because Miss Anderson broke her agreement," Merriman answered.

"Agreement with whom?" Garahan fairly growled the question.

"A very powerful man who doesn't like to be lied to," Merriman answered.

"What part of answering an advert to work in a shop in London, and being kidnapped and transported to Underwood's boarding house, is lying?" Garahan asked.

Merriman's eyes shot to his cousin before meeting Garahan's. "She promised to work at Scarlet Ribbons and The Scarlet Boudoir in exchange for transportation to London."

"That's a lie," Garahan said, his voice hoarse with the need to shout.

"There is the matter of her helping three others escape," Merriman added.

"Don't forget the little ones," Ambrose reminded him before shooting his cousin a warning glance.

Merriman ignored the look to say, "They were all to be trained first at the boarding house and then sent to Scarlet Ribbons and The Scarlet Boudoir."

"The two youngest lasses could not have been more than nine or ten years old!" Garahan barked. "Have ye any idea what would have happened to those wee lasses once they entered the door to either brothel?"

When no one answered, Garahan shouted, "They would have died at the hands of those filthy, buggering bastards who'd pay a king's ransom to satisfy their twisted appetites with a lass that young!" When the prisoners could no longer meet his gaze, Garahan lowered his voice to just above a whisper. "'Tis bad enough the older lasses had been forced to watch a performance of what would be expected of them. But by God, the younger ones were little more than babes."

He shoved away from Ambrose and spat on the ground in front of the man. "May yer soul rot in Hell's eternal fires for attempting to drag me wife back there!"

The sudden silence had Garahan realizing he'd inadvertently blurted out the truth of what he'd rescued Aimee from. "Praise God, I was able to rescue me wife and the others before they transferred the lasses to those brothels as they planned...or we'd never have found them in time."

"Then you admit that is where they were headed?" Ambrose sounded pleased with the idea.

"Nay, 'tis where they would have been *forced* to go. Know this—His Grace the Duke of Wyndmere has a connection at Bow Street who has the letter me wife received from the advert she answered to work as a *shopgirl* with the added opportunity of becoming a milliner's apprentice. The transportation to London was included."

"What proof do *you* have, Ambrose?" Tremayne asked.

"Other than the coin ye received to steal me wife from me?" Garahan demanded.

Ambrose clamped his jaw shut and shook his head.

Merriman asked, "Do you swear the information the duke's contact on Bow Street isn't a forgery?"

"On me ma's grave."

Coventry looked to Garahan, who gave a slight shake of his head. Coventry would know the lie about his ma was necessary.

"And the others?" Merriman asked.

"All received the same letter—however, their letters were found and burned, leaving no proof other than the words of those lasses."

"Ambrose, this changes everything," Merriman said. "We have to tell Garahan and the others the truth!"

"I don't think—" Ambrose began.

"And that's why we are in this fix, cousin." Turning his attention to Garahan, Merriman asked, "If we give you the name of the man responsible for luring young women from the country to London, will you promise not to mention Ambrose's name or mine?"

Garahan didn't pause to think it over—he agreed immediately, "Aye. Ye have me word. Once given, 'twill never be broken."

Merriman drew in a deep breath and exhaled. "A man named Farrell."

"The *Honorable* Mr. Farrell," Ambrose reminded his cousin.

"Aye," Merriman agreed.

Bile churned in Garahan's gut. This was the name of the man originally linked with two others threatening Baron Summerfield. That was, until Farrell went to Bow Street with information that he could not go along with Ashbrook and Robertson's plans. Had the bloody turncoat lied to King to cover up the fact that he was involved in something far more sinister—the highly lucrative supplying of innocents from the country to fill his brothels in the bowels of London?

This information had to get to Bow Street immediately!

"Thank ye, Merriman. Ambrose." Garahan turned to Coventry and asked, "Who is escorting this lot to Bow Street?"

"Hennessey and Masterson," the captain replied.

"Will ye tell King what ye heard, and ask that he not mention Merriman and Ambrose's names until he has Farrell in custody?"

"Aye, Garahan," Hennessey replied.

"With pleasure," Masterson added.

Bayfield and Tremayne flanked Coventry, watching the wagon pull away. "Nice work, Garahan," Coventry remarked. "King will be pleased with the information. Now all we need is for him to round up Farrell and for the men we sent to Wyndmere Hall to be ready for the impending attack."

"Baron and Baroness Summerfield have arrived safely?"

"They have," Coventry replied.

"Then ye have no worries, as they'll have traveled with me brother Ryan, Dillon Flaherty, and Thomas O'Malley," Garahan reminded the captain.

"Aye," Coventry agreed. "And Patrick and Eamon O'Malley, Rory Flaherty, and your brother Aiden are stationed at Wyndmere Hall."

"Faith, ye have nothing to worry about. Ye've got seven of the guard protecting the duke's family."

"Don't forget the five men from the new London guard and four of King's men," Tremayne said.

Garahan grinned. "Care to place a wager, Coventry?"

"What are you thinking?" Tremayne asked.

"The bloody buggers don't realize they're outnumbered until they arrive…and give up without a fight."

"I'll take that wager," Bayfield said.

"Did you forget the duke does not allow wagering?" Coventry asked.

Garahan glanced from Tremayne to Bayfield and back. "Nothing's stopping the two of *ye* from wagering. What do ye say, Tremayne?"

Tremayne smiled. "I say they'll attack, but give themselves up after Rory fires the first shot from his Kentucky long rifle from the rooftop."

Garahan snorted with laughter. "Now that's a wager I would love to be in on. Rory never misses a target with that fine weapon. But faith, I like me job, so no wagering for me, lads."

"Why don't you take your wife home?" Coventry suggested, then chuckled. "It's not a long walk, just across the hall from where I live. I hope Emma's fussing won't keep you awake. I have a feeling I'll be up for a few more hours trying to convince her to shut her eyes."

"Ma used to sing us to sleep when we had bad dreams," Garahan replied. "Ye might give that a try if Emma has them tonight."

Coventry placed his hand on Garahan's shoulder. "Thank you, Garahan. Oh and tell my wife I'll be in shortly. I need to speak with the men."

Garahan bade the others goodnight, entered the building, and headed straight for Coventry's apartment. He knocked and waited to hear Michael ask, "Who is it?"

"Yer worst nightmare, Michael Coventry—now open the door."

Michael was laughing when he opened the door. "You didn't even try to disguise your voice, Garahan. I knew it was you."

"Thank ye again for helping us protect yer family and me heart tonight."

Michael frowned. "Your heart?"

"Aye, me wife."

Aimee rose from where she sat at the table and walked over to put her arms around him. "Can we go home now?"

"Sure and 'tis a long journey. Are ye up for it?" She giggled, and he smiled. "The captain said he'd be in shortly, so I'll bid ye goodnight, Miranda. Is little Emma asleep?"

Miranda sighed. "Almost, but I don't expect that to last too long with all that's happened tonight."

"I told the captain Ma used to sing us to sleep when we had bad dreams," Garahan said.

Emma's eyes popped open when she heard Garahan's voice. She rubbed her eyes and stared at him.

"Do you remember the song?" Aimee asked.

"Aye, lass. I used to hum it to meself as I got older and me dreams were"—he glanced at Emma—"stronger."

"Would you sing to Emma for me?" Miranda asked.

"Aye—'tis an easy tune and a lovely lullaby."

⇥⟫⟪⇤

AIMEE LISTENED AS her husband's smooth baritone wove its magic around those gathered at the Coventrys' kitchen table. His lilting rendition of the age-old lullaby brought tears to her eyes while it soothed Emma to sleep.

When he was finished, Aimee heard a footstep behind her and spun around. But it wasn't an intruder—it was Captain Coventry, who walked over to Darby and placed a hand on his shoulder. "How does a man who is an expert with weapons—and his fists—have such a beautiful voice?"

Garahan chuckled softly. "Any Irishman worth his salt can carry a tune. We Garahans can charm the birds out of the trees if we're inclined to."

"Thank you, Garahan," Coventry said. "Your wife looks tired. Best take her home."

"Happy to oblige. Goodnight, all."

He held the door for her and closed it behind them. With his hand at her waist, he steered her across the hall to their door. "Home safe, lass."

"Home safe, Darby."

◇◈◇◈◇

CHAPTER TWENTY-FOUR

THE KNOCK ON the door surprised Garahan. He was planning to spend the rest of the night with his wife in his arms. "Coming!"

He opened the door, surprised to see Coventry. "Something wrong? Hennessey and Masterson only left a quarter of an hour ago."

Coventry stepped inside and nodded to Aimee. "I need to borrow your husband for a little while. I know you just left our apartment, but would you mind sitting with Miranda and Emma until I get back? Emma's asleep. I'll have Tremayne and Bayfield guarding the perimeter. Michael on the inside."

"Of course," Aimee replied. "Let me get my wrap."

Garahan frowned. "Do ye have reason to believe we'll need the men standing guard?"

"I prefer to err on the side of caution," Coventry said.

"I'm ready," Aimee said, rushing toward them from the back bedchamber, hastily donning her shawl.

Garahan placed his hand to the small of his wife's back and followed in Coventry's wake. Entering the captain's apartment, he wasn't surprised to see Emma cuddled on Miranda's lap, fast asleep. It had been a difficult day for the women in their lives. He hoped the poor little mite wouldn't end up with vicious nightmares.

Coventry kissed his wife. "We should return in a few hours. I shall send word if we expect to be longer than that."

"Thank you, Gordon. I do worry."

He brushed a lock of hair out of her eyes. "I wish you wouldn't."

Garahan pulled Aimee into his embrace and whispered, "I'll be home as soon as I can. Thank you for staying with Miranda and Emma."

"I would rather stay with them than be alone across the hall."

He nodded and pressed a kiss to her forehead before dipping his head to capture her lips in a kiss filled with promise.

"We'd best be off, Garahan."

"Coming." He nodded to Michael, who would guard the women from inside the apartment. "Guard them with your life, lad."

"I will, Garahan."

With a nod, Coventry closed the door to his home and walked toward the front door to the building. Tremayne and Bayfield were waiting for him. "I know I don't need to tell you to guard our families with your lives."

Tremayne shook his head. "Make sure King has had a chance to listen to Ambrose and Merriman."

Bayfield agreed. "They supplied the name of the man behind luring all of those young women to London."

"Aye, that bloody *bugger*, Farrell." Garahan curled his hands into fists, wishing he had his hands on the man. He'd teach him what happened to men like him who profited from buying and selling women and children to those with enough coin to pay for their perverted pleasure!

"Garahan!"

He spun around and wobbled on his feet, but caught himself. "Aye, captain?"

"I received a message from King. He needs to speak with us." Coventry hailed a hack and waited for the coachman to slow the carriage to a halt before opening the door and settling on the seat facing backward. Motioning for Garahan to take the forward-facing seat, he said, "Until your vision clears, and your balance settles out, I wouldn't ride with my back to the horses. Might unsettle your stomach."

"Thank ye. I'll keep that in mind."

As they rode through the night, Coventry said, "I hope King has had a chance to encourage the men we sent with Hennessey and Masterson to talk."

Garahan chuckled. "I'd like a crack at it."

"If King didn't need you to verify Merriman and Ambrose's claims, you would be resting."

"'Tisn't me fault that those bastards converged on us tonight. Would ye have me stand aside and watch while yer wife and daughter, and me own wife, were threatened?"

Coventry was quick to respond, "Of course not. But if we are going to keep Lieutenant Sampson and your wife happy, we'll have to see to it that you continue your balance exercises with me, but that's all. No more chasing after miscreants and thugs—you are to rest for the next three days."

Garahan snorted with laughter. "Faith, have ye forgotten who we work for?"

Coventry chuckled. "You bring up a salient point, Garahan."

The closer they got to Bow Street, the more Garahan shifted on his seat. He felt torn leaving his wife behind. Although she and the captain's wife and daughter were in good hands, he felt he was the only one who should be protecting her. Unrealistic thought. When he returned to full duty, she'd be under someone else's protection until he returned home at night.

"Problem?" Coventry asked.

"Nothing I cannot handle," Garahan answered. He waited a beat and said, "I'd like to get me hands on Farrell."

"Get in line," Coventry said, as the hackney slowed for the tangle of carriages in front of them. "After we meet with King, I'll send an urgent missive to His Grace to apprise him of this latest development. He should be well pleased."

"And able to keep Summerfield in check," Garahan added. "His Grace will need to know of the family connection Ashbrook has to the bastard who bargained with Squire Honeycutt's wife, and me sister-in-law's own ma, to abduct her!"

Coventry agreed, "Aye. Though between your brother, Ryan, and Prudence, they managed to rout the dastard and rescue the two young women abducted with Prudence."

Garahan smiled. "Aye, all of me brothers have married feisty women."

"As have you," Coventry remarked.

"That I have, captain." The hack arrived on Bow Street and slowed to a stop in front of the building.

The men alighted, nodded to the Runner stationed outside, and entered the building. Making their way down the darkened hallway, they were immediately shown into King's office.

"Coventry, Garahan," King greeted them. "I take it your wives—and your daughter, captain—are unharmed?"

"Aye," Garahan replied. "Ye should have seen the way me wife protected little Emma, fierce as a mother bear—beaning one of the intruders with the ceramic chamber pot."

Coventry shook his head. "I didn't see it, but have no doubt Aimee will be able to hold her own being married to Garahan."

Garahan did not take offense—he grinned. "Aye."

King motioned for them to be seated, but Garahan couldn't sit still—he was still feeling the aftereffects of the altercation with the intruders.

"As you know, we have three separate sources that confirm the involvement of Robertson, Farrell, and Ashbrook," King said. "Ashbrook is the only name directly tied to the threats against Summerfield, and the abduction of Prudence Garahan, the blacksmith's daughter, and the vicar's daughter."

"Have the boarding house owner and her thugs spilled their guts yet?" Garahan asked.

King nodded. "A few hours ago, the owner identified the Honorable Mr. Farrell as the man who offered her a percentage of his take from those he lured to London."

"While she was responsible for grooming the lasses before sending them to those two brothels," Garahan added.

"And what of the intruders my men dropped off?" Coventry asked. "Do they have ties to Robertson or Farrell?"

"Both, actually. Half the men were hired by Roberston, the others by Farrell, both of whom have been brought in and questioned and are currently cooling their heels in our luxurious accommodations."

Garahan frowned. "What of the Scarlet sisters and their escorts? They should be behind bars for what they forced those innocent lasses to observe, then forced them to participate in."

"Unfortunately, the sisters have ties at the highest echelon within the *ton*," King advised.

"Prinny," Coventry said.

"Can ye not do anything about the man? His corrupt connections trickle down and bring harm to those who have lost their way," Garahan said, "and worse to those who are trying to better their lives by coming to London, only to end up trapped, unable to escape a situation far worse than the poverty they left behind."

King shook his head. "He's the prince regent...untouchable."

"Give me five minutes with the man—" Garahan began.

Coventry interrupted him, "And a fine wake your new bride will be giving you after you are drawn and quartered."

"Treason." Garahan shivered at the very idea of being executed for treason. "I guess I'll stick to going a few rounds with me brothers and cousins."

"Wise decision," King said. "I have already sent a missive on to His Grace. With the mastermind behind the threats to Baron Summerfield behind bars, I expect to receive word from the men I sent to Wyndmere Hall by tomorrow that they have rounded up those who are under orders from Ashbrook to strike at the baron at Wyndmere Hall."

"Ye won't forget about O'Malley's contact, Leach, will ye?" Garahan asked.

"Ah yes, the behemoth who rescued a young woman. I've spread the word that he is one of O'Malley's trusted contacts—as O'Shaughnessy is yours—and neither are to be rousted again."

"Thank ye, King."

"By the way, Garahan, my thanks to you and the others who recommended their contacts when the duke decided to expand his guard. Coventry informs me the duke's London eyes and ears were instrumental in gathering the information we needed to expose and apprehend Farrell and the others."

"I'll be sure to let me contacts know, and pass it along to O'Malley so he can tell his as well."

"How is the eye?" King asked.

Garahan touched his eyepatch and shrugged. "I'm getting accustomed to having the use of one eye. Coventry's going to help me work on me balance. Lieutenant Sampson said every injury is different, and he could not predict how quickly it will heal."

"Good man, Sampson. He's been my personal physician since he retired from the King's Dragoons." He nodded to Garahan. "Keep me informed of your recovery."

Garahan nodded back. "I will." He turned to Coventry. "Are ye ready to return home?"

"I am." The captain rose. "I'll be in touch, King."

The Bow Street Runner shook Coventry's hand and then Garahan's and bade them goodbye.

Walking along the hallway, Garahan, murmured, "Do ye think Farrell has a connection to Prinny, too?"

"Time will tell, but I do believe his crimes will cause enough of an uproar among the working classes that the prince regent may wash his hands of anything to do with Farrell."

Garahan prayed that would be the outcome, but others with that royal connection had managed to escape paying for their crimes. He hoped Farrell would be tossed behind bars.

They bade the Runner outside goodnight. Coventry managed to flag down another hack without waiting, entered the carriage, and settled back against the seats for the ride home.

CHAPTER TWENTY-FIVE

FOR THE SECOND time that night, Garahan escorted his sleepy wife across the hall to their apartment, arms linked to keep her from stumbling. Poor lass was exhausted. Inside, he paused in front of their door and stared into eyes so blue, he wondered if mayhap she truly was an angel sent down from Heaven to guide him through the rest of his life. Hadn't Ma said that ye should always treat others kindly because ye never knew if they were an angel in disguise?

"There are times when I look at ye and wonder if ye're an angel."

She sighed. "I'm just a woman."

"Ah, ye're not just a woman—ye're *my* woman. Are ye tired, lass?"

"After all that has happened tonight, I don't know if I'm ready to close my eyes," she confessed.

Before he lost his head entirely and wrapped her in his arms to plunder her lips, he opened the door and ushered her inside.

She jolted at the snick of the lock, and as tired as he was, he wished he could find the man who'd compromised her, taking her virtue without qualm—*the buggering bastard!* He'd not be satisfied until the man was bleeding from his mouth, his nose, and trying to find his bollocks...after Garahan kicked them hard enough to lodge in the blackguard's throat. It would be satisfying to watch the man curl into a tight ball, gagging and moaning.

He savored the image for a moment longer before deciding it was best not to share his thoughts with his wife. "Me shoulder's a bit stiff—would ye help me with me coat, lass?"

She blinked, and she was once more the Aimee he admired—not the one he feared would never accept him as husband because of her past. "Yes, of course."

His heart began to pound as the heat of her hand seared through his coat sleeve. Unsure whether he would frighten her more if he spoke, he kept silent. Watching her, he nearly groaned when she bit down on her bottom lip—something he noticed she did when she was about to ask a question or was nervous. "Ye can ask me anything, lass. I'll always answer ye truthfully. Ye may not like me answer, but that cannot be helped. I'll have honesty between us."

"I would have us be truthful to one another too. I was wondering if you were able to get a name from the men who were in Emma's room."

"Aye, lass," he replied as he undid the buttons on his frockcoat while she watched. The interest twined with worry was unmistakable in the depths of her eyes. He placed the coat across the back of the chair by the window.

When he turned around, she was reaching for the buttons of his waistcoat. "Let me help. You don't want to strain your shoulder."

He dropped his hands to his sides and watched her fingers tremble until she slipped the first button free. "I haven't seen such a light in yer eyes as when ye held Emma."

Her hands still worked the rest of the buttons free, but her eyes were locked on his. "A light?"

"Aye, lass. 'Twas there for anyone to see. Holding her in yer arms brought a smile that spread from yer heart to yer lips...and yer eyes."

She nodded. "She is beautiful. I couldn't help but wonder what she was thinking when you started to sing to her earlier, before she closed her eyes and fell asleep."

"I can tell ye one thing, lass. She was thinking how pleased she was be in yer arms and feel the warmth of yer love and protection surrounding her."

"Love?"

"Aye, lass. Everyone in that room—except for mayhap yerself—could see the love pouring out of ye for the wee lass."

"I… Well, that is to say… It has been some time since I have held a babe. I used to take care of my cousin's children—as well as the household chores I was responsible for."

Whenever she spoke of her cousin, he could not help but think the man abused his hold over her by adding to her duties. "How old were they at the time?"

She smiled. "Harold was four years, Katherine was two, and baby Henry was four months old."

"Did they not have a nanny?"

She sighed. "They had trouble keeping one once hired."

He didn't bother to ask why. Her cousin probably treated the nanny the same way he treated the lass—as if she were a beast of burden, able to carry far more than her own weight in responsibilities and duties.

Aimee kept her eyes level with his chest as she slipped the waistcoat from his shoulders and carefully folded it. He reached for the garment. Where their fingers brushed against one another, his tingled. From her quiet gasp, he knew she'd felt it too. Without asking, her fingers trembling once more, she began to unfasten his cambric shirt.

"Would you like me to help you take it off? I don't want you to strain your ribs."

He sighed. "Lass, I know ye are having a bit of trouble believing me, even after I handled meself tonight against the intruders, but me shoulder and me ribs are not as much of a bother—or as painful—as ye seem to fear. I have had worse." He whipped his shirt off and was more than pleased with her response—her mouth gaped open, and her eyes widened.

Was it the slashing scar that began over his heart and disappeared beneath the bandage that bound his ribs that caused the reaction? Mayhap the width and breadth of his chest. He knew it was impressive—hadn't a legion of women said as much? He stepped back from her and asked, "Are ye needing assistance with yer buttons?"

"I think I can manage."

He had no doubt she could reach the top two buttons but was skeptical that she could reach the other three.

By the time he'd counted to twenty-five, she admitted, "I was wrong. Would you please help me?"

"Of course." When she presented her back to him, he quickly undid the remaining buttons and pressed his lips to the nape of her neck. Her shudder had him feeling bolder, but he did not want to break his word to her. "Shall I help ye remove yer gown? I wouldn't want ye to get tangled up in the length of it."

"I have to confess, I have never undressed in front of anyone before—let alone a man."

He put his hands on her shoulders and slowly turned her to face him. "Ah, lass. I never thought ye had." Bringing her hand to his lips, he kissed the back of it. "Take yer time, lass." He lowered her hand, taking hold of the other, and pressed his lips to her cool flesh. There were a few faint scars on both of her hands. While she held still, but did not pull away from him, he turned her hand palm up and traced the calluses he discovered. "Ye've worked hard, lass."

She snatched her hands away. "I know it's unfashionable."

"I don't give a bloody fig about that. Yer calluses and scars show yer strength, lass. That, more than anything fashionable, only adds to yer beauty."

"Scars aren't beautiful, and calluses get snagged on my clothing."

He slipped his arm around her and slowly reeled her in until there wasn't a breath between them. Her curves fitted to his as if they were designed—nay, destined—to be together. "That's where ye'd be wrong. Any Irishman I know would find the calluses—aye, and yer scars—attractive. We know the value of having a wife beside us ready to face anything and willing to work beside us. 'Tis worth more than any dowry a wife could bring to a marriage."

When her eyes met his, her vulnerability showing, he searched for the words to tell her how much she meant to him...the promises he intended to keep...the love that grew inside of him more each day. But he wasn't gifted like Da, who'd won Ma's heart with words. He was like Ma's people—the Flanagans—and would have to stumble with words and hope the lass would see clear to his heart.

"Ye matter, lass. In me eyes, ye're everything. Let me show ye, for I haven't the words."

While she considered his words, he lowered his head and captured her lips in a kiss that began softly...tenderly...persuasively...until her lips softened beneath his and she kissed him back.

DARBY'S WORDS TOUCHED Aimee's frozen heart. As he deepened the kiss, she tentatively parted her lips. He groaned and swept his tongue between them to tangle with hers. Shock had her opening her eyes, but he soothed her with the gentle touch of his hands that contradicted the pounding of his heart.

She could feel his strength—and the power he held in check to keep his word to her. Her mind spiraled back to the night she'd tried to forget. As if Darby had the power to read her mind, he rasped, "I would rather cut off me arm than hurt ye, lass. We'll go slowly. Ye need to trust me and to relax—not stiffen at me touch—or yer body won't accept me, which will only cause ye pain."

She buried her face in his broad chest as fear slinked up her spine. How could she tell him without hurting the man who'd opened so much of himself to her with but a look, a touch? Aimee owed Darby her life. In her heart, she knew she would have died if she'd been sent to that brothel.

"I do trust you," she whispered. "But there's a part of me that fears what lies ahead."

"Yer honesty means more than I can say. Faith, I'm weary of standing—would ye lie on the bed with me?"

She lifted her head and met the intensity of his gaze. "I know you won't force me, but I've seen that look in your eyes before."

"Ye should not mistake what I feel for ye as lust, lass. 'Tisn't.'"

"What is it, then?"

"'Tis hard to describe without ye fearing that I'm after making love with ye. Which I am, but I'm not after causing ye pain or leaving this bed with ye harboring even the tiniest bit of fear."

When she saw need and hope swirling in the depths of Darby's dark brown eye, another part of her heart thawed. She'd given her word and taken vows with this man. He was not the man who'd professed to love her a heartbeat before he offered the position of mistress—and, when she refused, had taken her virtue. She'd lost everything that night. But now she'd been offered a second chance with this man...her husband, who wanted to gift her life back to her. All she had to do was lie with him.

What was the difference between being taken against her will and making love?

"I'd need to show ye, lass."

"Show me?"

"Aye. Ye asked what the difference was between making love and being forced. 'Tis hard to explain when words can be twisted around to any man's advantage to get what he wants. I want to show ye how much I treasure ye and love ye, lass."

She hadn't realized she'd whispered that question aloud. Mortification tensed her throat. She forced herself to relax enough to reply, "I... Would you... Can we?"

"Aye, lass. I will and we can."

"I know it isn't necessary to undress"—she paused and swallowed her fear—"to do what we must."

"Well now, ye have the right of it, but I'm after showing ye how making love to ye is different from yer memory. I will wipe it clean, and then we will begin the rest of our lives together. Will ye let me, lass?"

She placed her hand over his heart and felt it pounding still. He was her husband, and she desperately wanted to trust him with her body as she had with her heart. She nodded.

"Will ye help me undress ye?"

Together they removed her gown. He pulled her flush against him for the second time, and the heat of him scorched through her thin chemise. Instead of tearing it off her, he kissed the tip of her nose, the apples of her cheeks, and finally pressed his lips to hers. "Ye're beautiful, lass. Will ye let me remove the last barrier between us?"

"What about your trousers?"

"Well now, I'd be more than agreeable to losing them, but am afraid me need for ye may frighten ye."

"Your need?"

"Ye unman me with yer innocence and the passion I know is waiting for me to unlock within ye. I'm fair to bursting with desire to make ye mine."

Uncertainty had her trembling again. "I'll turn my back to you, and you can remove your trousers, while I take off my chemise."

"Ye'll be getting an eyeful of me *arse* if ye turn around before I do."

A burst of laughter escaped before she could hold it back.

He studied her for a moment before admitting, "I've been told I'm just as handsome from the back as I am from the front."

Her eyes widened at the thought, and her courage nearly failed her. Throwing caution to the wind and placing her full trust in her husband, she tilted her head to one side and said, "As I am to be the only one from this moment forward who sees you that way, I'll be the judge of that."

"Turn around, then, or be prepared to be overwhelmed by one of me best assets."

She did as he bade her and removed her chemise. She heard him taking off his trousers and could not help but look over her shoulder to sneak a peek. Hand to her breast, she rasped, "Oh my!"

He was laughing when he swept her into his arms and carried her over to the bed. "Now then, me darling, let me show ye what's in me heart."

CHAPTER TWENTY-SIX

DARBY DUG DEEP to call on every last bit of his control not to rush his bride, but the need to bury himself inside of her had him by the throat. Choking back on it, he covered her with his body. Leaning on his elbows, he looked into the deep blue of her eyes and felt more of his control returning. She wanted to trust him—and he needed to show her that she could.

He brushed her lips with a tender kiss, then trailed a line of kisses from her lips to her jaw. When he reached her chin, he nipped it and took advantage of her gasp to delve into the sweetness of her mouth. With lips and teeth and tongue, he showed the depth of his feelings for her.

When she moaned against his lips, he poured his heart into the kiss, hoping she would understand without words what she meant to him. When the tip of her tongue tentatively touched his, he knew she understood and broke the kiss. "Lass, may I caress ye?"

"Caress?"

"Aye." The word sounded like a growl to him, but she didn't seem to notice. "I've a need to touch ye, to worship ye until ye're writhing in me arms, begging me to fill ye to the hilt."

His heart flew when her face flamed, and she bravely nodded. He eased off her to lie on his side and begin the discovery of her bounty—her shoulders, her breasts, the dip at her waist, and her womanhood. When she stiffened, he whispered words of encouragement. When she relaxed, he pressed his mouth where his hands had been.

Her moans were music to his ears. He wished he could see her with both eyes, but had promised to leave the blasted eyepatch on. Even with one eye, she was a beauty to behold. "Lass, I need to stretch ye so as not to cause ye pain. Will ye let me?"

Her brow furrowed a moment before she said, "I don't understand."

Tenderness filled him. "I'll start with one finger and then two, testing and teasing yer passage until I've eased the way for me to slide home."

"Home?"

"Aye. From this moment forward, ye'll be me home. The heat of ye—the heart of ye—joined together until I'm touching yer womb."

As he spoke, he showed her gently, and with each moan of her desire, he began a rhythm that would remain once she was ready to accept him.

Finally, finally, she cried out and begged, "Please?"

"Please what?"

"Make love to me, Darby."

"Faith, I have been, lass. Do ye want more?"

She was writhing beneath him when she demanded, "I want all of you inside of me."

He kissed her deeply as he settled between her thighs. Poised at her entrance, he rasped, "I need ye to say the words *mo ghrá*—now and forever, me love."

"*Mo ghrá?*"

"Aye, ye are me love. Say it," he urged. "Now and forever."

"Now and forever, Darby."

He filled her to the hilt, swallowing her sharp intake of breath with plundering kisses while they began a rhythm as old as time. She did not hold back anything from him, humbling him with her courage, her generosity, her love. And he gave his to her in return.

When she cried out in ecstasy, he thrust home one last time and emptied his seed inside of her, praying for a miracle—nay, two.

Lord, please let this begin her healing…

And in yer mercy, grant us a babe with angel-blue eyes and hair of gold.

They fell asleep tangled together—her legs wrapped around his waist, and him buried deep inside of her.

⇒⇒≪≪

AIMEE WOKE WITH a start, surrounded by her husband's heat and the musky scent of their lovemaking. She opened her eyes and saw the face of the man who'd thawed the ice in her heart. "It wasn't a dream."

"Nay, lass. 'Twas far better than any dream I've had in me life. I know I gave ye pleasure, but I'll have the truth from ye now—how much pain was twined with it?"

She cupped the side of his face. "Not enough worth mentioning."

He stirred inside of her. She moaned and stroked along the length of his spine until the tips of her fingers brushed his buttocks. "Darby?"

"Aye, love?"

"You do have an amazing *arse*."

He rolled them over and brushed the hair from her eyes. "Faith, I'm thinking yers is as well."

Eyes wide, heart pounding, hope tangled with love for this man, giving her the courage to ask, "Would it be all right if I change my mind?"

Confusion was quickly masked with a neutral expression on his handsome-as-sin face. "Aye."

He started to ease out of her, and she realized he'd misunderstood. She clamped her hands on his buttocks and held on for dear life. "Don't leave me. Make love to me now…and every day for the rest of our lives."

"I'm thinking ye'll have to convince me ye won't be changing yer mind again, lass."

She tightened her grip on his *arse*, lifted her hips, and plundered his mouth.

They came together in a flash of passion that rivaled a summer storm. Afterward, he pressed a kiss to her forehead, the tip of her nose, one eye, and then the other, before claiming her lips. "There's no going back now, lass. Ye'd best prepare yerself."

"Prepare myself?" she asked.

His smile was lethal. "We've sealed our vows—thrice over now. I'll be making love to ye every day for the rest of our lives."

She kissed him with all of the love he'd unlocked in her heart. "Do you promise?"

"Ye have me word. Do I have yers?"

"You have my word—and my heart."

"'Tis all I ask, lass."

When exhaustion began to claim her, she heard her husband whispering what sounded like a prayer. Rousing herself from her doze, she asked, "What are you praying for?"

He pulled her more snugly against him and answered, "I'm praying for ye, lass."

She sighed. "My prayers have already been answered. God sent you to save me."

The last thing she remembered, before sleep claimed her, was the sound of her husband's deep and even breathing that nearly matched the steady beat of his heart beneath her cheek.

The next time she opened her eyes, he was smiling at her, and her heart melted all over again as she recalled all that they'd shared the night before. He'd been so gentle and patient with her, asking her permission before he showed her yet another way a man and wife could make love. The memory warmed her heart.

Feeling more awake by the moment, she flashed him a smile

and had the pleasure of watching his eye darken with desire, as it had last night.

"Ye'd best stop looking at me unless ye want me to continue yer lessons in lovemaking this morning."

Immediately contrite, she apologized. "Forgive me, Darby. I had no idea that smiling at you would give you that idea."

"Now that ye do, lass, I'll be knowing when ye're using yer wiles on me."

She shook her head. "I'm afraid I do not have any wiles. I was thinking of last night and could not help but smile. Have I properly thanked you?"

"For what in particular?" he asked, wrapping his arms around her.

She felt her face flaming again but ignored it to be honest with her husband. "Marrying me."

"'Twas me pleasure. Is that all?" He sounded disappointed.

"No. You treated me as if I were fragile and easily frightened. You showed me what I had experienced before was as far from making love as we are from the sun. You made it beautiful for me… You made me feel loved."

"Well then, lass, ye should know that I do consider ye fragile, and ye were nearly white as a sheet when I laid ye on this bed last night." He pressed his lips to her forehead. "As far as making love, I've more to teach ye. Never doubt that ye are loved, lass."

She reached for his hand and held it to her heart. "You saved me from a fate that would have killed me. You showed me compassion and tenderness when I now realize you must have been beyond eager to make love…but you did not force me."

He pressed his lips to hers and rasped, "As God is me witness, lass, I'll never force ye or take ye in anger."

Emotions strong and true for this man swept up from her toes. When he grinned, she handed her heart into his keeping—and she would never take it back.

"Remember, good things come to those who wait, and if ye've had a change of heart now that the passion has cooled, I am willing to wait until ye invite me into yer bed again. I won't be rushing ye, even though I could be very convincing."

She laughed softly. "And yet here you are."

He laughed. "Are ye kicking me out, lass?"

"Not in this lifetime, Darby. I want to fall asleep in your arms every night and wake in your arms every morning."

"I'm thinking that could be arranged, lass." He kissed the tip of her nose, one eye, and then the other before easing back. "Now then, why don't ye close yer eyes and get a bit more rest while I fire up the oven and put the kettle on?"

"Darby?"

"Aye?"

"I love you."

"I love you too."

He got up then paused in the doorway and reminded her, "Rest."

"Aye, Darby."

He was laughing at her mimicking of his brogue when he walked into the kitchen.

She was smiling when she closed her eyes.

THE SCENT OF ginger and spices had her opening her eyes and pulling on her chemise and dressing gown. Standing in the doorway, she observed yet another hidden talent her husband had, as he opened the oven door and pulled out a small loaf of gingerbread.

"When did you have time to bake that?"

He turned and smiled. "Well now, seeing as how ye slept for another hour, I've had the time—though in truth, Miranda sent it over with instructions for warming it up."

"It smells heavenly."

"And will taste of it as well, if memory serves. I heard you stirring and set the tea to steeping. Would ye like a cup?"

"I should be waiting on you, Darby."

"Ye can do so later. I'm having a turn and enjoying it." He

served her tea and gingerbread warm from the oven. "Can I ask ye something, lass?"

"Of course."

"Are ye sore this morning?"

She buried her face in her hands.

"Well? Are ye?"

"A bit."

"Can ye be more specific?"

"Why do you want to know?"

He sighed, rose from his chair, and plucked her out of hers and sat back down with her on his lap. "Because, prickly wife of mine, I would not want ye to be suffering in silence. We're man and wife now, and I would have us be able to speak of anything."

"That is an intimate question," she whispered.

"Making love is as intimate as it gets, lass." When she didn't say anything else, he kissed her cheek and tucked her head beneath his chin.

"Not so sore that I wouldn't let you talk me back into bed, Darby."

"Well now, that's a proper answer from the woman I love. But unfortunately, I've a meeting with Coventry in half an hour, so I won't have time until later. What did you have planned for this morning?"

She felt her cheeks flaming again and tried to bury her face in her hands, but her husband was too quick. He held her hands to his heart and kissed her softly at first, as if she were made of glass. When he deepened the kiss, she melted against him.

"If I could miss the meeting, lass, I would, but I cannot. The captain received two missives early this morning, and he has been firing off a few of his own."

"About last night?"

"Aye. Will ye be all right by yerself?"

"I've been alone before. I can keep busy."

"Doing…?"

"My, aren't *you* full of questions this morning," she teased him, and it felt wonderful.

"How else will I get to know me wife better?" He stood with her still in his arms and set her on her feet. "By the way, Madame Beaudoine sent word that she will be here in an hour."

"Whatever for?"

Darby chuckled. "The usual, I would guess. She *is* the most sought-after modiste in London."

"I know that, but why is she coming *here*?"

He brushed a lock of hair out of her eyes. "She feels responsible for your getting injured in her shop and wants to do something special for you."

"Oh." What else could she say that would not sound ridiculous? She'd never been to a modiste before the other day, and that was to pick up dresses Mrs. Plumton had ordered for the staff.

"I mentioned that you look beautiful in blue." He tapped the tip of his finger to her nose. "It brings out yer freckles."

"I don't have any freckles."

"As I'm looking at them, I'm thinking ye may not have noticed."

She rubbed her nose and whispered, "Freckles are ugly."

Darby wrapped his hands around her waist and swung her around twice before setting her back on her feet. "Ah, lass, I can see it's going to take more than a long night of making love to ye to convince ye ye're the most beautiful, desirable woman I have ever met."

Her heart swelled at his words. "Am I?"

"Aimee-lass, ye take me breath away."

"You've already stolen my heart—it's only fair if I've stolen your breath."

He pressed his lips to hers and plundered.

The knock on the door had him ending their kiss and taking a step back. "That'll be Michael reminding me it's time for the meeting. If ye need me, I'll be upstairs."

"I'll always need you, Darby."

"'Tis a lucky thing, because I feel the same way. Don't fret over the gift Madame Beaudoine is bringing for ye. Promise me?"

"I promise."

"Ye look as if ye just got out of bed, lass."

"That's because I did."

"Best get dressed, or else ye won't be ready when they arrive."

"They who?"

"Madame Beaudoine and Mademoiselle Augustin. I've asked her to fit ye for a gown or two and some other essentials."

"Darby, I do not need any more gowns."

"I need to give them to ye, lass. Indulge me by accepting me gift and Madame Beaudoine's."

"Just this once."

He grinned. "Aye, just this once."

"Darby?"

He paused with his hand on the doorknob. "Aye, lass?"

"Remember I love you."

"I won't be forgetting."

She waited for him to say the words back. Instead, he strode across the room and pulled her into his embrace. "Ye're the other half of me heart, lass. I'll always love ye."

His kiss gave her the courage to admit, "I've never been fitted for a gown before—what if I do something wrong?"

Resting his chin on her head, he asked, "Do ye know how to stand still?"

"Well, yes, but—"

"Do ye know how to follow instructions?"

"Of course, but—"

"Ah, and the last question: do ye know yer left from yer right?"

She was laughing when she answered, "Yes, Darby, I do."

He leaned back, and the expression of love and patience on his handsome face filled her heart to bursting. "Well then, lass, ye'll do fine. I have faith in ye."

He kissed her one more time and promised to return with news from the captain.

CHAPTER TWENTY-SEVEN

A N HOUR LATER, Aimee was ready and waiting for Madame Beaudoine and her seamstress to arrive. The teakettle was hot, waiting to be poured into the pot she found in the cupboard. Miranda's gingerbread was sliced and arranged on the pretty plate she'd found with the teapot.

She'd enjoyed setting the table with the teacups and saucers that matched the teapot. Had another woman lived in the apartment before them? If not, then Miranda had been even more thoughtful than Aimee had already realized. If only she'd had the time to bake, she would have been able to offer cream scones with the gingerbread.

Just thinking of how Darby had roused her at dawn and made love to her again had her pressing her hand to her heart to hold in the joy that spread to the tips of her fingers. Hadn't the scent of gingerbread woken her from a deep sleep? The sight of her broad-shouldered husband pulling the bread from the oven had been such a paradox. The man she married was a wonder. Strong, yet gentle. Quick to defend, yet also to laugh. Kisses that drained every thought from her brain, and hands that roused her to a fevered pitch she had not thought possible.

The knock on the door brought her back to the present and the experience she planned to savor. Rushing to the door, she opened it and smiled. "Madame Beaudoine, Mademoiselle

Augustin, welcome! Please come in."

The women entered with a grace Aimee hoped to someday possess. What surprised her were the two gentlemen who swept in behind them, one with an elaborate dressing screen and the other an armful of gowns. Staring at the color and fabrics, she was overwhelmed and had to clear her throat twice to speak when Madame Beaudoine asked where the men should place the gowns.

"The settee and chair by the window," she managed to say. Thankfully, she was saved from answering any more questions when someone knocked on the door again. She opened it and nearly wept with relief. Miranda and Emma were standing there smiling.

"Garahan thought you could use company during your first fitting."

She reached for Miranda's hand, instantly buoyed by her calm demeanor and strength. "I am so happy to see you!"

Emma clapped when she saw the two beautiful Frenchwomen and the gowns they'd brought with them. "Pretty!" The little one's happiness was a balm to Aimee's nerves.

"Madame Beaudoine, Mademoiselle Augustin, please meet my dear friend Mrs. Coventry and her daughter Emma."

"*Alors!* Madame Coventry, Mademoiselle Emma, how lovely to see you again. I am working on the captain's latest order for his two favorite women. Wait until you see, *non*, Yvette?"

"*Oui*, madame," Mademoiselle Augustin replied. "The captain has an eye for color and what is fashionable."

"Except where necklines are concerned," Madame Beaudoine grumbled. "Ah well, let us begin."

They were soon chatting as if old friends, which eased the last of the tension from between Aimee's shoulder blades. The gentlemen bowed to Madame Beaudoine and promised to return in a few hours.

Aimee leaned close to Miranda to ask, "Do fittings really take that long?"

Miranda smiled. "Do not worry about the time. Enjoy being pampered—it is what both Madame Beaudoine and Yvette excel at."

"But I'm not a member of the *ton* to be pampered... I'm—"

"Mrs. Darby Garahan," Miranda told her. "The beloved wife of one of the Duke of Wyndmere's personal guard. The cachet that accompanies the duke and his guard is far more important in the upper circles than you would imagine."

When Aimee frowned, Emma scooted off her mother's lap, held her hands in the air, and said, "Up!"

Aimee was happy to oblige and cuddle the little one in her arms. Emma laid her head on Aimee's shoulder and closed her eyes. "Did she have trouble sleeping last night?"

"She only woke once or twice, and fell back to sleep when Gordon sang to her."

She should not have been surprised that the captain would sing to his daughter. "My papa did not have a soothing voice. Mum used to joke that it sounded like crows calling. I'm not accustomed to hearing a man sing, and was surprised at how soothing Darby's voice was."

Miranda agreed. "Gordon's is a bit lower, but just as soothing. As soon as he sang Darby's lullaby, Emma sighed and closed her eyes."

"Even without the Irish brogue?"

Miranda laughed. "Even without it."

"We are ready, Madame Garahan," Madame Beaudoine announced. "Are you?"

TWO AND A half hours later, the gentlemen had returned to collect the dressing screen, the fitted gowns in an array of blues—from silvery to a deep midnight—a nightrail and dressing gown in cotton as soft as a cloud that were to be altered and returned, and other items that were not acceptable in the modiste's eyes once Aimee had tried them on. Madame Beaudoine and Yvette bade her goodbye, promising to have the gowns delivered in three days.

"Let me help you straighten up, Aimee," Miranda said. But Emma had other ideas and started to whimper.

Aimee reached out to brush the tip of her finger over Emma's cheek. "I think someone needs to lie down and dream of faeries and butterflies."

"Faeries," Emma murmured, half asleep already.

A loud thump from above them had Emma blinking but settling down even when a few more followed. "What *are* they doing up there?" Aimee asked.

Miranda smiled. "My husband is tutoring Garahan in adjusting his balance. Compared to what I remember Gordon going through all those years ago, I'd say your husband is doing well."

A crash accompanied the loud thump and jarred Emma into tears, while Aimee gasped. "I'd better go help."

Miranda placed her hand on Aimee's arm. "Let Garahan keep his pride intact, and remember to be calm when he returns. Do not ask if he injured himself. If he offers an explanation, accept it. If not…"

"Accept that as well," Aimee finished.

"You and Garahan will find your rhythm, and before you know it, you'll wonder how you ever existed without him."

"Was it like that for you?"

Miranda smiled. "Yes. It was magical, but we had a decade as friends—both of us hiding what we felt for one another until the day… No, I won't tarnish the happiness we shared today while you were feted as if you were a princess. Madame Beaudoine and Yvette were charmed by your reactions."

"Did I appear too gauche?"

"Not at all," Miranda assured her. "They found your delight and wonder charming. I know I did." With her daughter sleeping against her shoulder, Miranda rose gracefully and reached for Aimee's hand. "I'll put Emma down for a nap and will be working on the mending. If you need me, just come over."

"I will, and thank you…for everything."

"My pleasure. You should probably sit down. It's been a busy morning."

Drained, but happily exhausted, Aimee dropped onto the settee by the window, curled her legs beneath her, and laid her head on the back of the settee.

⁜

GARAHAN HAD NOT planned on being gone as long as he had, but needs must. As one of the duke's guard, he was used to spending more hours working than not. Rubbing at the ache in his backside, which he'd landed on more than once, he thanked the captain. "I'm not as sure as yerself that I've improved, but I appreciate the time and instruction. I never thought about balance before, but faith if the lot of us don't use it when we widen our stance, bend at the knees, and put our weight on the balls of our feet."

"Aye," the captain agreed. "Prepared to leap in any direction in a fight. An excellent position. You should try it now that you're wearing an eyepatch."

"I don't want to frighten the lass when I fall forward on me nose. I'm thinking she's partial to me face."

Coventry snorted with laughter. "She's in love with you."

"I think I rushed things, but—"

The captain frowned. "I disagree. You would never have asked for her hand if you were not already half in love with her."

Garahan blew out the breath he'd been holding. "'Twas her angel-blue eyes and bruise on her cheek that tugged at me heart."

"Is that all?"

"Nay, 'twas her insistence that I go back to rescue the other lasses that had me falling *arse* over head in love with her."

"She'll be pleased to hear the news that after we left Bow Street last night, King extracted the confessions required. Farrell, Robertson, and Ashbrook will remain behind bars and be brought

240

to trial. As will the men who tried to break into our building last night, and the boarding house owner and her thugs."

"What of the two who gave us his name?"

"Merriman and Ambrose," Coventry said with a nod. "I believe their sentence may be more lenient, but it is not up either of us."

"I'm thinking they knew that, but still—"

"Let it go, and ask your wife how she enjoyed her fitting."

Garahan grinned. "She was nervous as a treed fox with a dozen hounds beneath him."

Coventry chuckled. "Best go soothe any worries she may be harboring. I'll have Michael fetch you if I need you. You haven't rested as prescribed by Sampson. Take tomorrow to do so."

"I have rested well…every night," Garahan said with a grin.

"The love of a good woman will ease more suffering and sorrow than any bottle. Remember that."

"Aye, captain."

Garahan couldn't wait to hear how Aimee's day went or to share his good news with her. He knocked twice and said, "It's me, lass. Open the door."

When he did not hear a sound on the other side, his gut churned. Ear to the door, he knocked again. Still nothing.

Tremayne entered the building and asked, "Why don't you use your key? That's what it meant for."

"Aye, the key." Garahan fumbled, pulling it from his waistcoat pocket, inserted it in the lock, and opened the door.

The late afternoon sunlight wrapped his wife in a halo of gold. He quietly closed the door behind him, walked over to the settee, and knelt beside her. Her beauty beguiled him, and the way she'd blossomed during their lovemaking lessons filled his soul, humbling him.

He stood and scooped his wife into his arms. "Faith, I'm a lucky bastard."

She roused when he placed her on their bed. Sitting up, she asked, "Darby? How did your meetings go with Captain

Coventry?"

He sat beside her, pleased when she reached for his hand. "Well, lass. The case I've been working on for His Grace ended surprisingly. The blackguards threatening the baron's life gave themselves up and confirmed the men we knew were behind the plot."

"That is wonderful news! I know O'Malley and the other men in the guard will be pleased."

"Ye have the right of it, lass. That's not all," he told her. "The man responsible for luring yerself, and God only knows how many other lasses, to London is behind bars."

"Thank God—then no one will try to come after Mary, Alice, or Beatrice?"

"Nay, lass."

"Sally and Jenny will be safe, too?"

"They all will—as will ye."

"Then you didn't have to marry me," she whispered.

He pulled her onto his lap and captured her lips in a drugging kiss. "Well now, lass, there's where ye'd be wrong. Me heart recognized yers the moment I saw ye. Ye were meant to be me wife and the other half of me heart." He hesitated, then asked, "Have ye changed yer mind?"

She drew in a breath and slowly exhaled. "I have."

His heart iced over. "Have ye now."

The tips of her fingers traced the line of her jaw. "I think I'd like to have my lessons, three times a day. Morning, teatime, and at night."

He slowly smiled. "Well now, I think I can arrange that. Why don't ye tell me about your time with Madame Beaudoine while I undress ye, lass?"

She slipped off the bed and presented her back to him. He made short work of the buttons and spun her around. She fell laughingly into his arms.

"Kiss me, lass."

Aimee pressed her lips to his and fell under his spell. One

moment they were dressed and the next lying on the bed skin to skin. She shivered, and he reveled in her reaction. "Now then, love of me life, I'll teach ye how a man can bring his wife to madness with lips and tongue."

Her eyes round with wonder—praise God, not fear—he kissed a path from the hollow of her throat to her belly, which quivered as he let his fingers soothe and excite. "If ye want me to stop, all ye need do is tell me." He traced a path with his lips to the inside of one thigh and then the other. "Do ye remember how I stretched ye, lass?"

Angel-blue eyes turned a darker blue. "Aye, Darby."

"I'm going to do the same with me lips and tongue." When she didn't tell him to stop, he rasped, "Like this." Her low moan of desire hit him in the gut and had him shaking with need to take what she did not realize she offered with each lift of her hips, each musical groan. It would kill him if he had to stop, but still he asked, "Should I stop now, lass?"

"Don't stop, Darby."

"I won't until ye're screaming me name and begging me to fill ye."

Darby kept his promise, teasing and retreating, nibbling and tasting her, until she was limp and begging. "Ye've yet to scream me name, lass," he said. The next thrust of his tongue was all it took to have her chanting his name...each time louder than the last. She inhaled, and he shifted until he settled between her thighs and swallowed her scream of ecstasy with his mouth, kissing her endlessly as he plunged into her. Surrounded by her damp heat, he filled her with his love and planted his seed. Together they shattered in one another's arms.

Later when they lay tangled together, he brushed a lock of gold from her face and kissed her gently, reverently. "Never doubt me love for ye, lass."

With a soft sigh, she laid her head on his heart. "I won't. Thank you for rescuing me, Darby, and for loving me."

"I had no choice."

She stiffened. "I see."

He chuckled and rolled until she lay beneath him. "I'd die without me whole heart, lass. As ye've got the other half of mine, and I'm not whole without ye, I'll never be letting ye go."

She wrapped her legs around his waist and lifted her hips. "In that case…"

They came together in a blinding surge that stole their breath. Hips and hearts pumping, they flew over the edge of reason into the abyss of pleasure.

When she stirred in his arms, he ordered her, "Give a man a chance to recover, lass."

She was laughing when their lips met and he tucked her against his heart. "I was going to thank you."

"Thank me later, lass—I need me sleep."

"Fine," she grumbled.

"Faith, me lessons in loving have turned ye into a lusty wench."

"Is that a bad thing?"

"Only if ye weren't married to an understanding man who is willing to give in and satisfy yer every desire."

"Every desire?"

"Aye, lass—but ye need to give me an hour to recover. Ye'll not regret it."

One hour later…

HE TOOK HER to the stars, and he was right… She didn't regret it.

EPILOGUE

Six months later...

A IMEE OPENED HER eyes and slowly smiled. "I was dreaming about you."

"Were ye, lass? Tell me more." Darby brushed featherlight kisses to her forehead, cheeks, and chin.

"We were lying in a field of wildflowers." She paused to press her lips to his before adding, "The sun was bright and warm overhead."

Darby shifted so he was poised at the entrance to her heat. "As warm as ye are right now?"

Aimee sighed and traced the tips of her fingers along the strong line of her husband's jaw. "Mmm."

He captured her lips in a devastatingly tender kiss as he slid home, filling her to the hilt. Her gasp of pleasure increased his. He plunged and retreated over and over until his wife cried out in ecstasy. He eased the leash on his control and drove into her again and again until his body took complete control. When she cried out his name, he poured his seed deep inside of her.

Lost in the power of their lovemaking, she came apart in his arms. He joined her spiraling upward to the heavens. When he felt her trembling, he roused from the remnants of their desire to place a hand to her backside, pinning her to him. He rolled them over until she was on top.

He brushed the tips of his fingers from the hollow of her throat to the tip of one very full and highly sensitive breast, and then the other. He marveled at the changes in her body—the size of her breasts, the swell of her belly, and, to his delight, the increase in her passion. "Do ye think ye're carrying our daughter with sunshine-gold hair and bright blue eyes?"

"I might be carrying a son with dark brown hair and warm brown eyes. Will it matter?"

"Nay, as long as the babe and ye are healthy." His lips claimed hers, igniting her passion. "Ye're going to be the death of me, insisting on having yer way with me every chance ye get."

She purred as he kissed a path along her collarbone, and sucked in a sharp breath when he increased the pressure of his hands on her backside, lifted his hips, and surged deeper within her tight sheath.

"I suppose I'll have to give ye what ye want, lass."

Caressing her sweet *derrière*, he drove into her until she shattered around him a second time, and he willingly followed her over the edge of reason into madness.

Before he lost the ability to speak, he rasped, "*Mo chroí*, I love ye."

"*Mo ghrá*," she whispered. "I love you more."

About the Author

Historical & Contemporary Romance "Warm...Charming...Fun..."

C.H. was born in Aiken, South Carolina, but her parents moved back to northern New Jersey where she grew up.

She believes in fate, destiny, and love at first sight. C.H. fell in love at first sight when she was seventeen. She was married for 41 wonderful years until her husband lost his battle with cancer. Soul mates, their hearts will be joined forever.

They have three grown children—one son-in-law, two grandsons, two rescue dogs, and two rescue grand-cats.

Her characters rarely follow the synopsis she outlines for them...but C.H. has learned to listen to her characters! Her heroes always have a few of her husband's best qualities: his honesty, his integrity, his compassion for those in need, and his killer broad shoulders. C.H. writes about the things she loves most: Family, her Irish and English Ancestry, Baking and Gardening.

C.H.'s Social Media Links:
Website: www.chadmirand.com
Amazon: amazon.com/stores/C.-H.-
Admirand/author/B001JPBUMC
BookBub: bookbub.com/authors/c-h-admirand
Facebook Author Page: facebook.com/CHAdmirandAuthor
Facebook Private Reader's Page ~ C.H. Reader's Nook:
facebook.com/groups/714796299746980
GoodReads:
goodreads.com/author/show/212657.C_H_Admirand
Instagram: c.h.admirand
Twitter: @AdmirandH
Youtube:
youtube.com/channel/UCRSXBeqEY52VV3mHdtg5fXw